Previously published Worldwide Mystery titles by
LISE McCLENDON

THE BLUEJAY SHAMAN
PAINTED TRUTH

NORDIC NIGHTS

Lise McClendon

NORDIC NIGHTS

A Worldwide Mystery/October 2000

First published by Intrigue Press/Philmont Publishing Company, Inc.

ISBN 0-373-26364-4

Copyright © 2000 by Lise McClendon.
All rights reserved. Except for use in any review, the reproduction or utilization of this work in whole or in part in any form by any electronic, mechanical or other means, now known or hereafter invented, including xerography, photocopying and recording, or in any information storage or retrieval system, is forbidden without the written permission of the publisher, Worldwide Library, 225 Duncan Mill Road, Don Mills, Ontario, Canada M3B 3K9.

All characters in this book have no existence outside the imagination of the author and have no relation whatsoever to anyone bearing the same name or names. They are not even distantly inspired by any individual known or unknown to the author, and all incidents are pure invention.

WORLDWIDE.®

TORONTO • NEW YORK • LONDON
AMSTERDAM • PARIS • SYDNEY • HAMBURG
STOCKHOLM • ATHENS • TOKYO • MILAN
MADRID • WARSAW • BUDAPEST • AUCKLAND

To my mother and father with love

NORDIC NIGHTS

A Worldwide Mystery/October 2000

Published by arrangement with Walker Publishing Company, Inc.

ISBN 0-373-26364-3

In this fateful hour,
I call upon all Heaven with its power
And the sun with its brightness
And the snow with its whiteness
And the fire with all the strength it hath
And the lightning with its rapid wrath
And the winds with their swiftness along the path
And the sea with its deepness
And the rocks with their steepness
And the earth with its starkness.
All these I place,
By Heaven's almighty help and grace,
Between myself and the powers of darkness.

—Traditional rune

Author's Note

Evidence of Viking explorations in the New World is both indisputable and suspect. Ruins of ancient camps in Newfoundland, a swampy meadow near the village of L'Anse-aux-Meadows, have been verified as dating from around the year A.D. 1000. But all written Viking evidence has been disbelieved by some scientists even while proven authentic by others. The Vinland Map in the British Museum, an accurate drawing of Viking lands including the coast of North America, and dated A.D. 1440, has been debunked and, just recently, deemed authentic again by Yale researchers.

In 1898 a Minnesota farmer discovered a slab of rock covered with runic characters that reportedly proved that Vikings had been bushwhacked by local Indians in the year 1362. The stone became known as the Kensington Runestone and is now on display at a museum in Alexandria, Minnesota. My thanks to the museum for supplying me with information about the runestone. Controversy still swirls around the stone's authenticity.

Hoaxes about Viking explorers have a long history on the continent. The Viking Tower in Newport, Rhode Island, once owned by Benedict Arnold, was found to be built no earlier than 1640. In 1952 a drinking horn carved with figures and an inscription found on the shore of Lake Michigan was first thought to be from A.D. 1317. Later it was revealed to be a tourist trinket from the Reykjavik (Iceland) Museum.

Did the Vikings sail up the Red River and explore middle America? Your guess is as good as mine. It's certainly possible.

For more information about runes, I suggest the book *Runes* by R. I. Page, published by the University of California Press in association with the British Museum.

Most verses heading chapters are from *The Poetic Edda*, a rich collection of Norse mythology, culture and verse, attributed to Icelandic scholar Snorri Sturluson (1178–1241) and other chieftains, storytellers and priests who kept the pagan traditions alive by writing them down. My translation is by Lee M. Hollander, University of Texas Press. Other quotations are from various Welsh, Scottish and Scandinavian sources of traditional verses and songs.

Thanks to Kipp, Evan and Nick, for keeping faith.

ONE

Wealth causes strife among kinsmen,
The wolf lurks in the forest.

FINE WHITE FLAKES sifted across the sallow slash of the spotlight in the town square. Callous gift of a coldhearted Mother Earth: a hard blessing of snow that fell and fell and fell. The sculptures carved of brittle ice looked small, insignificant, in the wavering, jaundiced holes in the night. Above it all the clouds hung like dirty laundry.

Artie Wacker poured coffee. It was obscenely late, or early. The town slept. We sat in the Second Sun, my Jackson gallery, with the track lights off, in our own pools of weak light, waiting for word from the police station. Thinking, I should be there, I got up to pace. I thought about the postcard I got from Erik yesterday, the one with the joke about the end of his marriage: *Only the Ice Man has his pick.* Prophetic now. All is prophetic in hindsight. I picked up the telephone and dialed Erik's number in Tucson. It rang six times before he picked it up, sleepy.

"It's Alix."

"Hey, little sister." A click, the light. "It's three in the morning."

"I know. Listen, Hank's been arrested."

"Who?"

"Hank Helgeson, our mother's husband? Chubby little ornery cuss, more Swedish than meatballs?"

"Oh, Hank. The meatball. Did he leave his socks on the floor or something?"

"Mom didn't arrest him, Erik. The cops did. For murder. Can you come up here, by any chance?"

"Whoa, whoa, back up. Murder?"

"The weird thing is he really liked this guy. A Norwegian artist, same kind of twisted Norsky pride."

"A real Norwegian?"

"From Norway, just got here today, and tonight he's dead. The Chamber of Commerce is going to love this."

"Was he in a rental car? Never mind. Why was Hank arrested for it?"

"Something about him being there in the room with the body. Can you come? I don't think I can handle Mom by myself."

"Who are you kidding? You're the youngest, her fair-haired girl. Ever since I called her a freeze-dried pickle at the reunion—"

"You did have too much to drink."

"She hasn't spoken to me since. You think she's going to want to see me in her hour of need? After I sang that little ditty about Hank—A Norse is a Norse, of course, of course—"

"She's going to be humiliated."

"She married the meatball."

"Oh, Erik. Come for me, then."

He sighed, long and hard. "Tomorrow the Over-Eighty Tournament starts with a bang. I've got a staff of a hundred for these geezers, with that many golf carts. I can't, X. But let me know what happens. Like if Mom gets her revenge. That was always fun."

"Hank was supposed to show his Viking longboat in the parade tomorrow—tonight—for the winter festival. Nordic Nights."

"The thing he's been building in the garage for the last five years?"

"His pride and joy."

Erik sighed again. "How are you doing?"

"Business is great. Couldn't be better. Christmas was fabulous."

"No, you yourself. Personally."

"Fine."

"Still the stoic Norsky. I thought that business last summer might have changed you."

"It did, Erik."

"I know, kiddo."

"It meant a lot to me that you came up then. I'll get through this. I will."

"I always said you had bigger balls than Odin."

"Thanks, I guess."

"Give the meatball my best."

ARTIE WACKER AND I finally bundled up and walked the five blocks to the police station. The night sky huddled close overhead, unwilling to let us forget the grip winter had on us, body and soul. My slouch hat wasn't much protection from the snow and biting cold, but Erik's faded red down jacket, dotted with duct tape to keep in wayward feathers, still held winter at bay. Artie hailed from Alabama. He was no doubt regretting his decision to take a semester off from LSU and come north. His teeth took up a singsong chatter before we got to the corner. At least he had a butternut-brown goatee to keep his chin warm.

The town hall squatted, lonely and dark with its fancy cedar siding and moss rock, its modern clock tower announcing that we should be in bed. Picking our way through the drifts, we found the back door. I had to knock loudly, twice. A policeman opened the door and recognized me.

"What's going on?" I asked, searching the cop's chest for his name tag. He wasn't wearing his uniform. Out of luck. And not for the first time tonight.

"Your mother's in there with Mr. Helgeson and Roscoe Penn."

"Roscoe Penn? The lawyer?" Artie grabbed my sleeve to peek around me, struggling for a view of the lawyer through the blinds in the hallway window. "I saw him on *Geraldo* last summer. He's really something, isn't he?"

Out of my foggy brain came the policeman's name, Elmer: tall, fifty-five, going to fat. He leaned into me and whispered in my ear, "Who's the elf?"

"Artie Wacker, works for me at the gallery. Artie, meet Elmer."

They shook hands. Artie wasn't too interested in the policeman. He squatted down to look under the blinds.

"Hank wanted Roscoe," I said, still sorting it in my own mind.

"Damn fine representative of the legal profession," Elmer said. His gray mustache twitched.

"And to think he could have had Uncle Lars's stepson, Eugene. Or a lawyer who wears three-piece suits. Did you see Roscoe on *Geraldo?* The Indian blanket around his shoulders and a coonskin cap? He looked like Davy Crockett rolling out of the sack."

"He's gone to the cowboy hat tonight," Elmer said. "With a big feather, though."

"Is Charlie Frye in there?" I asked. Elmer nodded.

"Here comes Roscoe Penn!" Artie said in an excited whisper, standing up.

The door opened, and the lawyer stepped through. Smiling, his gray cowboy hat sitting back on his head, Penn cut a grand figure through the cold, bland corridors of linoleum and fluorescents with his taupe gabardine cowboy-cut suit and shiny black boots. He looked Artie, Elmer, and me in the eye like he was running for office, then turned back to take my mother's arm, gentleman-like.

Una smoothed her indigo velveteen tunic, her hand shaking. Her short cap of gray-blond hair hung neatly over her tired blue eyes. Roscoe dwarfed her with his height. She looked up from listening to his whispering and saw me. She reached out her hand and squeezed mine.

"You really should be in bed. It's late, isn't it?" She looked at her watch. "Dear me."

"I couldn't sleep, Mom." I peered around them. "Where is he?"

Penn rubbed his square jaw. His face had the rugged appeal of the Marlboro Man, whom he had represented once: a match made in litigious heaven. The feather in his hat was striped and extravagant, like the man himself. He needed a shave (a little salt-and-pepper there), but who didn't at four a.m.? "We can't get a hearing on the bail until morning, and the authorities, in all their wisdom, think it's best to keep him here." Penn gave

Elmer a dismissive look. "This will all be over in the morning. It's a simple mistake."

"They're keeping him overnight?" I asked. Una nodded, flashing her expressionless eyes at me, then Penn.

"Believe me, Mrs. Helgeson, honey," Penn turned to her and said, "I'm going to straighten all this out in the morning. He'll get a wicked night's sleep." He glanced at his watch and raised his eyebrows: not much night left. "Then ol' Roscoe here will get Judge Foss to send him home in the morning." He straightened his broad shoulders, to reassure us of his manly confidence, then declared: "There is nothing worse than a small man with authority."

Charlie Frye came out of the room on cue, holding Hank by the arm, wearing his all-weather trademark wrinkled gray suit, his crew cut fresh above sagging eyes. Chief of Police Charlie Frye's dislike of me had solidified last summer, and the fact that I put a slew of his arson cases to bed had done nothing to affect his attitude. I made work for him, I have an intrinsic disrespect for authority, and I made him look like the political-appointee-with-shit-for-brains that he was. Come to think of it, I might dislike me too if I were Charlie.

This was my first look at Hank since his arrest, since he left for a nightcap with Glasius Dokken and Una earlier this evening. Glasius, who was now dead. What had they done after I left the gallery? Hank, my stepfather, looked terrible. His ragg wool sweater had crept over his large, round belly to reveal the un-buttoned blue oxford cloth shirt underneath and curly gray hairs, much more than grew on his head. At sixty-four he was three years younger than Una—and nearly bald. His gold wire-rimmed glasses, framing small gray eyes, were bent, sitting askew on his bulbous nose. His mouth hung open, and spittle clung to the corners. His wrists were in handcuffs. He looked so different from our tall, lanky father, whose flaxen hair and James Dean coolness was seared into my memory, that my brother's description of Hank as a meatball sprang to mind.

"Did you hear that, honey?" Una said to him. "Mr. Penn says we'll have you out in the morning. Do you want me to bring over your Metamucil?"

Charlie Frye and Elmer exchanged looks. I stepped up: "Mom, I don't think Hank's going to need that tonight." My mother blinked viciously. "He'll be out before you know it. And you have toothbrushes and stuff, don't you?"

"Come on now, Helgeson," Charlie barked with excess authority, ignoring me. "Elmer, take him to the lockup."

The policeman was gentle with Hank, guiding him, shuffling, past his wife and lawyer, down a dim corridor. Elmer flipped on a few switches as he went. We watched from the hallway for a moment, then Una turned away, a flicker of pain across her still-blond eyebrows. She lifted her apple-red chin, chapped by the winter wind, and turned to the lawyer.

"Eight o'clock, did you say, Mr. Penn?"

"Nine will be fine, Mrs. Helgeson." He helped her slip on the navy pea coat, putting his arm around her shoulders as we walked to the door. Penn, ever the gentleman, offered us a ride in his Cadillac.

We climbed into the car, a turquoise cruiser from the early seventies sporting longhorns on the hood like a cartoon villain's sinister mustache. The crushed velvet backseat swallowed us up, bringing back memories of the Thorssen-mobile, a '62 Plymouth station wagon. I could barely see out the windows. Artie pulled his feet up under him. Penn drove carefully on the snowy streets, back fins swinging around each corner. Having a car like this in Jackson Hole was even more deranged and impractical than owning, as I did, a '67 Saab with bad tire karma and a squirrel-powered engine. I had to admire him for it.

He was giving us a little legal pep talk, telling us about his clout, dropping names of judges, politicians, backstage with Call-Me-Phil Donahue in the early days, later with Oprah. My mother was eating it up, hanging on every word.

Penn took a breath. I asked, "What exactly do they have on Mr. Helgeson, evidence-wise?"

"Squat, Miss Thorssen. They don't have jack. There's nothing to link Mr. Helgeson to the ice pick in the deceased. He says he didn't even touch it when he found the body. It's another case of Big Fucker Charlie Frye—pardon me, Mrs. Helgeson—thinking he can solve a case because somebody's handy to pin it on. He doesn't have anything, he doesn't know anything. It'll all be over in the morning.''

Una sighed raggedly in the front seat. I stared at the dark, snowswept boardwalks of Jackson, Wyoming, through the crystallized glass. Unrelenting winter: a good night for Skadi, Viking goddess of snow. If the Thorssens of a millennium ago had sailed the fjords, tracked the barren snowfields on two spruce planks, and sent their children far west across endless seas to distant, unknowable dangers, what did that make me? A bloodthirsty adventurer, a foolhardy seeker of knowledge, a risk taker? I didn't know. I didn't know if I ever would know. Maybe the journey to find out who you were was what spurred on the Vikings—and me.

Glasius Dokken. It wouldn't be over for him in the morning. He would still be dead. I shut my sandpapered eyes. Shit, why did I bring him here? Why couldn't I have let him have his flyover, go directly from Seattle to Minneapolis without passing Go, without collecting his two-hundred-dollar ice pick between the ribs? Why couldn't I have been satisfied with a simple ice sculpture contest? Why did I always complicate things to the nth degree, as my ersatz boyfriend Carl Mendez would say? *Tangle, tangle, endless thread, Find the finish then you're dead.*

A kindred spirit, Glasius. His moody, complicated murals of Viking legends were hanging at the gallery. Yesterday morning there was an air of excitement in Jackson. The first day of Nordic Nights. Not an average day in the gallery, not at all.

But I hadn't thought it would end in murder.

TWO

Need constricts the heart,
but it often serves as a help
and salvation to the sons of man,
if they attend to it in time.

"ALIX THORSSEN." He let the two words trill across his tongue, thick with the flavors of Norway. "You know that is not a proper Norwegian name."

Glasius Dokken had already explained to me that the government in Norway won't let you name your baby just anything, it must be a proper Norwegian name. Parents who try to be original, opting for Butch or Susie or Latoya, are ordered to rename the baby at once. Alix is not acceptable for a girl. "Alix Thorssen," he muttered again under his breath, shaking his head sadly, feeling so very sorry for me. Poor, poor child with an improper name.

"Sigrid. Katja. Sonja maybe," he mumbled off and on all day, squinting at me. "Ve vill tink of a proper Norwegian name for you." It sounded more like *Norveejun* when he said it, a little like Lawrence Welk. *A-vun and a-two.* He had a habit of tapping his finger against the side of his nose, to think. "Agneta? Agna for short? How about Steine?" He floated many name trial balloons, all of which I shot down. I was rather partial to Alix after all these years, *Norveejun* or not.

A thousand years ago the Norsemen made a culture of winter. They tamed it with their ferocious tempers, their adventurous hearts. But this particular Norseman wasn't brawny or bold or even very enamored of the cold that we had in abundance. He did think the mountains, soaring like adolescent hormones from the sagebrush plain, were magnificent. I invited him to come back and paint them, to stay with me or Luca or one of my artist friends, to capture the grandness of the jagged rocky points we call the Tetons. He captured so much history in his murals, I had no doubt his Teton paintings would show a new facet in an oft-recorded scene.

"I will paint those mountains," he said. "Just for you, Alix Thorssen. For the Second Sun Gallery, where you shine as bright as the midnight sun. To show ever'body no one knows the snow and mountains like a Norwegian. No one can feel the many colors of snow like a Norwegian."

Glasius Dokken, very proper, was an art professor at the University of Scandinavia in Oslo, painter of Viking murals, chronicler of myths. His hair was like snow, a white fluff on the peak of his head, a sprinkling of dandruff on his lower slopes. With rounded shoulders and long, artistic fingers, he viewed the world from behind smeared steel-rimmed glasses. His eyes were as bottomless as the sky, his nose beaky and thin, his bottom lip full over a double chin. He walked slowly, examining everything with his eyes, with a light brush of his fingers, a gentleness of subtlety and ambiguity. Except when it came to Things Norwegian. Like the running gag about my name, which was much more serious to him than me, Glasius Dokken believed that some things were sacred.

It was, that January, a dangerous belief.

THE WIND BLEW steadily, full of ice, the day Glasius Dokken flew into Jackson Hole. The airport sits in the eastern shadow of the Grand Teton range, on a flat bluff above the Snake River and the cluster of dramatic rocky peaks. A Frenchman's wet dream, the Tetons: cross my heart. The American Airlines jet came in sleek and smooth through hard, cloudless skies, carrying the painter and his crates.

The Norwegian artist was on a nationwide tour with his Viking murals. He had squeezed the Nordic Nights festival in between a showing at the Scandinavian Museum in Seattle and a special event at the Walker in Minneapolis. I felt lucky to get a man of his caliber, a famous artist from the homeland, into the Second Sun Gallery.

Dokken set to arguing in unintelligible Norwegian with the

air cargo people about his crated paintings. The artist insisted on riding with the crates in the back of the pickup truck I had arranged to transport them to the gallery, even though the temperature hovered near zero. He wore only a gray turtleneck, green wool scarf, leather gloves, tweed sports jacket, and slacks as the snow swirled around him. I followed them back into town in my rattletrap, the Saab Sister, watching the road for black ice and Glasius's nose for ice crystals as he held tight to the crates. The Nordic festival: Let the games begin! Tomorrow's headline: Glasius *Dokken Wins Frostbite Contest by a Nose.*

The highway was barely distinguishable from the landscape around it. Tall sagebrush poked blackened twigs from the drifts next to the cross-buck fence that marched along, half buried in snow. A perfect weekend for the Nordic Nights, a perfect season. Goddess Skadi had blessed us with a snow year unsurpassed in recent memory. Teton Village and Snow King ski resorts opened at Thanksgiving, fully groomed, freshly painted, and fingers crossed. Christmas had made the merchants' year, with rooms booked, skis flying, restaurants cooking, and car batteries jumping. At the Second Sun Gallery, I wrapped, crated, boxed, and mailed for three weeks straight, barely coming up for air a week after New Year's. Now, just two weeks later, the festival pumped up the volume again. The Chamber of Commerce of Jackson Hole was having a group orgasm.

My own contribution to the winter celebration was the exhibition of Glasius Dokken's Viking murals and coordinating the ice sculpture contest opposite the gallery in the town square. I wondered what had possessed me to get involved in this nonsense. I wasn't a joiner; I couldn't even finish college properly, as my mother sometimes liked to point out. (Una liked an orderly life, with one step leading logically to the next. Her daughter Alix, who had a penchant for plunging in if not swimming out, felt nothing could be duller.) At meetings, and there had been many, the Chamber guys and gals plotted and planned in gung-ho glee. But they gave me my due as a longtime business owner in Jackson; there was satisfaction in that. I took a deep, chilly breath inside the Saab, jiggling the knob on the new radio

I had treated myself to for Christmas, trying to get something besides static.

So this was what it had come to. I was a Businesswoman. Well, I could live with that. For a long time I had let my partner, Paolo Segundo, carry the money mantle. I was above that sort of thing, into pure art and artists, finding forgers for the FBI and uncovering art scams. But that had changed, abruptly. Now I am Alix Thorssen, business owner, dealer of fine arts and crafts of the modern West. Strange without the Argentine, yes, it still felt strange. Not bad but foreign, as if I was just filling in for him for a vacation and he would show up through the front door at any time, tanned face, flashing smile, tight pants, and all. Sometimes in the late afternoon, when the sun came through the plate glass at a certain angle, I could feel his breath on my neck. I would turn, and only the dust motes floating in the sunshine were behind me.

Since Paolo had died, I realized how dear this place was to me, and planning the festival had helped crystallize that feeling. I glanced left at the bridge and saw two white trumpeter swans gliding in tiny circles in a pool of open water surrounded by ice. My world sometimes felt that small; living in Jackson could get claustrophobic. The paddling circles might shrink and expand with the seasons, but it was at least *my* pond, where *I* paddled.

The center of the Jackson town square lay cloaked in the white waiting of winter. Blocks of ice, each six feet tall, stood upright like a frozen Stonehenge, ready for the chisel. I parked the Saab in front of the gallery and got out, pulling close my old down jacket. My black wool turtleneck sweater, bulky and comfortable, scratched my chin as I pulled in my neck from the cold. My jeans were clean but hardly adequate winter wear, and I felt the chill on my knees. I should have dressed better today: Glasius's opening was tonight. I had been scrubbing floors before the sun came up, in that glamorous manner of the art world. Hopefully I would find a spare moment to change.

The windows of the Second Sun Gallery were frosted and opaque. I smiled proudly at the tidy storefront, its overhanging roof with icicles and boardwalk planks, brass doorknob, gold lettering on the panes. I had thought of moving the gallery, changing its name, or even closing its doors after Paolo's death, but I was glad now that I hadn't. From its windows I could see the heart of the town, the open square I so loved, with its quaint antler arches on the corners I tried never to take for granted, twinkling with tiny lights now in the shadows of the evergreens, sending sparkles onto the blue-white snow. Under the tall elms and magnificent firs I could keep my mind clear when things got hectic. I could stand there anytime and feel centered again.

As for changing the name of the gallery, or closing its doors permanently, neither was a long-lived consideration. I loved it too much, the space itself and the need for beauty in the ordinary life it represented. Right now I needed the action it provided too, the constant command to get out of bed, to work, to plan, to organize. Changing the name of the Second Sun (which was a combination of the English equivalent of Segundo and the last part of Thorssen) was just too damn complicated. It stayed more from inertia than anything else.

Artie Wacker met us at the door. He skipped over the snow-drifts to help with the crates. Glasius Dokken wrung his hands. I held the door and shouted orders (up, over, left, watch that corner, don't drop it!): a couple of my finer talents.

Half an hour later I left Artie deep in negotiation with Glasius about the placement of the murals in the back third of the gallery. The creamy white walls were barely big enough for the four-by-eight-foot murals. There was room for the gallery cards between them, and that was all. Glasius wasn't particularly happy about that, but I had already moved everything I could to the front, stashed away tons of stuff, and rearranged the rest. The murals would bring in customers, but Glasius's paintings weren't for sale. With all the tourists expected for the festival, I wanted to have something out for them to purchase. That was the idea I had. Call me crazy.

I set to work on the account books, a daily adventure that helped me get a grip on reality each morning. Today I had to get things straightened up before my mother came down from my apartment upstairs. She and my stepfather had arrived on Monday to visit and display Hank's prize Viking longboat in the parade. So far I'd only ''volunteered'' to help paint the prow one evening. I made a new pot of coffee for Wacker and Glasius—and myself—and hunched over the account book.

"YOU DON'T LOOK any blonder than yesterday."

Artie Wacker's soft drawl was a welcome interruption from bookkeeping. I turned to find my salesman grinning his sprite grin at the door to my office.

"Same ol' dishwater." I ran my hand through the mess of shoulder-length locks that stood in for a hairstyle. Yesterday my mother had tactfully offered to spice up my tresses with a home highlighting kit from the drugstore. It was guaranteed, she said, to lighten up my attitude—mother's euphemism for one's social life—as well. "We watched slides instead."

"Something titillatin', I suppose."

"Mmm." I couldn't even remember the slides for a moment. Some archaeological dig Hank had dragged my mother to last summer. I must have fallen asleep promptly after the lights went out. I spun in my office chair. Wacker's boundless energy and crafty smile made him a joy to have in my employ. He wore the college uniform: hiking boots, oversize trousers, and flannel shirt. "All done out there? I made some fresh coffee."

"He's already wired, man." Artie rolled his eyes.

"Problems?" I stood up, set down my pencil.

"Just bein' a little temperamental," he said. "Come take a look."

We walked out into the gallery area, spots from the track lighting warming up the wood floors I had so lovingly scrubbed. I glanced at my watch; time to open up. "Better unlock and let in the masses struggling to break free from their hard-earned cash."

"Right, boss." Wacker left me and the professor a little too eagerly. I smiled my congenial smile at Glasius Dokken, who was hunched over, tapping his left nostril madly. He didn't even see me, so intent was he at staring down his canvases.

Two of the murals hung against the end wall, with each of the last two at the end of the adjoining walls, making a "U" of the most elaborate and fantastical mishmash of Viking warriors and maidens, gods and goddesses, giants and ogres, heavens and hells, that you've seen since the Edenic jungles of Hieronymus Bosch. My jaw dropped as I took in their lush, dark grandeur.

"Vell?" Professor Dokken asked, impatient and probably jet-lagged. "Vat do you tink?"

I looked at him quickly and shut my mouth. "They're wonderful, Glasius. I'm blown away."

He frowned at me behind his opaque glasses. "About the level. Is it straight?" He waved his long fingers. "I am not so good at straight lines. I think it is from living at the top of the world." His shoulders rose and lowered as if a silent chuckle were at work.

I looked at the tops of the massive frames, cocking my head. Artie had done a fabulous job, considering the size of the canvases and their close proximity. The two on the back wall, the most conspicuous to errors, looked great. But I walked over to them, touched the corner of each one briefly, and stepped back again. "Okay?"

"Okay." Glasius waved his hand at them again, dismissive. "I can look and look and look, and still I see crooked. The people will bump them anyway, you tink?"

"I certainly hope not." I touched his elbow and turned him toward the coffeepot on Paolo's old sales desk. Forever and a day it will always be Paolo's desk. Now it held the coffeepot, cream and sugar, stirrers, napkins with Matisse cutouts, and the brochures for the show. "Would you like some coffee? Have a seat?" I pulled the wooden chair around to the side of the table.

"I been sitting all the day." He rubbed the small of his back, stretching. "But coffee, now, that is a proper Norveejun ting to do."

His mention of the Proper Norwegian began his search for a new name for me. He began that day with Tyra, since it would go so well with Thorssen, or as he said it, *Torson.* "You have a sister?" he asked during his second cup of coffee.

"Melina."

"What? *Melina?*" He shook his head. "What was your mother tinking?"

I smiled. "You can ask her yourself. Here she is."

Una Helgeson walked into the gallery through my office,

wearing her pressed blue jeans and a red blouse with white edelweiss embroidered down the placket. After a near lifetime of
dressing in the neutrals some blonds prefer, Una had discovered
color in her clothing. Her gray hair was coarser now, not the
fine spun gold my father had loved. Soft wrinkles creased her
cheeks as she smiled.

"Mom, this is Glasius Dokken. Coffee?" I backed away as
they began to pour and talk, hesitant and overly polite at first
like true Scandinavians.

"Did you see the messages I left last night?" Wacker called
as I moved toward my office again. "On your desk by the
phone?" He followed me into the office I prefer to think of as
cozy.

"My mother cleaned my desk last night," I explained, running my hand over the top of the old railroad desk with
scratched-in names. "It smells good, but it sure makes things
hard to find."

Artie pointed at a suspicious pile of papers. The tiny room
was windowless, more closet than office. It was orderly, painted
a creamy buttermilk with bookshelves over the wooden desk
holding reference books and the Rolodex-from-Hellodex. Under
the shelves hung paintings. I rotated the pictures over my desk,
choosing works from the storeroom off the office; right now a
small oil painting by the deceased Ray Tantro hung next to one
by a contemporary Teton County artist, Fish Blixxen. Both were
winter scenes of the Teton Range, frigid, ethereal, and full of
violent purples, curdling blues, and dead white.

"Here they are." Artie handed me a stack of pink While You
Were Out slips. The top one was from Carl Mendez. He'd called
at seven-thirty last night and again just before closing. I was at
a Chamber meeting last night, then went to a late dinner with
Una and Hank before the memorable slide show. I fingered the
form and wondered if it was urgent.

"He didn't say," Artie said, trying not to smile at his mind
reading. "But he didn't sound like he had his jaw wired shut."

Carl Mendez, sometime boyfriend, had taken leave from the
police department in Missoula to take helicopter piloting classes.
He was in California, out in the Mojave Desert. I was glad I

didn't have to see it; learning to fly a helicopter can't be pretty. But I was happy he was doing something he wanted to do. He'd go back to the MPD after three months of classes and be an assistant pilot for the emergency units. At least, that was his plan.

I rubbed the knot on the bridge of my nose. Carl bugged me about it. I broke my nose last summer during unauthorized contact with a kayak paddle, and it looked it, a bend midway, a knotty bump on the bridge. My breathing had improved, but it was still less than perfect on one side. It gave me character.

"He didn't say what he wanted?"

Artie shook his head and pointed to the next form. "This guy did. He's the TV guy you sold that big vase to at Christmas. He wants another one just like it."

"Ah, the matching vase syndrome strikes again. Used to be matching lamps beside the sofa, now it's vases. He didn't mention peacock feathers, did he?"

Artie chuckled. "You want me to take care of it?"

I handed him the pink slip. "Deal." I glanced through the other messages. They were all business except for Carl. "In fact, take care of the rest of these, will you? Until Monday, I can't talk about anything but this wild and crazy Norsky thing." I closed my eyes, trying not to feel the tug of fatigue, and the anticipation of more of the same. "Tell me again why I agreed to this?"

Artie tapped his finger against his chin. "Let's see. I quote from memory, such as it is: 'I'm Norwegian, I'm in business, I'm a member of the Chamber of Commerce, and a loyal local. How can I say no?'"

"No mention of brain damage? Amnesia? Next time will you please get out the gag and rope? Better yet, send me to Tahiti this time of year."

I sighed and tried in vain to picture my tan-resistant body baking on a South Seas beach. It was hopeless. I could joke, but nothing could get me to leave Jackson this time of year. For one thing, the business was too important to me; I had no partner now to fill in, so I had to be here and get the job done. Thank

God for Artie Wacker and the part-timers who came and went; they kept me sane.

The other reason I'd never leave in January, despite record snowfall and cold temperatures, is that I love winter. Its purity, its simplicity, are things anyone who dislikes snow finds it hard to understand. But there it is. Snow is good; snow cleanses and renews. It reduces living to the basic necessities: food, warmth, shelter. Winter sets your priorities straight, gives you direction, and provides a framework for the day. Okay, some people don't like framing their day with block heaters and snow shovels and rock salt. Myself, I thrive on a change of seasons. It must be that Viking blood. I must have winter in my soul.

I dialed Carl's number at the helicopter school in the old military barracks in the desert. It rang ten times, and I hung up. He would be out trying to break his neck about now. I pulled on my pac boots, grabbed my coat from the hook, and went to get the mail.

Mostly bills, and the *Jackson Hole News,* which featured a half-page photograph of ski-jorring, a wacky combination of chariot racing and ski jumping. The skier was midair, his cowboy hat flying out behind him, headed for disaster. A postcard slipped out, and I picked it up off the boardwalk. The picture featured a golfer trying to play his ball, which was stuck into the side of a saguaro cactus. Arizona Hole-In-One, it said. I turned the postcard and read it quickly: *Dear X, How goes the far north? Thx for the sox but this is AZ, remember? Sox is 4 cold.* I blew Christmas again. He continued with news of his two-year-old son, Willie. He liked the trucks I sent. Well, that was good news. *Joanne is gone to Peru, don't know how long. For good, I hope. Willie is here with me. Life is good. E*

Erik had a rocky marriage, and it looked like it might be over. Una had been mortified by his unsolicited opinion of her at the family reunion as a freeze-dried pickle, and who wouldn't? It was such a colorful description, and true enough that no one in the family would soon forget it. I had forgotten what he called me, something about being as buxom as a carrot, and Melina, our sister, had only suffered his abuse of her stubby legs.

We forgave Erik, but Una never had. She swept all the bad

stuff out of her mind, out of her life. She had never seen her only grandson, and that must hurt. She just kept on keeping on, in true Norse fashion. I admired her for that. She had suffered a great deal when my father died, both emotionally and financially, and struggled to finish raising me, the only child left at home, working in the school cafeteria and then cooking for a caterer. When I looked at Una, I saw a survivor. But is the only way to survive with your good humor intact to pretend everything that doesn't agree with your worldview doesn't exist?

Good humor was something Erik knew about. On the edge of the postcard, in tiny lettering, he summed up his failing marriage: *Ole says, Any man can have a wife but only the Ice Man has his pick.*

THREE

I know a third: in the thick of battle,
If my need be great enough,
It will blunt the edges of enemy swords
Their weapons will make no wounds.

ON THE WAY BACK from the post office I stopped to admire the ice sculptures in the square. The sculptors had begun yesterday; the blocks were still little more than hunks of frozen water. The sky had cleared, now crystalline blue in the cold. The reflection of the sun off the snow was blinding; even with my Ray-Bans I had to stand on the boardwalks for a moment to let my eyes adjust.

I was ostensibly in charge of the ice-carving event but had delegated my authority to the chef of the Snow King resort, Dieter Moritz. Dieter was Swiss and had more experience in ice carving than all Wyomingites combined. I found him bundled up in a red knit cap and brown Carhartts, helping adjust the tilt on a six-foot-tall chunk of ice. Grunts and groans from the four men finally resulted in a slight alteration of its lean. When Dieter saw me and came over, his round face was flushed.

"Good day for ice." Dieter's breath made a cloud in front of him as he clapped his mittens together.

"I heard the weather forecast," I told him. "We're due for a thaw on Saturday."

"One more day, that's all we need. If we can make it to Sunday, it will be perfect." Dieter pointed to the other slabs of ice standing upright around the square as if waiting for the pagans. I had the odd sensation of my nose hairs freezing up, collecting ice crystals, and rubbed the broken protuberance gingerly.

"All are spoken for," Dieter said proudly. "Had to twist a

few arms. No one really wanted to be out here in zero weather for days on end.''

"Thanks, Dieter. Do you know what they're going to be carving?''

Dieter shook his head. "We never tell. That is the fun of ice carving. You must see the form develop out of the formless ice, like a mermaid emerging from the sea.''

"Hmmm, do you think anyone will be carving a mermaid?''

Dieter laughed. "Only if they put some clothes on her. She will freeze her little tetons off out here today.''

I smiled and shivered, feeling like a mermaid in January myself, despite being well clothed. Of the eight blocks of ice, seven were now occupied by carvers with picks and chisels and spray bottles. All around the sound of tapping clattered on the hard, cold air. It had the effect of being in an old shoemaker's shop.

"Where's that one?'' I nodded toward the unoccupied block of ice, sitting untouched.

"That's Merle's. He'll be here, he said he would.'' Dieter didn't sound too convinced. "Merle Tennepin. He cooks for the Rockefellers when they're in town.'' The Rockefellers once owned the Grand Tetons, just one of the small family holdings. When the park was formed, they kept the homestead inside its borders.

"Don't think I've met Merle.''

"You would remember. Only cowboy with Cordon Bleu diploma.''

"A real cowboy? Like from Wyoming?''

Dieter nodded. "He met Skippy or Muffy or whatever her name is in Paris, and they brought him back to cook. He should be here tonight.''

"I'll look for him.'' I picked my way across the trampled snow, dodging flying ice chips, across the street to the gallery. I should have wondered when I saw Una and Hank flanking Glasius Dokken, their heads together. I should have seen they were up to something. Instead I hung Erik's old down jacket on the hook, let my boots drip on the mat, and poured another cup of coffee to warm me. I settled into the mail, entering the checks received on a deposit slip, the bills received in the account book.

The gallery was warm and cozy, the murals were hung, the ice sculptures under way, I had lunch plans with Maggie. Nothing could spoil the sense of accomplishment I felt just then. I was on top of things. Neither my mother nor my demanding artist wanted anything from me.

I was so grateful I didn't pay attention.

MAGGIE BARLOW OWNED an insurance agency in Jackson, an independent outfit that did a booming business in the second- and third-home insurance racket. She was a hometown Jackson girl, played ice hockey with the guys, and was the current care-taker of my wild horse Valkyrie. When I slipped into the booth in the bar at the Cadillac Grille, she had a glass of wine waiting for me. She was that kind of friend.

"I thought I was going to have to drink that myself." Maggie smiled, putting aside the *News*. "Not that I wouldn't have sac-rificed myself for you, honey."

"Am I late?"

"You're always late. But we love you anyway." Maggie's black hair swung over her shoulder, dangling on her menu. "Now don't be mad, but some male types are joining us."

I frowned over my wine. "Maggie, you didn't."

"It's not like that. Not a setup or anything." She looked up and straightened, smiling. "Oh, shit, here they are."

I took one gulp of wine and turned to get a gander at them. From first glance it was obvious they were both athletes; their Lycra gave them away. There is very little more thrilling than a man in Lycra tights. Well, there is my mother's dumpling soup.

"Alix, you know Carter Reineking," Maggie said, rising half-way out of her seat, then thinking better of it.

We shook hands. Carter was the director of the cross-country ski area at Teton Village and served as the Nordic Nights chief ramrod. "We've been seeing too much of each other inside stuffy rooms," I said, smiling.

"Amen to that." Carter grinned through his brown beard. He was handsome in a hairy kind of way that Maggie apparently liked. She was salivating, checking out his Lycra. "This is Bjarne Hansen."

Tanned with a thatch of blond hair flopping over his forehead, Bjarne looked every inch the Olympic-class Nordic ski racer that he was, lean and strong. Best in Norway, Carter had told us at meetings for weeks. Now he was here to race and promote Nordic Nights.

We ordered lunch, Bjarne next to me, Carter next to Maggie. I smiled at my friend, hoping the points of my teeth were glimmering. As the food came, I realized Bjarne hadn't said a word; he was probably feeling as awkward as I was. Maggie and Carter were whispering. I wondered how long this had been going on.

Bjarne was eating an avocado sandwich with sprouts and a cup of minestrone. "How's the course?" I asked.

He almost spit out his soup. Swallowing, he nodded. "Very nice. Lots of good snow. And of course, we like it cold." He smiled at me, his blue eyes suddenly meeting mine. It gave me a jolt, and I quickly took a sip of wine.

"You speak very good English," I said.

"Norway is a small country. Most of us speak four or five languages." He shrugged. "It is necessary."

"Glasius Dokken—the artist—is over at my gallery. His English isn't nearly as good as yours!"

"Dokken. Yes, I've heard of him."

"He paints those big murals with the Norse gods on them, warriors and battle-axes and ships. You should come see them."

"My mother took me through his studio once when I was small," Bjarne said. "He is quite famous in Norway."

"Oh, you've seen the murals, then."

Bjarne shook his head. "It was long ago." There was something sad in the way he said it, as if both Norway and his youth were so very far away. Carter must have heard it too.

"Why don't you go over and meet this Dokken, Bjarne? We can take the afternoon off."

I touched Bjarne's arm; he tensed in the nylon windbreaker. "Yeah, that would be great. I'm sure Glasius would like meeting you too."

"Wait, wait." Maggie held up her hands, traffic cop. "I have a special treat for us after lunch. There's this mysterious woman who reads fortunes. I've got it all set up. She's over at Cosmic

Connie's." Carter gave her a look: Do I know you? "Oh, come on." She put her arm through his. "It'll be fun. Connie told me you encouraged her to bring somebody in for Nordic Nights. So she found this woman. She reads the runes."

Bjarne perked up. "The runes? Like Viking runes?"

"Yeah, you'll see. It's fun." I looked at my watch and opened my mouth. Maggie preempted me. "No excuses. You work too damn much. Call Artie and tell him you'll be an hour longer."

So I did.

COSMIC CONNIE'S real name was Doreen MacAllister, but like many people in Jackson, she had shed a skin along the way and reinvented herself. Now she wore her wavy hair past her waist, streaked with green and purple, and had a tiny moon-and-star tattoo on her left cheekbone. Her bead shop was lined with strings of exotic African and Czechoslovakian beads of every color imaginable, from globulous gold beads the size of golf balls to transparent seed beads the size of a pinhead. Red polka dots, flower child designs, blue, black, green, and orange. The back wall of the shop was decorated with a mural of the universe with flying saucers, shooting stars, comets, Saturn with rings, a tiny green Earth. There a table had been set up, covered with purple velvet. A small crowd stood around the table. We walked slowly to the back of the store, Maggie dragging us with invisible cords.

Connie came out of the group, wearing a drifty assortment of blue-green scarves, and hugged Maggie. As her insurance agent, Maggie was privy to much of Connie's personal history. Such as that she was supporting an ex and their sixteen-year-old daughter, who still lived in Kentucky, and that the reason she was now Cosmic Connie of Jackson Hole had to do with a role as an extra in a movie that led to a hot fling with a well-known actor. She appeared to be still playing a role.

She shook hands all around, giving Bjarne an extra-long handshake and a little arm squeeze. "Norwegian? You must know all about the runes, then."

Bjarne frowned a little, causing Connie to reach over and pinch his cheek. I thought he would jump at the touch, but he actually seemed to warm up a little. "Well, don't you?" she asked.

"Sure, the runes are all over Norway and Sweden," Bjarne said. "On old memorial stones and stave churches."

Maggie and Carter worked their way into the crowd, mostly women, who stood around the table. The voice of a woman behind the table was low and indistinct; I could see only the top of her head through the people. Behind her, though, a tall man stood out, a very dark African wearing a black tunic. He held a large wooden box with brass latches, like a flat trunk.

"Are we talking about the runes like letters?" I asked.

"The Viking alphabet," Connie said, acknowledging me briefly before snuggling closer to Bjarne. "Mistress Isa uses the old letters to find the messages to your future. Come, you must be next." She pulled him around the women, slipping her chiffon-encased arm through his. His blue eyes caught mine briefly, and then he was gone. I moved around to the other side of the group to watch.

Mistress Isa, the fortune-teller, was holding both hands of a young woman in the audience. The woman looked like a Texan—don't ask me why, but after a while in a tourist town you just start guessing. Half the time you're wrong, but it's more a feeling you get from people. This woman, wearing a jean jacket decorated with sparkly puff-paint dots, had a Texas-size sense of wonder on her face as the fortune-teller told her the end of the story.

"To pick this rune for your future position is a sign of great things, new beginnings in your life. A time of fertility—" The woman getting the reading couldn't have been twenty; her friend, with a nose ring, poked her and laughed. "A time of great power. Do not take this sign lightly," Isa counseled. "Finish projects you have begun, and begin anew. You have been closed in a bubble. Now the bubble has burst, and you are free. But take your flight in a full mind. Be centered and alert, and anything is possible."

"Wow. Cool." The Texan was grinning as she withdrew her hands from Isa's. "What do you call that one?" She pointed at the rune on the purple table cover, one of three small wooden squares inlaid with turquoise and silver.

Isa picked it up and laid it in her palm. "Inguz. The goddess of the vulva."

The girl with the nose ring guffawed; titters were heard throughout the crowd. Cosmic Connie pawed Bjarne's arm and whispered something in his ear.

"Anything is possible?" the Texan asked, her voice squeaky with anticipation. Isa closed her eyes and nodded. She was a very pale woman with platinum hair pulled straight back into a tight bun at her neck. Her colorless face was punctuated by eyes clearly enhanced with purple contact lenses. She wore a creamy white cloak, matching angora sweater, and slacks. Around her neck was a blue leather thong connected to a small leather bag, also sky blue.

"Wow," the Texan said again. "Thanks." She handed back the small rune and backed away, eager to begin her adventure.

"Find your center. A full mind possesses the will to succeed," Isa called in parting. A full mind probably wasn't in the cards for Miss Texas, but one could always hope.

"Mistress Isa?" Connie stepped up to the table, a death grip on Bjarne. His face was expressionless, tanned, and smooth. If anything, he looked tired; he must have come straight to lunch from a workout. "This is Bjarne Hansen. He would like a reading."

Isa had picked up the three runes on the table and turned to the tall black man beside her. He opened the box as if he were selling cigars, revealing many more wooden squares inside. The backs of them were inlaid in silver, the smoothed wooden corners more visible against the satin lining. The assistant moved his large hand over the pieces as if blessing them. When he moved his hand away, I realized he had been mixing them up. I perked up. This was just like Scrabble. Maybe Bjarne would get a triple word score.

The woman next to me, with beaded dreadlocks, had one finger raised in anticipation of being next. She wagged it a couple times, then sank back, rejected. To her friend she whispered, "At least he's cute. Maybe *I'm* in his future."

I pushed closer. A painted wooden sign across the front of the table read "Mistress Isa, White Queen of the Runes." Where had Connie found this woman? I glanced back at Maggie, who winked at me, grinning. She had her arm through Carter's and looked quite pleased with herself. Carter stood stoically in the athlete's at-ease position, wrists crossed in front of him. This was sure to be a test of the newborn relationship.

Bjarne was picking runes from the box and placing them one at a time on the velvet. Isa laid her hand on each of the three, straightening them into a line square with the front edge of the table. She had numerous silver rings on her fingers, some with gems, some with what looked like rune lettering, a pointy sort of crude alphabet that Vikings used to hack into stones when they wanted somebody to remember them. A step up from pictographs of the Bronze Age, with a little help from the Italian and Germanic tribesmen of premedieval days, they later evolved into Old English and Old Germanic lettering. I had read about runestones in the old country but had never had any contact with them. The first letter on the rune Isa turned over was a funny sort of jagged S.

"This rune is your past. Sowelu stands for the sun's energy, the wholeness that comes from a complete nature." Isa suddenly went rigid and closed her eyes. She lifted both hands up toward the ceiling. Her voice was formal, hypnotic: "You who are the source of all power, whose rays illuminate the world, illuminate also my heart, so that it too can do your work."

Bjarne had his eyes glued to her. She lowered her hands, opened her eyes, and looked at him. "In the past you have felt the need for wholeness but not felt whole. You have felt the need for power, for strength, but the power necessary to complete your goals was not there. You retreated from your goal because you were not whole. Is this not true?"

Bjarne squirmed, shifting his feet and swallowing. His jaw muscles clenched. He gave a curt nod.

"Then let's see where you are today." Isa turned over the center rune. It was the shape of a pointy *P*. She reached out and extracted one of his hands from Connie, stroking it with her other hand. "Thurisaz," she said in a throaty whisper. "The

sign of Thor, a sign of enormous power and energy." Isa looked
Bjarne straight in the eye from a distance of only a few feet.
"Thurisaz can be good energy or bad, good power or destructive. The old ones have written, 'In the thick of battle, if my
need be great enough.' Then Thurisaz will come to your aid. If
your need be great enough." She looked at the crowd, holding
them in the palm of her hand, sweeping her pale-painted nails
across the air. "Thurisaz is a call to your inmost soul. Can you
use the power? Will the power of this rune destroy you and all
you love? Or will you find a place for it in your dreams?"

Connie scratched her nails up and down Bjarne's arm excitedly. She smacked her lips and stared up at Bjarne's chin, stuck
out stubbornly. His eyes, however, held something akin to fear.
I wondered if his being Norwegian had made him more suscep-
tible to the charms of this witch. She was charismatic. Isa
dropped Bjarne's hand.

"Let us see how Thurisaz relates to your future, the final rune
of this casting." Isa turned over the last rune. It was shaped like
an *H*. She closed her eyes; her outstretched hand shook for a
moment, then she clenched it. She stood like this for what
seemed like a long time, as if getting signals from the runes.
The black man in the shadows behind her began to stir, looking
closely at her, his fingers squeezing the rune box. He licked his
lips and shifted his weight. It was the first time I had seen him
move during the reading, as if he was supposed to stay still and
unobtrusive. His apparent anxiety made me uncomfortable. What
had been just in fun suddenly seemed twitchy and strange, and
I wished it were over. I looked at my watch; I hadn't been here
that long, but I really wanted to go now. I looked at Maggie.
She had her lips close to Carter's ear and was whispering sweet
nothings, oblivious to the vibes I was feeling.

"Hagalaz," Isa said loudly, opening her eyes. "In your future
Hagalaz will protect you from bad weather. You have to use the
power of the previous rune outside, in the weather. This rune
will make sure the weather will be good." She scooped up the
three runes quickly and said to the assembled, "That is all for
today." She turned to the black man and deposited the runes in
the box. Pulling the white cloak tighter around her shoulders,

Isa pushed through the crowd toward the door. Connie stared after her, mystified.

"Um, Mistress Isa will be back at four o'clock," Connie announced to the disappointed women in the crowd. I cut across the departing group toward Connie and Bjarne in time to hear Connie talking to the black man.

"Is anything wrong, Peter? Mistress Isa left so quickly."

Peter kept his eyes down, gathering up the items left on the velvet cloth: a stick with letters carved in the side, a seashell, a section of a birch limb, an old coin. He put these in a leather pouch.

"No, nothing is wrong." His voice was very low, and he had a Caribbean accent.

"Where did she go?" Connie frowned out her front windows into the cold sunshine. The store had cleared out except for Bjarne, Maggie, Carter, and me.

"Sometimes the power of the wyrd becomes too strong for her and she must be alone," Peter said.

"Ah," Connie said, nodding. "I understand."

Bjarne looked whiplashed. As Connie went to look down the street for Isa, I touched his arm. "Are you okay?" I asked.

He nodded, focusing on my face as if snapping out of a revelation. "Oh, sure." We walked toward the door.

"Was that just me, or was that a little weird?"

"Weird?" He shook his head. "It was all in fun, right?" He smiled at me, a great smile. Maggie and Carter joined us, and we went into the street. I must just have a vivid imagination, I thought. It was fortune-telling, for heaven's sake. Nobody was bending spoons.

"So you're going over with Alix to meet that artist?" Carter asked, backing away as if it had been decided. What had Maggie been filling his head with? I gave her my best I-know-where-you're-going smirk, and she winked at me again. That woman. I was going to have to get full details of her afternoon delight. She and Carter walked backward down the boardwalk, out into the street, turning and laughing as they ran, hand in hand, in the direction of Maggie's apartment.

"Looks like you're stuck with me," Bjarne said, watching them go.

"And vice versa."

We walked slowly down the boardwalk, across the alley, looking in the windows of leather shops, T-shirt stores, and jewelry emporiums. I dragged Bjarne into the bookstore and searched the shelves for a paperback to read tonight so I wouldn't have to watch Hank's slides again. We were all to go to dinner at Luca's, but it would break up early enough for Hank to bring out the slide projector. He'd done it every night this week. I found a Marcia Muller mystery I hadn't read yet and paid the bearded proprietor. Tucking the book into the pocket of the down coat, I pointed Bjarne across the square, passing by the ice carvers hard at work making mermaids and undisclosed ice maidens. Dieter was up on a ladder at his own block; I waved at him, but he was concentrating on something that looked like a cornucopia full of grapes, of all things.

The afternoon warmed a little, with the sunshine and the hum of tourists. I pulled the slouch hat lower over my face to keep the sun off, pushing the Ray-Bans up my battered nose. Bjarne walked next to me until we got to the camera shop next to the gallery. I stopped him by the arm.

"If you have something else you'd rather be doing, now's the time to say it," I said, taking off the glasses now in the shadow of the overhang. "Please, tell me."

He had his hands deep in the pockets of his windbreaker. "Miss Thorssen, all I have been doing for the last two weeks is skiing. I can think of nothing I would rather be doing than strolling with you." He smiled, his blue eyes lit up. "We Norwegians have simple needs."

I laughed. "I heard once that Christ's last words to the Norwegians were 'Stay simple until I return.'"

His turn to laugh. "Yes, and we are very religious."

We stepped up to the door of the Second Sun. Inside I could see Glasius Dokken gesticulating wildly about his murals to a group of elderly tourists that included Una and Hank. Artie was behind the display case showing jewelry to two women. No chaos, no panic, nothing gone to hell in a handbasket just because I took a couple hours off for lunch and a fortune-telling interlude with the White Queen of the Runes.

"One last thing," I said. "You must call me Alix. Even though it is not a proper Norwegian name."

Bjarne looked at me with those damn eyes. "Are you a proper Norwegian girl?" he asked.

"Of course not. Simple but not proper."

"I doubt you are simple," he said, flashing that smile again, then putting one hand over mine on the door handle, the other on the small of my back. "I doubt that very much."

FOUR

Have thy eyes about thee when thou enterest
be wary alway
be watchful alway;
for one never knoweth when need will be
to meet hidden foe in the hall.

"DID THEY LOSE his luggage?"

At the back of the small crowd gathered around Glasius Dokken and now including Bjarne Hansen, my mother stared at Bjarne's bright blue Lycra tights, which showed every minute contour of two very muscled legs. He did look a little underdressed next to Glasius's baggy tweeds. I'd made the introductions. Glasius and Bjarne spoke a little Norwegian to each other, then Glasius launched into his lecture about the mural to a curious tourist adrift in turquoise.

"No, Mom, he came from a workout. He's a Nordic ski racer," I said. "Cross-country skiing. Stop staring. He and Glasius are getting along fine, aren't they?"

"Anyone could get along with Glasius," Una said. "He's such a dear. Did you have lunch, honey? I could go up and get you some dumpling soup. It's still on the range."

"We ate with Maggie. But thanks." I wondered how much time Maggie had for middle-of-the-day rendezvous. "Did you go out?"

"We ate the soup, of course," Una said, wandering away from Glasius's lecture to look out the plate-glass windows at the passersby. There weren't many in the middle of the afternoon. It would pick up again after skiing. "Glasius was looking at your mythology books. I hope you don't mind."

"No, of course not." I couldn't imagine that he would find anything he didn't already know in them. His mural of Odin hanging from the ash tree, the one he was now explaining in halting English, was the creation myth of the Viking people. In it the nine worlds are created, along with eighteen of the runes. I peered over the heads of the people and saw a gathering of small sticks under the bearded, inverted figure of the Allfather, Odin. Those must be the runes. Odin was nearly three feet long in the mural, with a spear piercing his side. Must have been a long nine days, hanging there, bleeding.

"You don't have anything original in Old Norse, do you?" Una asked. She was staring out the window still, her face away from me.

"Well, no, I don't think so. Does Glasius read Old Norse?"

Before she could answer, the artist let out a bellowing *"Tank you fer comin'"* and the lecture broke up. Hank came over to Una and quietly said something to her. I stepped up to Glasius. Bjarne stood by as if waiting to be useful.

"Coffee, anybody?" I asked. Both Glasius and Bjarne looked relieved at the suggestion, as if they were unable to come up with any conversation on their own. We poured and stirred, and we all felt better. Una and Hank put on their coats and took off for the heated garage, where the longboat awaited its final decorations. They asked Glasius to come along and look at it. I told them about the fortune-teller, thinking they might get a kick out of it if they ran out of things to do. After they left, I had time to sit down in the back and work on a brochure for my next show for a few minutes. I almost forgot about Bjarne; he and Artie were swapping jokes in the gallery.

"Miss Thorssen? Alix?" Bjarne rapped lightly on the doorframe. I turned in my seat, putting my finger on the spot in the copy that was giving me fits.

"Come in. I'm sorry, you're probably ready to go back, aren't you?"

Bjarne sank into the chair wedged into the corner of the cubbyhole space and rubbed his face with his hands. "I am pretty tired. I usually take a nap in the afternoon after my workout. But I didn't even ski this afternoon."

"I'll call Maggie and see when Carter's going back out to the Village." I dialed Maggie's home number and let it ring. I hung up and dialed her office. Her secretary Crystal put me through. "Back at work so soon?" I smiled at Bjarne, but he just looked bushed. I turned to admire the paintings on the wall under the shelves, my usual phone pastime. "We're looking for Carter. Is he there?"

"Carter? Carter who?" Maggie's tone was acidic.

"Oh, I see. What happened?"

"He called in to the center as soon as we got to my apartment. Jerk. There was an emergency. A guy from North Dakota lost control and whacked a tree."

"Is he okay?"

"Concussion. Broken arm. Carter had to go. I'm looking over his liability policy right now."

"I'm sorry, Maggie."

"Not as sorry as I am."

"Well, I'll get Bjarne back myself, then. And we'll have to have lunch again soon."

"Right." She ruffled some papers on her desk. "Will you be at the parade tomorrow?"

"Of course. We're watching from in front of the gallery. Come over and join us."

She agreed, now sounding more hurt than angry. She recovered enough to ask me how Bjarne was doing and did I like him. I assured her he was fine. She chuckled and hung up.

It was four-thirty. We were due at Luca's at six. It would take me the better part of an hour to run Bjarne out to Teton Village. At seven I had to have Glasius back at the gallery for the reception. Bjarne was sitting with his head resting on the wall, eyes closed. His hair flipped insolently over one eyebrow. I put my chin on my palm and just looked at him for a minute after hanging up the phone, until I realized what I was doing.

"Bjarne?" I whispered, standing next to him. "Why don't you go upstairs and lie down?"

He roused himself and straightened. "Um, okay. Upstairs?"

"Are you doing anything for dinner? Because we're invited out for a quick bite, then back here for Glasius's reception. Would you like to come with us?"

Bjarne stood up. He was only an inch taller than me, but then I was wearing my clogs. "Sure," he said sleepily.

I leaned my head out into the gallery. "Artie? I'll be right back." Artie waved, engaged in deep conversation with three coeds.

I took Bjarne's hand and led him up the back stairs to my apartment. I flipped on two floor lamps, illuminating the small space that functioned as a combination living room, dining room, and kitchen, with a counter separating the kitchen from the rest. The dark blue walls rose to a spangle of stars I had spent weeks stenciling just below the ceiling. The deep, dark blue was more than a bit morose to me now, but the thought of the time it took to paint the stars, and the time it would take to repaint the whole shebang, made me tolerant. I had once shared this apartment with Paolo, years before, and after he left it had seemed so spacious. Now, with my mother and Hank staying here, it felt intolerably cramped. The smell of dumpling soup filled the air, an old family odor with memories of the kitchen with the red chrome table, endless Monopoly games played on rainy days, chicken pox and measles, and Grandma Olava's bony, loving hands.

I dropped Bjarne's hand, but he squeezed mine quickly before he let go. "Do you want the sofa? Is that okay?"

"Anything." He sat down and pulled off his running shoes. When he stretched out, his feet went up over the arms.

"Well, that won't work. Come on." I motioned him to the bedroom. "Take the bed. I'll wake you in about an hour."

He didn't make any cracks about plumping the mattress for him or try to squeeze my hand again, I noticed as I went back downstairs. Was that really disappointment I was feeling? I shook it off and went back to work. The after-ski crowd streamed in, cackling and smelling fresh, their skin glowing. I poured coffee, sold earrings, passed out brochures about Glasius's murals, and talked up the Nordic Nights festival. Two good-looking guys from New Jersey told me that one of the ice carvings was quite interesting. The carver had rolled two huge snowballs up to the base of his cylindrical ice sculpture. The Jersey boys got quite a kick out of describing it to me. I promised to look into it. If the carving was what these boys thought it was, I was going to catch it from the Chamber of Commerce.

Just before I was going to wake Bjarne, the phone rang. It was Carl. "You're a hard one to catch." His voice was tense, almost angry.

"Hi yourself. I called you this morning, but you were out." I seemed to remember having this conversation last week, identical down to the semi-hostile breathy pauses. "You caught me now. How are you?"

"Okay. Good, really." He didn't sound convincing.

"Yeah? What'd you do today?"

"Flew the chopper. That's what we do every day. Fly the chopper. Eat, sleep, fly the chopper."

I frowned. "Well, that's why you're there." Why did he sound so angry? And the big question: Did I really want to know? "So, how's the weather?"

"Sunny. Same every day."

Okay. Well, that about shoots my conversational skills. I waited for him to say something else. Behind me Una and Hank came into the gallery, talking to Glasius. I needed to gather up the troops to get to the next venue. Carl wasn't saying anything, but I could hear him breathing into the phone. Finally I couldn't wait any longer.

"Is everything okay?"

"Why wouldn't it be?"

"I don't know. I just thought maybe you had something to tell me."

"Like what?"

"I don't know." I rubbed my nose, feeling the bumpy cartilage of the break, remembering those shiners without fondness. "Carl?"

"Yeah?"

"I gotta go. I'm sorry." He didn't want to hear about dinner parties and foreign guests and stepfathers and wine and cheese. It would just make him feel worse, more lonely, more isolated. So I wouldn't tell him.

"S'okay. Just wanted to make sure you were all right."

Had I told him that? No, he hadn't asked. But now the phone call was done. We said goodbye and hung up.

PAOLO'S SISTER LIVED in the clapboard bungalow in the shadow of Snow King Mountain, where he had lived until last summer. When he died, he left me the house and his share of the gallery, along with some executor jobs that I would have preferred not having. But he trusted me, and in his way, he loved me. A friendship, yes, even a love like Paolo's didn't come along often in life. I didn't expect it to ever come again.

But there was no way I could live in his bungalow, with its creamy siding, rose-colored door, lavish gardens in the back (now covered with snow)—there were too many memories here. So I sold it for a nominal amount to his sister. In exchange she gave me the old, listing garage in the back. I had been transforming the building into a studio over the last few months. Christmas had derailed the process, but so far I had painted it inside and out, installed a woodstove, bartered for and stacked a cord of wood, and bought art supplies. I had painted a couple pictures before Thanksgiving but hadn't had time since to get back. I was hoping to at least check the mousetraps tonight.

The small living room had changed since Paolo's tenure, but not much. The mauve leather sofa still dominated the room, but now plants and flowers were perched everywhere, in the small bay window, hanging from the wall, on stands and end tables. Luca missed the lushness of Costa Rica, where she and her mother had lived after exile from Argentina, so she did her best to re-create it here. I spied two orchids blooming in the jungle, long sprays of waxy bright flowers.

"Good evening, hello," she said, holding the door open for the group. Una and Hank filed in first, then Glasius Dokken, who hesitated at the door, dumbstruck by Luca in her pink silk tunic and slacks. I came in next, followed by Bjarne.

"Bjarne Hansen, Norwegian skier, Glasius Dokken, Norwegian painter," I said quickly. "Our hostess, Luca Segundo."

"Come in, come in, oh, it is so cold tonight," Luca trilled, sweeping us into the room and closing the rose-colored door. "But not if you are Norwegian, I suppose."

Glasius nodded, wide-eyed, apparently baffled by Luca's accent. Bjarne wandered into the kitchen, where my mother and Hank stood next to a large kettle of hot cider, ladling the steaming drink into cups. Luca took the painter's arm; she led him into the living room, where they sat down together on the leather sofa. Grateful someone had taken a fancy to old Glasius, I joined the others in the small kitchen. A forties gas stove dominated the space: the Big Mother, Paolo called it. Una scurried past me with two cups of cider, intent on delivery.

"How is the longboat coming?" I asked Hank over my teacup.

"Almost finished. Just a little more painting, a little gilding on the prow," Hank said.

"Will it have a sail?" asked Bjarne, his lips curling mischievously.

Hank frowned, pulling his eyebrows together. "It has a sail, a full, square one made from old parachute silk. But we'll have to wait until the night of the parade to see if I can unfurl it. If there's no wind, you know."

"It would be quite a sight against the flare of the torches, and the fireworks," I said.

"Torches?" Hank shook his head. "Oh, there's a fire hazard, then."

I laid my hand on Hank's arm to reassure him. "We can line up the parade so there aren't any torches near you. I can't wait to see it all finished. Is it big enough to ride in?"

Hank scoffed. "Ride in? No, no. The main body is only twelve feet long, the oars are like toothpicks. No, I'll be pulling it with the pickup."

"I am supposed to ride in the parade," Bjarne said, making a face.

"In a boat?" Hank asked.

"As King Harald." Bjarne struck a pose of the fierce warrior, one hand on an invisible battle-ax, the other over his heart. "Carter has some costume for me."

"One of those awesome horned helmets, I bet. I went to a Minnesota Vikings game when I was in college at St. Olaf's. They're quite attractive," I said.

"Minnesota Vikings?" Bjarne asked.

"Football team. Professional. Lots of crazy fans with those helmets on."

"Oh, football. ESPN," Bjarne said, nodding.

"No, no. NFL," Hank corrected. Bjarne frowned at him, sipping some cider.

"You mean Norwegians Fond of Lutefisk?" I asked.

Hank shot me a look that was worth every second of boring slide shows over the week. He put more cider in his cup and escaped into the other room. I leaned over a big gunmetal gray pot, lifting the lid to peek inside. The smell of black beans with cinnamon and chilies engulfed me, taking me suddenly back to the last meal I had with Paolo. He had made this dish too, from his mother's old family recipe. I shut the lid and blinked in the steam.

"Smells terrific." Bjarne stood beside me, ladling more cider into his cup. "Is everything all right? Did I say something?"

"No, no. I said something. My stepfather takes everything so seriously." I looked into the other room where Glasius sat next to Luca on the couch, regaling the group with stories of Norsemen of old. Una was laughing, covering her mouth. It was good to see her so happy; I often wondered about her and Hank, such a humorless fellow.

The conversation drifted to Bjarne's ski race. He had an easy day tomorrow, with the race coming up on Saturday. I promised to come out and cheer him on. It was an easy promise; I wanted to see him in action.

"Do you think Mistress Isa will be right about gathering your power, or whatever she said?"

Bjarne shrugged. "Sounds like dumbo-jumbo to me."

"Mumbo-jumbo," I said, laughing. "But dumbo isn't bad either. Where do you suppose she gets that stuff?"

"The runes are very powerful," Bjarne said seriously. "I didn't mean they were dumbo-jumbo. But interpreting them without knowing someone? That means she thinks she can read my mind, feel my, what do you call them? My vibes." He shook his head. "I don't know about that."

"What do you mean, the runes are powerful? I thought they were just an alphabet."

"They're more than an alphabet to some people." Bjarne rubbed at a chapped spot on his lower lip. "Have you heard of Wicca? The Anglo-Saxon magic?"

"Yeah, I guess."

"There are those who believe in the Norse gods just the same, who find magic in the runes as followers of the sky gods or the earth gods." He raised his eyebrows. "I have heard tales of great quarrels between the believers of the two. The Aesir and the Vanir. Earth and Sky."

"Wait a minute. You lost me."

"Pagans," Bjarne said, raising his eyebrows in mock horror. "Witches, covens. Not black magic, most of the time. But not your average churchgoer, either."

"You sound like you know some of these people."

"I have friends. Only a few in Norway, but many in Canada and the States."

"And you?" I asked. "Are you a pagan?"

Bjarne laughed and threw back that gorgeous hair. "No, no. Not me. My mother would disown me."

"I have a mother like that myself." I looked back into the other room. Luca was standing, motioning everyone to the table. "So is that fortune-teller one of those witches?"

"I don't know," Bjarne said. "I don't like people twisting minds, it isn't fair. It isn't good sports, to play with somebody like that. I just have to wonder about someone like Isa Mardoll, who thinks reading meanings into the runes can tell the future. It's foolishness."

"Mardoll—that's her name?"

Bjarne didn't answer. We sat around the table Luca had decorated with a large bouquet of gladiolus, their yellow-and-orange lushness a welcome tonic on a gray winter night. I forgot about witches and runes and enjoyed the special warmth of eating with people I loved, and liked. It was a feeling deep in my bones, in some primal place that harkened to the smorgasbord, the groaning board, the hunt board full of game and the spirit of survival for all the clan. We ate for the coming battle, the new harvest, the morrow, whatever it would bring.

Well, we ate quickly, for it was soon time to go back to the reception.

ARTIE WACKER HAD everything ready: wineglasses and wine on Paolo's desk, Brie and cheddar and jack cheese on another table brought out from the storeroom. I could tell he'd taken a minute to vacuum the rug, and I thanked him quickly before I forgot. He was such a conscientious employee, I couldn't believe my luck in hiring him, even if he stayed only a few months, like all the others.

The reception began with my introduction of Glasius Dokken and his short speech. The crowd was small, only twelve or fifteen people, most of them over sixty. I was mildly disappointed by the turnout but hoped more people would come in before the reception ended at nine.

"Dogsled races," Artie whispered to me at the cheese table. Somehow I had a big glob of Brie on a cracker aimed at my mouth. And in my own hand too.

"Pardon?" I lowered the Brie and eyed it.

"The dogsled races are going on right now," he said. "That's why the crowd's so wimpy."

I devoured the cheese and cracker, finding a space for it after the black beans and rice at Luca's. Dessert, I told myself, French dessert.

"When are the races done?" I asked.

"By eight. So there's hope."

Una and Hank listened attentively to Glasius's talk about the mural, which featured a Viking longboat and Leif Eriksson discovering America a thousand years ago. It was difficult to imagine the courage of these men, braving the storms of the North Atlantic to venture into unknown lands where they had no idea of the grave dangers that awaited them.

My stepfather had been talking about the Viking discovery of America almost nonstop for the last year. His slide show of two nights ago was about their trip to the Runestone Museum in Kensington, Minnesota, where a slab of rock was found a hundred years ago, engraved with a story of another Viking adventure to the New World. This time the Vikings supposedly got all the way to Minnesota, only to have half their group scalped by Indians.

It was an interesting tale, even amusing. The only problem with it was that it was dated about 1360, over a century after the end of the Viking era. The great voyages had ended by then, or so scholars thought. Hank had his own theories, like the possibility that there could have been explorers into the medieval ages after the Viking era. I knew better than to argue with him. Most of his "discussions" ended with a tirade against scholars who were too cynical for their own good. Hank was annoyingly loyal to anyone who thought the best about the early Scandinavians. And frankly dismissive to anyone who didn't agree with him.

Glasius moved on to the next mural, the Death of Balder. This fair-haired son of Odin was invincible until Loki tricked their blind brother into shooting a mistletoe arrow through Balder's heart. I had already heard Glasius's interpretation of this mural, so I decided to walk across the street to look at the ice sculptures for a minute. A cut-off barrel had a blazing fire lighting up the square, and spotlights shone on most of the ice carvings so the sculptors could see what they were doing. By now most of them had finished for the day, leaving their spotlights trailing orange and yellow extension cords. The spots shone on into the darkness, framed by the twinkle lights on the antler arches at each corner of the square.

I stepped out into the cold darkness—to get away from the Brie and crackers, I told myself. That wasn't exactly true. The gallery often got claustrophobic for me, as much as I loved it. Those four walls closed in, and I began to plot threatening notes to my accountant, who had spent so much time this fall teaching me to keep my own books. I missed being out in the field, or whatever you called it, driving the Saab Sister hither and yon, appraising stolen art for police departments, chasing forgers, hiking into the hills after strange cults. It all sounded wildly appealing just now, as inside the gallery a crusty, dandruff-laden art professor regaled the crowd with his tales of fifteen years mixing the paint to get the gray of Odin's hair just the right shade.

Picking my way over cords and snow piles, I found one carver still hard at work. The tall obelisk of ice he worked on had yet to reveal itself, unless you counted what those Jersey boys had imagined. Standing on two large rolled snowballs at its base, a man in a dark brown Australian duster and black cowboy hat worked at the ice, pounding it with a chisel and pick.

"You must be Merle Tennepin," I said, hoping not to startle him.

He turned briefly, his shaggy mustache covering his mouth and a good part of his chin. He nodded his affirmative and went back to work. I stepped closer, trying to get an idea what he might be carving. So far the block had smoothed-off upper corners, and that was about it.

"I'm Alix Thorssen. I'm the Chamber of Commerce person for this event. I have that gallery across the street." I waved toward the Second Sun. As I looked in that direction, I could see Bjarne standing on the front step, hands in his armpits, looking around desperately. I waved at him, and he started across the street.

"Congratulations, Miss Commerce," the cowboy/chef said, his back still toward me.

"Thorssen," I corrected. "I was just wondering what you'll be carving. I mean, if you don't mind revealing it."

Bjarne jumped a snow pile by the boardwalk and walked toward us. The cowboy never stopped his infernal chip-chip-chipping, even though his progress was invisible.

"I'll be carving ice just like everybody else."

"I know that," I said to myself, and to Bjarne as he walked up. Louder I said, "But what's it going to be?"

Merle turned and jumped down from his snowball. He stabbed the ice pick and chisel into the other ball of snow with a powerful thrust. Then, fingering his mustache and taking off thin leather gloves, he looked at me from under his black Stetson and said, "You, Miss Commerce, are on a need-to-know basis."

And stalked off into the night.

"Pleasant fellow." Bjarne stood next to me, watching Merle's back and shivering in his thin windbreaker. "And a helluva man."

I glanced quickly at Bjarne. He was staring up at Merle's sculpture, smirking with delight. It did bear an unmistakable resemblance—at this stage in its development—to a six-foot phallic symbol worthy of a state capitol building. I couldn't believe this was Merle's actual intention. No, it would develop into something else; he was only using the snowballs to stand on instead of carting in a ladder. The fact that they led the observer to a certain conclusion was a mere coincidence. They weren't balls, just snowballs, I told myself, cocking my head at the sculpture.

I stood frowning, hoping no one else got the drift. A group of tourists, laughing in high spirits, moved through the embryonic ice sculptures. Besides the skiers, I thought I saw the fortune-teller and her assistant; Mistress Isa in her white-on-white was hard to miss. They blended into the skiers, then the shadows.

Suddenly Bjarne started laughing. I reached over, pulled out the extension cord of the spotlight on Merle's phallus, and glared at Bjarne. He rolled his eyes helplessly, his dimples deep, and I had no choice but to laugh myself. I laughed until Bjarne pushed me into the snow to shut me up. Then I took him home.

WE WERE STILL laughing as I pulled the Saab Sister into the parking lot of the Tetonian Motel out on the commercial strip toward the turnoff to Teton Pass. The peeling, gray motel buildings stretched along a creek. The old car bumped into the potholes in the pavement, sending us bouncing. Bjarne was in Room 19, halfway down the string of identical doorways framed in dirty white with railings listing sadly by the rental cars. I pulled into an empty space as close to his room as I could find.

Bjarne paused, hand on the door handle, looking shy suddenly. "You will come out and see me race? Cheer me on?" he asked.

"Sure. What time?"

"Ten in the morning, while the ice is still fast—but not too hard—on the tracks."

"Ten. Got it," I said. The Saab chose that moment to die. "Damn!" I fiddled with the choke and turned the key again. The old engine refused to catch, protesting this cold weather. "I didn't mix the oil in the gas last time. That must be it."

"I know nothing about cars. You want to come in and call?"

Bjarne led the way to his room, unlocking the door and turning on the light. His bed was neatly made, and clothes hung in the closet, tidy and neat. He pointed out the phone, grabbed some clothes, and went into the bathroom. I called Artie, still at the gallery, and asked him to bring out the gas can and a small can of engine oil. The old Saab had a two-cycle engine, and I hadn't been taking proper care of it. Artie said the reception crowd was gone; Una and Hank had taken Glasius somewhere for a nightcap. He'd shoo out the last customers, lock up, then be right over.

When I looked up from the phone, sitting on the edge of a scratched plastic laminate desk in the dingy motel room, Bjarne stood in the doorway of the bathroom wearing a pair of loose flannel plaid pajama bottoms and a red sweatshirt. He had washed his face, I guessed, because it was reddened and he smelled like Dial soap. He stared at me, smiling, not saying a thing. I set down the phone and stood up.

"I'll wait in the car. Artie says he'll be over in a minute."

"Don't be silly. It's freezing out there."

"But you're ready for bed. I don't want to keep you up."

"Come, we'll watch some TV. Maybe those Vikings will be on." Bjarne sat on the edge of the bed and flicked the remote control. A rerun of *Cheers* appeared, much laughter.

The double bed was stiff, and the bedspread a worn floral quilt with its polyester threads coming loose. I eased down on it. "No," I said, "the Vikings lost in the playoffs. They're done for the season."

"Too bad." Bjarne stabbed the remote with his thumb, and the TV went black. He turned to me, causing me to blink. "What if I was to kiss you?" His voice was husky and soft.

"Oh. Well." I shrugged my shoulders. "I don't know."

"We could find out," he whispered. I didn't argue. He leaned toward me, pressed his lips against mine for a short while, and pulled back. "Well?"

"It was okay," I croaked. I touched his chin and pulled him back, this time longer.

"Better?" He pulled me close against him this time, the warm, clean smell of his skin, the laundered smell of his shirt, the masculine odor of desire rushing over me.

A car horn honked outside. I jumped out of Bjarne's grasp, standing, blinking in the yellow light of the cheap motel room. I swallowed and licked my swollen lips.

"That's—that's Artie."

Bjarne stood up and walked to the door with me. Just before I stepped out, he pushed my hair aside and kissed me on the neck. "I'll see you Saturday, then."

"Saturday," I repeated, touching his tanned cheek for an instant.

Artie had the hood open on the Saab and the gas and oil ready for my instructions. He looked up from unscrewing the oil cap, an elfin smile on his face.

"Keeping warm?" he asked.

AND THAT WAS WHY I didn't keep tabs on Una and Hank and Glasius that evening. I didn't know where they went, what they talked about, or how Glasius had managed to get himself killed. I didn't have the strength to interrogate my mother that night. It was four A.M. when we drove back to my apartment in the back of Roscoe Penn's Cadillac. I told Artie to sleep in and sent him home. It was too late to open the sofa. I collapsed on the bed next to my mother, a shadow of disapproval crossing her face before exhaustion erased it. Just before I drifted into a leaden sleep, I smelled Bjarne on the pillowcase. I should have been entertaining my resident artist, but I was fooling around with a skier instead. And what about Carl? I didn't even want to think about him just now.

As I drifted off to sleep, I comforted myself with the remembered sound of my brother's voice, his warm humor and strong sense that whatever happened, I could handle it. Bigger balls than Odin? Yeah, right.

FIVE

Runes wilt thou find,
and rightly read,
of wondrous weight,
of mighty magic,
which that dyed the dread god,
which that made the holy host
and were etched by Odin.

ROSCOE PENN CALLED at eight o'clock. Una and I sat at the round oak table, shell-shocked, with coffee. She startled, straightening. I set my hand on her shoulder as I rose to get the phone.

"Morning, Miss Thorssen." Roscoe Penn sounded awfully awake. But then he probably hadn't tossed and turned, his stomach in knots, visions of Glasius Dokken hanging upside down from an ash tree with a sword/ice pick in the ribs dancing in his head all night. That particular juxtaposition of Odin in the mural and poor Glasius would stay in my mind, Glasius in the face but fully clothed in his tweeds with a long gray beard and his own white hair trailing on the ground. The spear in his side trailing blood just like Odin's, his eyes open toward the ground where the rune staves were strewn.

"Good morning," I replied, clearing my throat. Una and I hadn't spoken yet, going about our morning rituals in silent shock.

"The hearing's been set for ten o'clock. If you and Mrs. Helgeson could come to my office about nine-thirty, we can walk over together."

I agreed, thinking that an hour and a half might be enough time to get both of us looking presentable. Una had bags under her eyes. Her hair was matted and uncombed. She wore my old yellow chenille robe, the one Carl had split down the back last summer. Her flannel nightgown peeked through the rip, its cheery roses only emphasizing our demoralized state.

I told Una the plan. She got up stiffly and went to the bathroom to get ready. I drank more coffee then took my turn under the shower, feeling more human. Downstairs in the gallery, I took a last look at Glasius's murals. They seemed silent and subdued this morning, their dark backgrounds fading into shadows, questions. Odin still hung suspended, getting the information about the nine worlds, the three norns, the eighteen runes. While many cultures venerated the four directions, the Vikings were fond of nines. Everything in nines.

The dream of Glasius hanging with a spear/ice pick in his side flashed in front of my mind, and I turned away from the paintings. I wrote out a note for Artie, for whenever he showed up to open the gallery. Crate the murals, it said. Rearrange and rehang whatever you can find. It wouldn't be easy for him to do by himself. But I didn't want to look at them anymore.

ROSCOE PENN, ESQ., held court in a low log building a block from the town hall, a building more suited to the Ponderosa of *Bonanza* fame than the legal profession. Inside, the well-oiled walls were hung with medicine shields and Indian blankets. The receptionist's desk was topped with a huge slab of red sandstone cut in a naturally uneven oblique circle. On this she tried to balance a computer monitor; a wadded-up tissue was wedged under one corner. She was a pretty girl with long blond hair that needed constant attention to keep out of her face.

"Mr. Penn is expecting you," she said, leaving the colorful padded chair to disappear into the back hallway. In a moment Roscoe Penn emerged. Una gasped slightly, coming out of her own haze to absorb the knee-high cowboy boots, pressed denims tucked into them, and fringed leather vest of our esteemed attorney.

"Ladies, ladies, come back and have a seat." He waved us through a carpeted hallway to a large corner office with a magnificent view of Snow King Mountain, the white runs and green fields of treetops crisscrossing its peak. We sank into buttery leather armchairs as Roscoe perched on a desk made from one huge slice of a tremendous tree that happened to grow not round but flat enough on one side to accommodate actual work. The side facing us, supported by trunk timbers, retained its thick, shaggy bark. If I had paid more attention to my biology teachers in high school, I could have identified it: Douglas fir, redwood, white pine? On the desk sat a lamp made from real arrows arranged in a tepee shape and topped with a painted hide shade. It cast a warm glow on the rings of the ancient tree, and on Roscoe Penn's silver bracelets.

"I need a little more information about last night, Mrs. Helgeson," Roscoe began, folding his arms. I frowned at him, experiencing a distinct chill from his warmth of last night. "What did you and Mr. Helgeson do last night? Give me a rundown."

Una sat forward, her hands tight in her lap. She wore the black slacks again with a white blouse and black jacket, almost funereal. Maybe she was mourning for Glasius, I thought, her friend of one day.

"We went to dinner at Luca's, then back to the gallery for the reception," she began.

"Luca Segundo," I said. "A friend of mine." Roscoe nodded, then concentrated on my mother, his dark eyes focused and serious. Without his cowboy hat, his steely hair was long and well-moussed, combed back off his elegant forehead.

"After the reception Hank and I wanted to take Glasius out for a drink. He seemed so wound up from the lectures and all. We were going to take him home after, since we couldn't find Alix."

I cringed inwardly, dropping my eyes.

"Where were you?" Roscoe asked. I looked up, surprised.

"I went outside to look at the ice sculptures, then I took Bjarne Hansen home. The ski racer. Back to his motel, I mean." What did he want to know my comings and goings for?

Roscoe nodded, satisfied. "Continue."

"We went to a little bar Alix told us about, kind of off the beaten path, isn't it, dear?" Mom smiled at me, indulgently.

"The Six Point. Over on Jefferson." I seemed to be the Just-the-Facts Ma'am.

Una continued. "Yes, the Six Point Saloon with all those dead animals staring at you. What did you call it?"

"Funky," I said.

Una pursed her lips. "We sat at a table. Hank and Glasius had a brandy, I had some hot cider. I had some wine at the reception, and that was quite enough liquor for one day for me." Her tone suggested that everyone should stop with one glass of wine because she did, a tone I was intimately familiar with.

"We were there about an hour, I guess, I'm not sure. Then we left, got into the pickup, and they dropped me off at the apartment. Then Hank took Glasius back to the Wort Hotel. I went to bed immediately, I was exhausted."

"And Mr. Helgeson?"

Una frowned. "I think he came soon after."

"You think? But you didn't see him come to bed?"

She cocked her head. "I'm pretty sure I did." Her voice was tiny now, unconvincing.

"And you, Miss Thorssen—"

"Call me Alix, Roscoe."

He recrossed his arms, amused by my informality. "All right, what time did you come home, Alix?"

"Eleven, quarter after, something like that." I had driven around a little, out to Wilson to whistle for Valkyrie and look at the stars and think about Bjarne's kisses. So sue me, Mr. Cowboy Lawyer, if you're going to get that out of me. I had a reputation as such a hardheaded pragmatist. I had heard it more than once from Gloria Worster, who headed up the Chamber of Commerce, as she exclaimed over my seeming coldness at the death of my partner. Little did she know. And little was I going to tell her. I let her think what she wanted, preferring to keep my emotions to myself, in true Norsky form. Erik would have been proud. I hoped I could reach him today, even with the Over-Eighty Tournament going down.

"And was Mr. Helgeson at home when you arrived?" Roscoe asked.

I shrugged, glancing at my mother. She was staring at her hands, strong but spotted with age. "I don't know," I said. "I didn't check."

"Did you see him come in?"

"No."

"What time did you go to bed, Mrs. Helgeson?"

She looked at me quickly, then back at her hands. "About ten-thirty."

Roscoe Penn rose from the edge of his massive desk and began pacing in huge, cowboy-boot steps, back and forth in front of the large window facing a snow-covered garden. A birdbath topped with ten inches of snow peeked out of a drift. The day was sunny and frigid, the sky a hard, cloudless blue, perfect for more dog races set for the afternoon at Teton Village, and more ice carving too. He stopped pacing abruptly, stuck two fingers in each of his jean pockets, and jutted out his jaw at the window.

"We'll do our best this morning," he said brusquely and looked at his watch. He pulled a leather-trimmed wool sports coat off a twiggy coat rack and slipped it on. "Time to roll."

I SLIPPED MY ARM through my mother's and back into my pocket, trying not to think about the sick feeling in my gut. Last night Roscoe Penn had been all bluster and confidence. Now he couldn't have been less reassuring if he had worn black and brought along a ball and chain. A look at Una was all I needed to see that she was not feeling bountiful hope. Her lips were tight in a line, her eyes squinting against the wind, her chapped chin thrust out in defense. I turned away so she couldn't see the worry in my eyes and tried to console myself by running through what I knew of Roscoe Penn's illustrious career.

He had successfully sued on behalf of an L.A. Lakers cheerleader with a legendary bustline who had been tossed into the air during a halftime routine. The male cheerleader who was designated as her receiver let her slip through his fingers to the hardwood floor. Her injuries weren't completely disabling, but Roscoe went for deep pockets. He sued the manufacturer of the hand lotion the receiver had put on before the game, alleging a warning should have been applied to the bottle: "Use caution when tossing cheerleaders. This product may cause butter fingers." Penn won $7 million in the lawsuit because the jury was distracted by the cheerleader's breast tissue.

Personal injury and product liability cases stuck in my mind, big decrees and much publicity. I could remember only one murder case Roscoe Penn had been involved in, a variation on the Twinkies defense. A runner had drunk gallons of red Kool-Aid before a marathon. During the race he became disoriented, then abusive toward several runners, hurling insults, paper cups, and the odd pebble as they passed him. He also spent quite a bit of time in the Porta Pottis. When the race was over and the athletes were standing around in silver space blankets, the runner went to his car, took out a .44, and singled out one of the runners who'd passed him with a single bullet to the back. Roscoe Penn argued that the red dye in the Kool-Aid had caused temporary insanity. The jury didn't buy it.

That was certainly reassuring to recall. Una started rummaging through her purse as we got to the door of the Teton County Justice Court. She seemed frantic suddenly.

"Did you forget your glasses?" I asked.

She looked up at me, stricken. "The Metamucil. He needs it."

I pulled her shoulders toward me and gave her a big hug, smothering her face in my nylon jacket. I knew the feeling: Hank wouldn't be getting out this morning.

IT WASN'T AS IF Roscoe Penn didn't try. He turned into a different beast in the courtroom, brash, effusive, charming, even coy with the judge. Judge Juliette Foss was blond and not quite forty, but she had plenty of experience with men like Roscoe Penn. She didn't smile as he brandished his way through the hearing, sweeping his long arm across the front of her bench like a caress. She wasn't impressed by the well-known Penn pyrotechnics, table pounding, hat waving, and foot stomping. When Hank Helgeson took the stand and couldn't explain his fingerprints in the hotel room of Miss Isa Mardoll, the judge frowned.

"It would be in your best interests, Mr. Helgeson, to explain to the court what you were doing in someone else's hotel room," Judge Foss said soberly. "Even if the information should appear embarrassing to you or your family."

Hank, looking pale and constipated, bit his lower lip, stared at the back of the brightly lit, modern courtroom, and refused to say. I grasped my mother's forearm and leaned toward her. "Why won't he tell her?" I whispered.

Una didn't answer, tears forming in her lower eyelids and spilling suddenly down her cheeks. She rummaged, found a hankie, and collected herself. I felt my throat closing; I couldn't ever remember her crying. She must love him an awful lot. I put my arm around her small shoulders.

"Mr. Penn, I suggest you have a small conference with your client and impress upon him the gravity of this charge," Judge Foss said.

Roscoe stepped up to the witness stand and spread his arms wide in front of Hank. We couldn't hear what he was saying, or see Hank's face. After a couple minutes, Roscoe stepped back and addressed the judge.

"My client has nothing more to say, Your Honor. He feels it is his constitutional privilege to remain silent. He does not have the burden of proof, the state does, Your Honor." Roscoe turned to the assistant district attorney, who sat smugly at his table, chin in his hand.

"Is your client citing the Fifth Amendment, Mr. Penn?" the judge asked.

"Not necessarily. Not at all, Your Honor. He—"

"If he's not citing the Fifth, and he refuses to answer, he is in contempt of court," Judge Foss said coldly. "Do I need to explain that to you, Mr. Helgeson?"

Hank was still, blinking his eyes once with no reply.

Judge Foss threw down her pen and looked at the DA. "Is that the extent of your evidence, Mr. Robbins?"

Robbins stood up suddenly. "Um, yes, Your Honor."

Hank's fingerprints at the scene and his opportunity—that is, not having an alibi—were the DA's evidence. It was more than weak. But that wasn't what Judge Foss was getting at.

"I'm going to give you more time, Mr. Robbins. We shouldn't have rushed into this hearing this morning. If I'd been thinking straight last night when you called, Mr. Penn, I wouldn't have agreed to it. But you, Mr. Helgeson," said the judge, turning to Hank, still in the witness stand, "need some time to think about the ramifications of your actions, both last night and this morning. I hold you in contempt of court until you can bring yourself to answer the questions put before you. I will reconvene this hearing on Monday morning at ten A.M." She slammed down her wooden hammer, an archaic leftover along with black robes. "This court is adjourned until that time."

ROSCOE PENN STAYED behind to knock some sense into Hank Helgeson. Mom didn't want to talk to him just then and needed to get the Metamucil. We were silent on the walk back to the log cabin legal center of Penn Enright Hacker, Attorneys at Law. The Saab Sister had been covered with a thick, hard frost in just the three hours it had sat on the street. I pulled out a scraper and began hacking away at it. Una looked at the log building and twisted her gloved hands. Finally I had enough frost off to see out the front and back. I just hoped the darn car started.

The seat was brittle with cold, slapping my thighs through the wool slacks I put on for my mother's sake. I shivered, turned the key, said a prayer. It wasn't necessary. Una straightened in her seat, her face set in the inscrutable way of Scandinavians, when you can't tell if they're about to burst into tears or laughter or venomous tirades. I squinted at her, checking the little tension lines around her mouth.

"Let's go, Alix. It's cold enough to freeze Hades in here."

At the gallery we trudged upstairs to the apartment. Una went directly to the bedroom and reappeared moments later in her jeans and a cotton shirt she had worn painting the longboat. It sparkled with dabs of gold paint. As I stood in the living room, still trying to hang up my coat and take off my boots, she went to the sink in the kitchen and started pulling out cleaning supplies. I knew better than to argue with her.

"I'll make a pot of coffee downstairs," I said, slipping on my clogs. "Come down in a bit and we can talk."

Una was busy attacking the sink by then, Comet and a sponge her weapons. She didn't turn.

I waited a minute, gathered up a clean cup and a tube of Chap Stick. "Mom? Did you hear me?"

She sighed, now rinsing the sponge and going for the cupboards, inside and out. "I heard you. I just don't think I want to talk right now."

"In a little while?"

"No, not in a little while either."

"Why not?"

She still wouldn't turn toward me. "I am so angry right now, Alix. I am too angry to talk."

"We can talk about anger."

She shook her head. "I can't."

"What happened last night, Mom? When did Hank come home?"

"You heard what I told Mr. Penn."

"Was that what happened?"

"I don't lie, for your information."

I moved to the end of the kitchen counter, where I could see at least a side view of her face. Talking to her back was getting nowhere. She wouldn't stop moving, wiping, setting aside dishes, wiping some more.

"So you went over to the Six Point and then came back home? That's it?"

Exasperated, Una threw the sponge in the sink. Still she wouldn't look at me, hanging her head between arms braced against the sink. "That's it. The only problem is, I didn't see him climb into bed. Is that a crime?"

"No, Mom, it's not a crime. It's a problem, though. For Hank."

She looked at the ceiling, no doubt contemplating wiping it with Lysol. Her voice was low. "I know."

"Are you going to go see him?"

"That depends."

"On what?"

"On how I feel."

Not wanting more details in that department, I left her to the Comet and Lysol. When a mother gets like this, there are limits to how much a daughter can help. A mother doesn't want to expose her frailties to her daughter, and a daughter really doesn't want to see them. We want our parents to be strong and take-charge and to know exactly what they're doing at all times. That was the way I thought about Una since Rollie died so many years ago. My father's death had been devastating. She deserved happiness with a man again. Maybe we didn't particularly like Hank. Maybe we thought Mom deserved somebody better. But she had made her choice, and at least earlier in the day I was sure she loved him.

In the gallery all was dark. Yesterday's sunshine had disappeared, leaving the blue-white scene of the town square out my front windows an eerie pale cloud punctuated by unformed icy blobs. It was almost noon, there were no customers, the gallery was shut, and the sun had gone into hiding. Oh, and my step-father was rotting away in a cell because he couldn't bring himself to speak up. That had never been *my* problem, at least when my ass was in a sling. Another day in paradise.

SIX

Men will quake with terror
Ere the seventy sea-oars
Gain their well-earned respite
From the labors of the ocean.
Norwegian arms are driving
This iron-studded dragon
Down the storm-tossed river,
Like an eagle with wings beating.
—King Harald's Saga

I CRADLED THE PHONE under my chin. "Any geezer hole-in-ones?"

Erik laughed. It was a welcome sound. "There's been a few hole-in-thirty-ones. Does that count?"

"Only in cribbage."

"How much coffee have you had, Alix?"

"I lost count. Is my voice getting squeaky?"

"No, but your synapses are charging. That's always a sure sign."

"I'm going to need all the synapses I can charge."

"What happened? Hank get out of the clink?"

"Hardly. Now he's in on contempt of court. He won't say why his fingerprints are all over the hotel room where the body was found."

"Has he told you?"

"Hell, no. I haven't even talked to him. Una won't say either. The hotel room belonged to a woman. Someone not exactly his type, whatever that means."

"You're saying you don't think Hank might have had a little thing on the side?"

"The Swedish meatball?"

"You're right. What happens now?"

"Another hearing on Monday. There wasn't really much evidence pointing to Hank. But he wouldn't defend himself at all. And there aren't any other suspects."

"Whose hotel room was it?"

"A woman named Isa Mardoll. She reads the runes, like a fortune-teller."

Erik snorted. "You get more flakes up there, Alix."

"It must be the altitude."

"So Hank went to get his fortune read? Was this woman in the room?"

"No, the cops showed up with Hank standing over Glasius."

"What—oh, Christ. I've got to go. An unarmed golf cart is heading for the lake. See ya, X."

I hung up the phone, set down my coffee cup, and opened up the gallery. The note I had left for Artie still sat on Paolo's desk. The murals still hung in the back, brooding, morose, and prophetic. One canvas drew me in as I waited for the first dawdling customers to seek refuge from the weather.

The mural was Glasius Dokken's interpretation of Asgard, the place of the gods. This wasn't the comic-book version, though. That one, in the *Mighty Thor* comics I had read for nearly twenty years, was my place of fantasy and escape when my father died.

Asgard in the mural was a cloudland where the golden gods lived and administered their blessings and curses. There was the Rainbow Bridge, a flaming stream of color called Bifrost. The bridge connects Asgard with Jotunheim, the place of the giants. On it stood Heimdall. In the comics he is the guardian of the bridge. He played the same role in Glasius's mural—strong, a son of Odin who created the different races of man—warrior, peasant, serf. Glasius had painted him sturdy and strong in a hide jerkin with a huge battle-ax at his side.

In the great hall Gladsheim were Odin, Freyr, Thor, and Freyja, goddess of fertility. Gold was everywhere in Asgard, from Thor's magic hammer to Freyja's tears to the bricks in the paved streets to horse bridles and chimney stacks. Everything was lovely in Glasius's Asgard, peaceful at first glance. Then outside the glow, beyond the stone wall, threats hovered. There was Loki, the Shapeshifter, who practiced deceit and devilment. There were the giants plotting revenge for some slight. And the dark elves, or were they dwarves? Hard to tell. Lots of them, though, blacksmithing and making magic.

What had Glasius written about this mural? I picked up the brochure and read his quote of a historian: "The great gifts of the gods were readiness to face the world as it was, the luck that sustains men in tight places, and the opportunity to win that glory, which alone can outlive death." The Vikings were keen on glory since they didn't believe in an afterlife per se. Fame and glory, and as much gold as one could plunder, were all that was left. It was a sorry fate, but the Vikings didn't despair. They filled their lives with adventure and courage and the great wonders of living.

Ready to the face the world as it was. Man, that was a hard thing to do. This morning, on my coffee buzz, the world seemed a pretty tough place to do business. The phone rang, bringing the world's business back to me.

It was Luca. "Oh, good heavens, what happened?"

"I wish I knew," I said, waving to three heavily made-up ski bunnies in million-dollar outfits. They stamped their feet on the rug to warm up, fannies jiggling in stretch pants. "And Hank. He's sitting in jail."

Luca made more upset noises; I spun more homilies. There isn't much to say when someone suddenly dies and you didn't really know them. We expressed our bewilderment and hung up. The phone immediately rang again.

"Miss Thorssen." The voice was deep and slightly accented. "My name is Harry Jorgensen. I am the Norwegian consul in Billings. I have been asked to look after Glasius Dokken's effects."

"Good," I said. "I've got his murals here, and I don't know what to do with them."

"We'll take care of it. It may take us a few days or even a week to gather together all the loose ends. I'm planning on coming down there next week."

"What shall I do with the murals?"

"For now? Leave them where they are. The gallery is secure?"

"Absolutely. Just put in a new alarm system."

"Good. The police chief tells me Mr. Dokken's personal effects are needed for a short time. For evidence, I suppose. So there is no point in getting the ball rolling too early. We can mail the paintings home soon enough."

"Mr. Jorgensen, do you know how big the paintings are? Glasius has—had—huge crates for them. I don't think they can be mailed."

"I see. How did they get to you?"

"With Glasius as excess baggage on his flight. I'm not sure I'd let them go home unescorted."

"Hmm. I'll think about that. Is there anything else I should know about? Other interests of Mr. Dokken's in Jackson?"

"I don't think so. He wasn't even here twenty-four hours." But he'll never really leave, I thought morosely, rubbing my nose bridge for what would surely be the first of many times today.

"I'm afraid this may cause quite a stink diplomatically. Glasius Dokken was considered a national treasure in Norway."

"So I gathered. I'm so sorry about all this."

"So am I. So are we all."

I had succumbed to rubbing my forehead now and staring at the desk, so that I didn't hear Una come into the gallery. She chatted with the ski bunnies until she saw me hang up the phone.

Mom looked a little haggard, but she had freshened her makeup to cover up the bags under her eyes. The hot pink lipstick was brazenly optimistic but matched the turtleneck sweater over her jeans. She fluffed her bangs. "I'm going over to the garage to check the longboat. I've decided to pull it in the parade tonight myself. I have to check the hitch and make sure I know how to work it."

I stood up. "Wait a minute. You're driving the pickup in the parade?"

"Hank wanted a little more gold around the inside of the prow," she continued quickly. "That'll only take a minute. Then I have to wipe down the sides once more. There was so much dust in that garage. You couldn't know about that when you rented it for us, Alix, but it did make for a lot of cleaning, then—"

"Time out!" I hollered. The ski bunnies stopped whispering about a set of green-glazed pottery and stared at me. I lowered my voice, moving closer to my mother. "What's for lunch?"

"Lunch?"

"Yeah, you know, food in the middle of the day." I knew nothing could stop her more easily than the mention of a needed meal. "I'm pretty hungry."

Una blinked at the still, white gloom outside, then at her watch. Her eyebrows drew close, then she shrugged. "The dumpling soup is in your refrigerator. Heat it up yourself. Don't wait for me, dear."

And with that she grabbed her navy wool pea coat and little white fur hat and was gone. The ski bunnies smiled big, perfect smiles at me, made a show of examining a print of a cowboy in sexy chaps, admiring his bulges, then loudly exclaimed about the time. As they left, Artie dragged in. His hair was frozen in spikes, his hiking boots untied.

"Sorry I'm so late," he muttered, hanging his head. He danced for a second in front of the desk, then bounded off to hang up his jacket.

"You're not late. I told you to sleep in."

He returned, rubbing his cheeks. "What's going on?"

"I need you to hold down the fort, Artie." I filled him in quickly about the state of Hank. "I've got some errands to run. I'll be back in about an hour."

SNOW BEGAN TO FALL as I walked the two blocks to the Wort Hotel. It began slowly but escalated to huge, thick flakes covering whatever wasn't already covered in no time flat. The ice carving in the town square went on unabated, the chipping creating a weird chorus flattened by the falling snow. I detoured through the square, unable to stop my fascination with the emerging forms. The first one I passed looked like Harvey the not-quite-invisible six-foot rabbit. That is, until you saw that between his big ears were a pair of pronghorns. The chef busy hacking away on the jackalope hailed from a famous steakhouse on the way to my favorite paddling spot on the Snake River. Well, last summer's favorite. Since the Big Kahuna whipped the paddle away from me and smashed my nose with it, my enthusiasm for kayaking has dimmed. I waved at the chef and gave him the thumbs-up.

I passed Dieter's cornucopia and what looked like a buxom lass jumping out of a cake, although the bottom of it was unfinished. Also a musher and dogs—in ice—and a couple of unidentifiable blobs that needed work. I was supposed to judge this group on Sunday; I hoped some of these guys got a move on.

And there, at the end, was Merle's phallus. It hadn't changed. Merle was nowhere to be seen. The two snowballs, each about two feet in diameter, still hugged the base. What was I going to do about Merle? I paused, contemplating the giant projectile, as the three ski bunnies, late of the Second Sun, trooped by. I tried to move to one side and blend in with the snowflakes, but they saw me. One of them squeaked and pointed out the phallus to her friends. High-pitched giggling ensued. I tried not to look over at them. They wandered off, still laughing. One touched me on the arm as she passed. I turned to her perfect skin and red lips and fluffy blond hair as she whispered: "This even beats that cowboy picture in your shop. God, I love this town."

Her friends burst into hysterics.

THE WORT HOTEL is an unpretentious brick square, about three stories high and stretching half a block on the back side of the Million Dollar Cowboy Bar and other squareside businesses. It doesn't have a fancy canopy or twinkle lights lining the drive, because there isn't any drive. If you're lucky, you find a spot to double-park and unload your bags, then proceed up the six or eight steps to a spacious, warm lobby. Since I had no idea what room Isa Mardoll was staying in, I dawdled a bit, looked into the restaurant, a classic red vinyl booth space with fancy glass partitions between patrons. I didn't see anyone I recognized, so I took the stairs to the second floor, looking for a sign of the police. It didn't take long.

Charlie Frye stood waving his hands in front of Tad Robbins,

the assistant DA at the hearing this morning. I stopped where
the hallways turned, backed up so they couldn't see me, and
tried to listen. I heard only snatches. Then the talking ended. I
peered around and saw Tad Robbins walking toward me, head
down, hands in pockets. I guessed he hadn't found anything new
at the crime scene. Charlie Frye turned back to the room, leaning
both potato-farming hands on the door frame. I passed Tad Robbins and came up behind Charlie noiselessly.

"Is Miss Mardoll in?"

Charlie Frye jumped out of his reverie. "Christ, girl.
Don't—" He began to make the usual noises, then remembered
he hated me. His face hung with disgust. He was a tall, thin
man with a steel gray buzz cut and jowls, political crony of our
esteemed mayor, who owned an Old West girlie saloon. The
mayor had somehow been reelected last fall. Charlie's eyebrows
pointed down his nose. "What do you want?"

"I'm looking for Isa Mardoll. Is she here?"

"What do you think? This is a crime scene, so scoot along."

"Do you know where she is?"

"No, I do not. Get out of here, Alix, before I throw you out."

"Mr. Frye. Is that a threat?"

He turned to face me, reddening. "No, sugar, that's a promise."

I took a step backward, content to goad him but not too san-
guine about violence on my person. "Gee, Charlie, you sure
know how to put the brute in brutality."

He clenched his jaw, then his fists, as I smiled and turned
down the corridor. As I passed the next door down the hall, I
saw a crack of light; then it closed softly before I could see
more. Room 219, I saw, filing it away.

I returned to the Second Sun through the heavy snow with a
white bag containing a takeout turkey-and-sprouts sandwich
from the Bunnery. The snow had changed the town, as it always
did, into a fairyland of white, clinging to pine needles and
fenceposts, to dog fur and windshields, to broken dreams and
lost chances. It covered everything ugly and old and used up
and made it new again. Snow had more power than God, I
thought in my irreligious moods. It made all the bad stuff at

least appear to be good again. A crystal blessing, a moment of purity that cleansed and healed. It didn't last long; soon it would be tracked up and dirty, like life. So I stopped for a second on the boardwalk and stuck out my tongue. I caught nine snow-flakes, licked my lips, and went inside.

As I shook my slouch hat over the mat and slipped off my boots, I saw Bjarne talking to Artie. The skier, wearing virtually the same outfit as yesterday but with black tights and a red jacket, was smiling at something Artie was telling him. They stood in front of Glasius's murals, moving to one side as a young couple maxed out in Gore-Tex edged by them. I picked up my boots, slipped out of the old down jacket, and padded into my office. Bjarne was there, in the doorway, when I turned around, fingering the wet ends of my hair.

"What are you doing here? Shouldn't you be training for the race tomorrow?" I asked.

"I heard about Glasius," Bjarne said, his voice soft. "It is terrible."

I sat down in my chair, all the airiness of new-fallen snow gone. "Yeah. And they think my stepfather did it."

Bjarne sat down on his heels in front of me, resting his hands on my knees. "But he didn't?"

"No, he didn't. He's a little excitable, but he's not a killer. Besides, they were friends."

"Well, don't worry. The United States is a fair country. The truth will come out."

I smiled at him, with his blond forelock dipping down to one eyebrow. His eyelashes were damp and clumped together. "Thanks for coming by."

He gave me a quick kiss, just a reminder of last night, patted my knees, and stood up. I had turned to offer him half the sandwich when the phone on my desk rang. Una was having trouble with the hitch on the pickup and wanted my help. I told her I'd be right over, as soon as I ate my sandwich. I turned back to Bjarne, who was leaning against the door frame and looking out at the snow through the plate glass.

"Turkey and sprouts?" I offered.

He shook his head. "I had a big lunch already. Thanks." He motioned toward the window. "Nice snow for the race."

"It's beautiful, isn't it? I love snow. It must be the Norwegian in me."

He smiled and walked around to the desk, perching his Lycra-clad fanny on it. "It's not really that Norwegians love snow. They understand it. They accept its good and its bad. They live with it. They know it the way a man knows the contours of his lover's body, knows what is enough and what is too much."

I stopped chewing for a second, staring at the painted snow in the painting over my desk, a warm flush rising to my cheeks. Finally I swallowed the bite of sandwich in my mouth and wrapped up the remains. "I—I have to go help my mother with the longboat. She's going to do the parade tonight. Unless I can talk her out of it."

"Mr. Helgeson is still in jail?"

I nodded. "I guess she feels like she needs to do it for him. He worked so hard on it." I stood up. "Do you want to go see it—or do you have to get back?"

"Lead the way."

HANK'S VIKING LONGBOAT was a living memorial to the genius and beauty of the ancient Norsemen. Authentic down to the iron rivets, or clinkers, that joined the overlapping wood sides, it curved to each pointed prow up from a keel plank that was shaped and coddled lovingly to provide a unique line. The prow arched in a graceful curve to a dragon's head etched in gold and black. The mast wasn't exactly authentic, because it was hinged near the bottom to drop flat onto the deck for transport. It was small, as Hank had said, only twelve feet long, whereas the famous Gokstad Ship (excavated from its burial mound in 1880, a thousand years after it sailed the North Sea) was sixty feet long. The oak hull of the Gokstad, lean and sleek, weighed seven tons and used sixteen pairs of spruce oars. Hank used spruce too, but had only six pairs of tiny oars.

Across the railings on the sides of Hank's boat were hung banners with the Swedish and Norwegian flags and several other colorful designs. The ship sat on a specially adapted boat trailer that cradled the sides with wood that matched the boat itself.

Bjarne stopped at the tall, heavy doors of the rented garage on Kelly Street near the hockey rink, and sighed. He gazed open-mouthed at the boat. "Is beautiful," he said quietly. He walked up and touched the finely sanded planks of lapped siding, then ran his hand along the railing that curved up to the prow. "A fine, fine ship. Fit for the high seas!"

"All we need is Leif Eriksson, but he's in the clink," I said.

Una poked her head around the business end of the trailer. "There you are. I'm having a devil of a time with this hitch." Bjarne and I stepped around the prow of the ship to inspect the problem. Una stood with dirty hands on her hips and a sheen of dampness on her nose. She blew at her bangs impatiently. "Look at me. I've gotten myself filthy already. Hank had this set so you just drove the pickup hitch under the trailer, released the wood block, and it would slide into place. I've helped him do it a hundred times."

Bjarne knelt next to the trailer joint. "This wood block?" A chunk of pine held up the trailer. Una said yes, then scurried off to wash her hands. Bjarne yanked on the latching mechanism of the trailer a few times.

"Is this the way it works?" he asked.

I gave the latch handle a few obligatory pulls. "I guess. My dad had a drift boat for fishing, but it's been too long since I worked one of these."

Bjarne stood up. "What happened to it?"

"Dad's boat? We sold it after he died. Nobody liked fishing like he did. I still fish sometimes, but not from a boat."

"I like to fish for salmon in the fjords," Bjarne said, mimicking a cast. "Big, big salmon."

"Every fish is big to a fisherman."

He laughed. "No, these are big salmon." He showed me a three-foot measurement, and I rolled my eyes.

"Did you figure it out?" Una said, dabbing her hands on her jeans as she walked back from the rest room.

"Is the latch broken?" I asked.

Una frowned. "I'm not very mechanical. That's Hank's thing."

I lay down under the trailer latch, peering into the gizmo that grabs the hitch ball on the truck, trying to see how it worked. "Wiggle it," I told Bjarne. I could see how it was supposed to move, but it wasn't. Una got me a screwdriver, which I jammed into the latch, trying to look creative in my blunderings. Bjarne wiggled the handle of the latch again. This time it moved past the previous blockage, making a scraping noise.

"That's it!" Una said, clapping her hands. "Then we just slip it over—"

"Wait!" Bjarne and I said at once. I lay at an angle, half under the hitch and half under the trailer itself, as the wood block gave way. The trailer groaned steel and shifted. I put my hands up to shield myself just as it clanged against the hitch and bounced off. Una gave a little screech as the weight of boat and trailer fell across my abdomen. My hands held it for a second, then collapsed. I felt the wind knocked out of me first, then two ribs took the shock.

"I've got it," Bjarne called out. "Don't move, Alix, I've got it!"

Too surprised to move, I was now concentrating on the intense and increasing pain in my ribs. I put my hands back under the square black metal of the trailer neck and pushed. It wasn't until later that I realized Bjarne had the whole thing off me by then, and all I did was give it an extra lift. With a clank and a clunk, he dropped the latch against the ball and pulled back the handle to lock it.

Una knelt beside me. "Oh, honey, are you okay? I'm so sorry." I grunted and nodded to her. "I don't know what happened. I must have kicked the block. It happened so fast, I— Are you sure you're okay? I'll take you to the emergency room."

I slid gingerly on the dusty cement floor, out from under the trailer. Una helped me sit up. I know I winced, because the pain stabbed me. "Does it hurt?" my mother asked. "Where?"

I grabbed the pickup bumper and hauled myself up. Bjarne

had stepped over the hitch and took my other arm. Between him, Una, and the bumper, I was standing.

"My ribs," I said. "It only hurts when I laugh." I tried to smile at them, but breathing also hurt. "I'm sure it's nothing."

"I broke a rib once skiing," Bjarne said. "Fell on a log in the trail. It hurt like hell for a few days."

"And then it only hurt like purgatory?" I croaked.

"What did they do for it, Bjarne?" Mom asked.

"Put the strip of cloth round and round." He demonstrated in the air. "Keep it still, secure, you know? And they told me to lie down and rest for a few days."

"Ace bandage," I said. "I have one at home."

"I'll take you back and get it wrapped up," Bjarne offered. "Unless, you, Mrs. Helgeson—?"

"I'd be glad to," Una said, her eyes shifting back to the boat and the pickup. "I just have to rig up the sail. It's ready to go. I just have to attach it to the mast. And I was going to stop over and see Hank and tell him about it." She peered into my face. "Will you be all right with Bjarne?"

"Sure, Mom. Finish up here. I'll be fine." I let loose a genuine smile now. Breathing had returned, more or less. "Really, it's not a big deal."

I headed for the door, relieved not to have my mother fussing over me like I was six years old again. Some people may get off on that, but it only makes me uncomfortable, embarrassed, and snappish. The last thing my mother needed today was to play nursemaid to a grouchy grown-up daughter.

Bjarne put his arm around my shoulders as we walked to the door. "Does it hurt too much?" he asked, his breath sweet with peppermints, his golden forelock grazing my ear as he bent to open the door.

Not that I had any ulterior motives for sending Una on her way. Not that I had anyone else in mind as nursemaid. Not at all. *Moi?*

We stepped into the new-fallen snow. "I guess I'll live."

By the time I stood in front of the tiny bathroom mirror and pulled up my sweater to get a look at my white midriff, I had decided that the ribs weren't broken. I had walked the stairs just

fine, taken a series of big breaths, and even gotten into and out
of the Saab without major pain. I was feeling a little silly about
having Bjarne dote on me. I rummaged around in the tiny
wooden cabinet, a former icebox, in my bathroom for the Ace
bandage. The flesh-colored cloth was covered with green fuzz.

I set the bandage on the sink and stretched to see in the mirror
the spot on my stomach where the trailer had hit. It was tender
to the touch, and turning bluish. A bruise, not cracked ribs. It
hadn't hit me hard enough, despite the weight of the trailer.
Catching it, however briefly, must have saved my ribs. I dropped
my sweater, fluffed my dishwater-blond hair, and peered closer
in the mirror.

The flickering fluorescent light made my eyes look bluer than
they were. Also my skin, which was in serious winter pale mode.
I rubbed my cheeks for a little color and bit my lower lip to
pink it up too. The bump on my nose hadn't gone away miracu-
lously, nor had the bend that sent the sharp tip of it off to the
left. My bangs were in my eyes, needing a trim. The earrings I
had put on last week, simple silver hoops, looked tarnished. I
rubbed them with a washcloth to shine them up, bared my teeth,
and decided they needed a brush.

Teeth clean, I picked up the Ace bandage and picked off lint.
The apartment was quiet outside the bathroom door. I wondered
if Bjarne was still there and realized that I was hoping he would
leave. I was wasting time in here, picking lint. Putting the bandage up to my nose, I suddenly smelled Paolo. He had worn
this bandage on his ankle for a few days last summer after he
twisted it. The green lint was from his socks. I could smell his
distinctive odor, a blend of musk and chili peppers and foot talc.
When I looked up in the mirror I began, inexplicably, to cry. I
hadn't cried for Paolo in months, but still his foot odor sent me
over the top! *Get a grip on yourself, Alix.* I wiped the tears.
Now my eyes were red and swollen.

"Bjarne?" I called through the door. "Are you still there?"

"Yes, I am here."

"I'm going to do this myself. You don't mind, do you?"

"Mind? No, but I can help." He was right outside the door.
"Let me in. I'll help you."

His voice was so close. I thought about his touch on my ribs, my neck, and shook my head. I leaned my forehead on the door and took a deep breath, testing the ribs again. "It's okay, Bjarne. Really. I know you have to go get ready for the race."

A pause. Then, soft: "Alix?"

"Hmm?"

"Are you trying to get rid of me?"

"No! It's—the bathroom. It's really dirty. I'm so embarrassed to let you see it." I glanced at the toilet, gleaming from Una's cleaning frenzy. Even the shower curtain had been scrubbed.

"Oh. The bathroom." I could hear his breathing. "Last night, Alix. I'm—it didn't mean anything."

It didn't? My eyebrows were crunching now. I cleared my throat and tried to mean it: "I know."

"You don't have to worry about me, Alix. I'm not the kind of guy who jumps women. You believe that?"

I rolled my eyes. Here I was, hiding in the bathroom like a weenie teenager. I turned my back to the door. "I believe you."

"Good, because I really like you. You know that?"

"Bjarne? Are you still going to play King Harald in the parade?"

"Unfortunately, yes."

"Then I'll see you tonight."

"Tonight, then," he said. His footsteps faded toward the door. It opened, closed. Down the stairs the footfalls dropped away. The bell on the front door tinkled. I held the Ace bandage to my cheek for a moment, then dropped it back in the old icebox. The bruise on my ribs was purple now, and swollen. I twisted at the waist a couple times; the pain was minimal. The ribs couldn't be broken. I patted some cold water on my eyes and went back to the gallery.

A half hour later the snow still fell thick and fast when I sent Artie out for food. Business in the gallery had been steady, if not fast; he had sold several prints. I stepped into the storage room after he left to look for some replacements. Picking out a woven hanging and two small pen-and-ink drawings, I pulled the string on the light as I closed the door behind me. Arranging the wall space of the gallery was one thing about the business I really liked. Much more fun than keeping the books. I got out a hammer and nails and the small can of touch-up paint for the walls.

I had the wall hanging almost up on the center of the side wall when Una returned. Silently she held up the corner of the weaving as I pounded in the last nail. Her face was gray and expressionless as I thanked her and stepped down off the chair.

"I saw Hank," she said. She didn't look at me or ask about my ribs. Her gray hair was damp from the snow, her fur hat peeking from her purse instead of on her head. Her pea coat's shoulders were still white.

"Did he say anything?"

Her jaw clenched. "Stubborn Swede."

I waited, turning the hammer over in my hands. The gallery was empty now, the lull before the après-ski crowd rolled in. Faintly the sound of chisels on ice pinged like a faraway, off-kilter clock. Una padded in stocking feet over to Paolo's desk and set down her purse. She turned to me suddenly. "He was there. Last night."

"In Isa Mardoll's room?"

Una nodded. "He won't tell it to the judge, he says. Because he didn't kill Glasius."

"If he didn't kill him, what difference does it make?"

She frowned. "There's something else, I don't know what."

"Like what?" I spun and gazed at the wall hanging, a woven mixture of mountains and clouds, not a monumental piece in my book, but salable. It hit me: "The reason he was there, you mean. Did he tell you?"

"I asked him. He said it was between him and Glasius. Now with Glasius gone, he's the only one to…" Her voice trailed off.

"To what? To keep the secret?"

She shrugged, nodded. "Stubborn, stupid Swede."

I put the hammer and jar of nails on the desk. "Mom, did you and Glasius and Hank go see Isa Mardoll yesterday afternoon?"

She looked me in the eye, then broke away, silent.

"What happened?"

"Nothing."

"Did you get your fortune read?"

"No. Nothing happened." She slipped out of her coat, hanging it on the back of the desk chair. "We went to that Cosmic place, like you said. We were there about ten or fifteen minutes, then we left."

"What did Glasius do while you were there?"

"He watched that Isa person. Hank did too. Maybe Glasius did talk to her. I thought she was silly, waving her hands around, such a pale, unattractive woman. I looked at beads. I bought one for you." Her face lit up for a moment as she remembered the gift. Her purse, however, was large and overloaded. She sighed in frustration looking for it.

"It's all right, Mom. Give it to me later."

"It's blue and white, with stars like your apartment. I got you a prism too, for your window. Now where—"

"Mom, please." I put my hand over hers, stopping the frantic search. "We'll look for it later."

She dropped her hands to her sides and shut her eyes. A second later they flew open. "How are your ribs? Did Bjarne wrap you up? Do they hurt?"

I waved my hands. "Don't worry about me. I'm fine." Artie opened the door, a small white sack in his hand. He shook like a bear, sending snow flying, and grinned at us.

Una continued: "I think you should see a doctor, Alix. An injury isn't something to fool around with. Just look at your nose, you—"

"Mom, please."

"What's the matter with you?" Artie said, getting into the act.

"Nothing, nothing's the matter," I said, a bit sharply.

"Whoa, sorry to be concerned, Miss Thorssen." Artie put his hands up in mock defense and backed away. "Anybody want a cookie?"

A welcome intruder, the floral delivery guy, stomped his boots outside on the wooden step. The bell chimed again, and in a moment I was holding a huge bouquet of yellow roses covered with plastic and dotted with snowflakes. The delivery guy, a college student like Artie, pulled off his cap and recited: "Yellow rose, remind me of my faraway love, the turn of his cheek, the sound of his laughter. Yellow rose, do not let me soon forget." He bowed grandly, snapped his cap back on. I could have sworn he clicked his heels together as he turned and exited.

Artie chuckled. "Drama major at Yale."

"First week on the job?" I asked, still smiling at the jaunty deliveryman now skipping across the street to his van.

"Second. I give him a month."

"They're beautiful, Alix," Una said, untwisting the tie that held the plastic. "Who are they from?"

I slipped off the plastic and wadded it in the trash. Una handed me the card, sitting on a little plastic holder among the perfect buds. The message was brief and to the point.

Miss you. Love, Carl.

SEVEN

From the grand old Viking centuries
Up-Helly-Aa has come
Then light the torch and from the march,
And sound the rolling drum;
And wake the mighty memories of heroes that are dumb;
The waves are rolling on.
—Shetland festival song

THE PARADE was set to begin at six. The ice sculptures, some finished, some half done, were lit dramatically against the black sky. High clouds from the snowstorm were easing off into the stratosphere but covered the stars. The snow stopped about five, making the day's accumulation about six inches. I spent a few minutes shoveling the steps and sweeping the windblown snow off the covered boardwalk in front of the store, and set up four old lawn chairs for Maggie, Artie, Luca, and me.

The shopping crowds swelled about an hour before the parade as tourists jockeyed for the best viewing spots and dawdled over trinkets. I was helping Artie ring up some jewelry when Maggie showed up. She gave me a big hug and slipped off her fur mittens.

"I hope you have some quilts we can toss over us. It's damn cold out there tonight," she said. Her cheeks were rosy, highlighting her shiny black hair.

"I made some coffee," I said, pointing over to the pot. "Warm yourself, girl."

Maggie didn't take off her long blanket coat as she poured herself coffee. I finished gift-wrapping a small earring box and handed it over to a sweet lady from Indiana. I checked the time and told Artie I had to run upstairs and change. I motioned Maggie to come up with me.

The apartment was quiet. I took a deep breath, enjoying its sanctuary, until the thought that Hank's incarceration was the main reason for the peace. Una, brave survivor, had bundled up in his heavy wool coat and two sweaters to pull the Viking ship in the parade. I tried to talk her into letting me or Artie go along, but the most I got was her allowing Artie to help guide her out of the garage. That took all of ten minutes, he said, and he was back at the shop selling his personal charm within a half hour. I hoped everything was going well at the lineup site in the big parking lot by the Chamber of Commerce building. Una was stubborn and independent, but I could hardly fault her for it, since I'd been known to be described that way myself. Arguing with her about needing help was a serious insult that only reminded her of her age.

"Need something to eat? Help yourself," I told Maggie, disappearing into the bedroom to pull on my woolies. I yanked off my jeans, pulled up the long johns, added a turtleneck and the big red sweater, found a pair of wool socks without holes, one gray, one red, and put the jeans back on. Maggie was cutting up the leftover cheese from Glasius's reception when I came out.

"So are the flowers from Bjarne?" she asked. "'Cause if they are, I've got to have a little talk with Carter about not taking me for granted. You know, I am still pissed about yesterday, and I never stay pissed." She shoved a cracker and cheese in her mouth and munched.

"Not Bjarne. They were from Carl," I said.

She raked her eyebrows and said something that sounded like "Oh?"

"He's not very happy at the helicopter school. He's always so grumpy when he calls. I guess he kind of realized it."

Maggie swallowed. "Not happy why?"

"I don't know. Maybe he doesn't like it."

"Or maybe he just misses his little honey bunny."

I smiled. "Maybe." I grabbed a stocking cap and my warmest mittens. "Ready?"

"Quilts," Maggie reminded.

I grabbed two army blankets and a ratty old quilt that had

been Grandma Olava's off the shelf in the closet. I handed the blankets to Maggie. As we opened the door to go downstairs, we saw Luca, halfway up.

"Come on, come on! It's starting." She waved us down as she turned. We clattered down the old wooden staircase, through the gallery, and out onto the boardwalk. Luca and I pulled our chairs close together and shared Olava's quilt. Maggie dropped a blanket on the extra chair for Artie and bundled up under the other. In the street, on the other side of the square, a torchlight procession led off the parade. The torches were held high by student athletes like Olympic flames. I recognized a couple of stars on the high school ski team who'd had pictures in the paper, a fellow who played on the farm league hockey team, and the Chamber of Commerce director, of whom I wasn't particularly fond. Maggie nudged me as they rounded the corner and she spotted the director.

"Look at that outfit. Doesn't she have any shame?"

Gloria Worster—rhymes with "booster"—was wearing the biggest, furriest après-ski boots this side of Aspen. Each one looked like a small English sheepdog. Above skintight black pants she wore a gold-sequined black jacket with red, glittery fringe down the arms and a big furry white hat, like Una's, only real fur and much more of it, almost a drum major's hat. She swaggered down the street, swinging her rear end with abandon.

Maggie stifled a laugh. "Where's her baton?"

Luca leaned over me, toward Maggie. "Is she one of those twirler girls?"

Maggie laughed again, unable to speak.

"In her own mind," I told Luca.

Artie stepped out of the gallery, turning to lock up, then scooting his chair closer as he sat down. "Cheez, it's freezing. Whose idea was this, anyway?"

"There she is," I told him, nodding to Gloria. "In all her glory."

"Look, here comes Bjarne," Maggie whispered. On a float pulled by a black pickup truck with four back tires, Bjarne stood on a flatbed decorated to look like—well, that was difficult to tell. It was all white; maybe it was just supposed to be Norway in the winter. He was wearing a huge fur coat, hide boots with long, crisscross laces, a fake metal breastplate that had the unmistakable sheen of aluminum foil to it, and a big metal helmet with horns. The outfit looked so bulky, it was a wonder he could reach into a bucket at his feet and pick up gold-wrapped chocolate coins to throw out. Children young and old raced to pick them up from the street. As the float moved right in front of the gallery, he looked up and gave an overhand throw directly toward us. The coins clattered against the boardwalk, and one landed right in Luca's lap.

"Nice aim," I said, standing to pick up two coins near my feet. I smiled, straightening up, and lifted the coins. Bjarne hollered, "Salut!" and blew me a kiss. I wiggled the coins and sat down under the quilt again.

"Ooh, he is cute, Alix," Luca teased. "Especially with horns."

"I know *I'm* partial to horny guys," Maggie said, smirking.

"You're partial to anything in pants," I reminded her.

"Actually I like them out of their pants," she said.

Luca had her hand over her mouth, shaking with giggles. The cold did that to you, made you have to laugh or cry to keep warm. Laughing was definitely better. The next participant in the parade was a herd of four tame reindeer on halters, pulled by their owner, a renegade rancher who looked nothing like Santa Claus.

Artie leaned forward. "That guy Bjarne doesn't wear pants anyway. All he wears is Lycra."

"Yeah, and he's not politically correct with all that fur on. Somebody's going to squirt ketchup on him," I said.

"But he has horns," Luca said, her voice veering upward. "Big horns."

I nodded to myself. He did seem to have big horns, if the way he kept showing up and offering to kiss away my troubles was any indication. I felt particularly cozy, under Olava's quilt, with two guys chasing my skinny little Norwegian ass. What could be better?

"Quit looking so self-satisfied," Maggie said. "Go get that

thermos of coffee. Make yourself useful. It looks like high school heaven for a while.''

The marching band was next, so I went inside to pour coffee into the thermos and find four mugs. I had to go upstairs and rinse out a couple we'd used for breakfast, so by the time I got back down, the last of the high school teams was just rounding the corner of the square and filing past with their banners proclaiming them the Wyoming State Forensics Champions for 1999.

''Where's your mother in the lineup?'' Maggie asked as I poured coffee into her mug around her rabbit fur mittens.

''Toward the end, she said. But the parade isn't all that big. It was a little hard to rouse enthusiasm to march around on a cold, dark January night at six thousand feet elevation in the Rockies.''

''There's a nice crowd, though,'' Luca remarked. ''Lots of customers.''

''That's the point,'' Maggie said. ''Of most everything in this town.''

''You sound so cynical, Maggie,'' Luca said. ''I just love it here. It is so beautiful, so clean. What would the town do without customers?''

''Good question,'' I said. ''You wouldn't be a tad cynical, would you, Maggie?''

''Luca, you have to understand I grew up in this town when it was a sleepy little western stage stop on the way to Yellowstone Park. Not an annex of an Aspen T-shirt shop.'' Maggie flopped backward in her chair. ''Oh, don't mind me. I think it's PMS.''

''Hey, the Clydesdales,'' Artie said. The Bud wagon went by, pulled by the shaggy-footed hulks. In the summer they were known to give away beer at the Fourth of July parade, but on this night a lone driver bundled in a long duster switched the big horses into action. The steam rose off their backs into the streetlights. Another group of torchbearers walked by next, looking bored and stepping around road apples of magnificent girth. Behind them two students, one with a wheelbarrow and one with a shovel, took care of the mess.

"Is that the boat?" Luca said, pointing to the far corner of the square. Hank's pickup was rounding the square, coming toward us now. The longboat's sail was unfurled, an ethereal white silk square, billowing and rippling in the light breeze.

I stood up to get a better view. "Wow. It's beautiful, isn't it?"

Maggie took my arm. "I'll say," she whispered. "Your mom is something else, doing this today of all days. My mom would probably be home in the fetal position."

I glanced at Maggie and smiled. "She is something, isn't she?"

The Viking ship's slender oars wiggled as Una crept around the corner by the Second Sun to move down the street in front of us. I saw her checking the mirrors, going so slowly, creeping along, so that the majestic sail didn't pull too hard on the mast and booms. Luca and Artie stood up to the railing with us, all awestruck by the eerie beauty of the longboat. By itself the wooden boat was a fine model, precise, to scale, and crafted with loving care. But with the sail it became a true ship, ready to sail the clouds to another time, another place.

The spirit of the Vikings moved past us, the gold prow glistening in the streetlights, the dragon head fierce. Luca pulled out her camera and took a picture. I watched it creep away, savoring the sight of the creamy sail and cataloging details to tell Hank of its beauty. I didn't see the next parade entry until Artie shouted: "Cancer sticks! Cancer sticks! Smoking kills!"

The man dressed as the Marlboro Man and his swinging cowgirl helper, who pulled a red wagon painted with the Marlboro logo and full of packs of cigarettes, looked up briefly and smiled. He had the look of a male model, handsome in a jawey way with dull eyes. He wore the chaps, hat, red shirt, and cowboy boots of the classic costume as he passed out packs of cigarettes, pausing only to shake his head benignly to little children.

"Don't get hooked! Cancer sticks will kill you!" Artie continued his tirade, cupping his mouth.

"That's right, Artie," Maggie said. She turned toward the Marlboro Man and shouted, "What happened to the last Marlboro guy? Lung cancer?!"

A couple of young men with packs of cigarettes in hand

turned and waved them at us gaily. Free stuff is free stuff, even if it kills you. "You sap," Artie called.

"They're bigger than you, Artie," I reminded him. I heard him jingling the keys to the gallery in his hand just before I heard the commotion down the street. A glance told me the news was not good. I dropped Grandma's quilt to the chair.

"Shit. The boat's on fire!" I ran down the steps, pushed aside tourists, and made for the Marlboro Man, where the running room was better, upsetting the wagon of cigarettes quite by accident.

Ahead the flames licked up the sail, rising higher in the night sky. The pickup was still moving the trailer forward.

"Stop, Mom, stop!" I called as I reached the boat. The wooden boom across the bottom of the sail was engulfed now, with flames moving all across the parachute silk.

Una stopped the truck, threw open the driver's-side door.

I grabbed her arm. "How do I get the sail down? Where's the rope?"

"On the other side." She scuttled around the stern of the longboat with me at her heels. "There."

She pointed to a loose lanyard running up the side of the sail just as the fire licked upward along it. "Oh, no." She covered her mouth.

Quickly I scooped some snow into my heavy wool mittens, soaking them to the skin. Waiting for the fire to die down wasn't going to help. I grabbed the rope, hearing the hiss of the wet snow against the flames, pulled the locking pulley out of position, and dropped the sail to the boat in a thundering heap. Instead of dousing the fire, the wind created by the lowering of the sail fanned the flames. Orange fingers of fire rose from the billowing silk close to the deck of the boat.

"We've got to get the sail off!" I threw a leg over the gunwales and felt my mother give me a last heave-ho into the boat. Later I would wonder how I thought I could just vault into a boat that stood six feet off the ground, but somehow, in the heat of the moment, it happened.

The deck was small, cramped with the handles of the oars, so I broke many of them trying to reach the mast. I stared at the boom, trying to figure out how to detach it from the mast, while the heat of the fire rose around me.

"There's a latch behind the sail," Una called, peering over the gunwales. "Do you see it? Push it upward, the boom will roll out toward you."

A bucket of snow came flying over the boat and landed near my feet, making sizzling noises but doing nothing to put out the fire. I patted more snow in my mittens. I didn't want to even look at my hands right now. I batted at the flames near the mast, pushing down the burning sail. Another bucket of snow flew in. Artie's voice came with it. "I'm coming in, Alix!"

"No, Artie, don't! Take care of Una." I picked up more snow. My eyebrows felt very hot. I blinked hard, squinting to see the latch. I hit the sail again, putting out a small flame. There was the latch. I rammed it with my palm. Nothing happened. I hit it again, harder. The boom crashed against the wooden gunwales.

"This way, Alix! Push it toward us," Artie hollered. I saw him and Una, helped by Maggie and some strangers, getting ready to receive the mast from me. As I looked over, the boom began to roll. Toward me, just as Una said. The flames continued to burn the big sail on both sides of me. The mast looked charred but intact. As the boom picked up speed, I sat down hard on the deck, splintering oars as I fell.

"Get down, Alix!"

I leaned back as the boom rolled over me, protecting my face with my wet mittens. Yelling from the street, indistinct, came over the gunwales as the heat went through my knit cap to my scalp. I peeked through my mittens; the boom and sail had stopped over me. I used my feet to scoot down toward the mast and twisted around to stand up.

"Tip up the far end!" somebody hollered. Two men, strangers to me, lifted one end of the boom. On the other side, Artie grabbed the end and hung on it. Maggie and Una pulled. As the boom rose higher and the two strangers let it go, I moved under it, found a spot untouched by flame, and pushed it up over the side.

The boom stood for a moment on its end, charred sail flapping around it, flames finding new fabric. "Watch out—it's going to fall!" I yelled to the small crowd who had formed to watch the drama. Slowly, gracefully, the boom tipped toward the prow of the ship, missed the pickup, and landed in the snowy street with a thud. Artie and Maggie began immediately to throw snow on the remaining flames and stamp them out. I swung my legs over the gunwales and jumped down, feeling a catch in my rib cage that made me suck air.

Una stared at the soggy, stinking mess, stunned. She had bits of black on her coat and hat, a dark smudge across one cheek. I looked back at the longboat. The mast was blackened, the gunwales dented and charred, most of the oars broken. Yet it hadn't burned. We had saved it. The sail could be replaced, I hoped. I turned and gave my mother a hug.

"What'll I tell Hank?" she whispered, rubbing her hands together. "He won't believe it—he'll think—"

"It wasn't your fault, Mom. The boat was so beautiful. It was magnificent." It seemed almost a sacrilege to say this now that it was ruined. But it had been magnificent.

Una took her eyes off the boat and looked me in the eye. "It was, wasn't it?"

"Absolutely."

"Ma'am?" The voice with a Texas drawl came up behind us. I turned, not sure if I was the ma'am in question or Mom was. A young man stood there, eyes wild from the excitement, in a homey cap and oversize dull brown snowboarder jacket. "Ma'am, I didn't get a look at him or anything, but if you need me when you talk to the cops and all, well, I'll do what I can."

I looked at Una and back at the snowboarder. He sported a scraggly goatee, mostly blond, and matching hair that stuck out the bottom of his cap. "A look at who?"

"The guy who threw the torch," he said, jumping from one lug boot to another. "He must have been behind me, because suddenly as you were chugging by, this torch came sailing over my head! I saw it in the air, you know? Like a frigging comet or something, you know? Zoom, over my head! Just like that." He demonstrated with hand movements.

"And it hit the sail?"

"Oh, yeah. Just the corner, you know? But it was enough to light the cloth up. Whoosh, just like that!"

I looked at the shadowy faces staring at us in the street. Artie and Maggie had stopped their stamping on the burning sail and were coming toward us. Una had her head cocked, frowning at the snowboarder's voluminous pants, then up at his face, uncomprehending. The scene, with the yellow porch lights under the eaves, the dirty snow, the ruined ship, the smoldering silk, the pickup still running with a wheezing sputter, was surreal. I looked closer at the young man. "Someone threw a torch? You saw him?"

"Not a good look." The snowboarder shook his head. "By the time I turned around, he was running. I saw his back, it was dark."

"What did he look like?"

The young man tried to smile. "Sorry. It was dark. He went down that alley." He pointed over the boat toward a break in the storefronts, an alley running the width of the block. "I mean, I'm pretty sure it was a guy from the way he was running. Dark clothes, that's all." He looked at Una. "Sorry, ma'am."

Artie stepped up to Una, touched her arm. "You want me to pull the boat back into the garage for you?"

Una agreed, gratefully. Some bystanders helped Artie get the soggy sail and boom back onto the boat. I checked it first to make sure the fire was out, then took Maggie's suggestion that we duck into the Six Point Bar down the side street. The bartender and proprietor, Rusty Pehrson, put a pot of coffee on and served free beer.

Maggie, Mom, and I crowded into the tiny rest room to clean up, and I examined myself in the pocked mirror. The bathroom had been paneled with barn siding back in the seventies in an effort to rusticate it. By now the cigarette burns, graffiti, and drunken kicks with cowboy boots had decorated the siding far past the rustic. I leaned over the small hanging sink and pulled my stocking cap off. My hair was all still there, but my eyebrows had curled with heat, singed just a little.

"Take off your mittens," Una said after scrubbing the black off her face. "I want to see your hands."

"I think I'll go home and clean up," I said. I didn't want to take off my mittens here. My palms had developed a low ache, especially my left hand. The wet wool kept them cool. "I'll just put a little more cold water on them." I ran the faucet and felt the cool liquid against my hands.

Maggie leaned over me and turned off the water. "Turn around," she said, pushing my shoulder back so I faced her.

"Let's see 'em." She picked up my right hand. The knit mitten was charred, black. I pulled it away.

"I can do this at home," I complained. "I don't want you fussing over me like a couple of old hens."

Una looked at Maggie, pursing her lips. "She gets like this when she really needs help. I'll bet they hurt, don't they?"

"Not really," I said.

"Then take it off," Maggie said, putting her hands on her hips and blocking the exit. Surrounded, I acquiesced. The knit fabric stuck slightly to my palm as I pulled the mitten off. Una took my hand.

"It's red but not too bad," she said.

"I told you that. Can I go now?"

"The other one, missy," Maggie ordered.

I sighed, then pulled slowly on the wet knit. The fire had charred this mitten badly, and it seemed to be stuck to my palm. "Okay, it hurts," I said. "You don't have to watch, though. I'll go home and do it."

"Let me, honey," Una said, taking my hand. Gingerly she lifted the knit up with pinched fingers. I clenched my jaw, blinked my eyes a few times, and finally the mitten was off.

"It's starting to blister," my mother said. "What have you got at home for burns?"

"I'll get some ice from Rusty," Maggie said, leaving the rest room in a rush.

Una leaned over my palm, picking errant fuzzies off the reddened, raised blister. "She's right, ice will help. What else do you have?"

"I don't know," I said, trying to remember the contents of my medicine chest. "Like what?"

"We'll just swing by the emergency room and get them to bandage it up," Una said. "And no arguing with me this time."

"Yes, Mom." I smiled at her, and her eyes smiled back.

LUCA WAS SITTING at the bar when we got out of the rest room, talking to Rusty, who stood behind the bar. I insisted on a moment of calm and a glass of wine before heading off to the hospital. Luca turned to me, her forehead a web of concern.

"Are you all right? Maggie said you had a burn?"

I held a bag of ice cubes against my palm. "It's not the important hand." I winked at Rusty. He poured me a glass of white wine. This was why I liked this place so much. Not that I drank here a lot. Not that I liked the decor, a jumble of dead animals with antlers and marble eyes, the creative Wyoming varieties of critters like jackalopes and the rear end of a white-tailed deer with eyes painted on its cheeks called a "Wyoming Jackass." But the guy behind the bar remembered what you drank and he left you alone to drink it. Or talked to you if you felt like it. Rusty, in his flannel shirt and lumberjack boots, looked more like a macho sawmill operator or hunting guide than a sensitive bartender. But that's what he was.

"Does it hurt awful?" Luca asked.

I shook my head. Luca still had her camera around her neck. "Did you get some pictures?" I asked.

"Oh, yes," she said, smiling. "Even of the fire. I took the whole roll."

"Pardon me." A man sitting on the other side of Luca peered around her. He looked local. "I work for the paper. Would you be willing to let us run some of your pictures of the fire?"

Luca's mouth dropped open. She looked at me, then the man, and gasped.

"Sure she would," I said. "For a price."

"Naturally," the man said. He extended his hand. "Conrad Baker. Call me Con." Luca shook his hand and introduced herself, blushing. He extended his hand then to me.

"And Danny Bartholomew has told me all about you, Miss Thorssen."

"Oh," I said, pulling my hand back. Danny worked at the *Jackson Hole News;* he had not forgotten how his tipping me to the whereabouts of an artist had gotten me, and him, into trouble. "Was it all bad?"

Con Baker laughed. He was dark and bearded, a man who got enough to eat at night. "There might have been a few choice adjectives, but almost all of it was good."

"Did you see her tonight? Saving the boat from the fire?" Luca said, patting his arm. "She is a hero!"

Con looked at her hand on his arm, then up at me. "I missed that. Parades never did much for me."

"Well, the pictures will show it," Luca said. "I will get them developed in the morning."

"If you want, I can do that for you," Con said.

Luca frowned, fingering her camera. "It's all right, I—"

"There's not an edition tomorrow, is there?" I asked.

"Not until Sunday," Con said.

"I think she wants to see them first," I told him.

"Time to go, Alix," Maggie announced behind me. "Your mother is beat, I'm beat, you're burned. Let's get out of here."

I stood up, still palming the ice bag, still in the old down jacket, now in need of more duct tape for the holes made by flying sparks tonight. My body suddenly felt creaky and sore. The adrenaline had fled, leaving behind the dregs of excitement, fright, and quick action: aching muscles, sore back, burned hand, general exhaustion. I took a final sip of wine and waved to Rusty. "Coming, Luca?"

"I think I'll stay another few minutes, Alix. My car is right outside."

I smiled at her, glad she was meeting people here in her adopted town she loved so much. Con Baker seemed nice enough, even if he was a little overeager to get his paws on those pictures. We walked out into the night that smelled like a smudge pot on a cold night in an orange grove, dirty, leftover heat butted against frigid air. Maggie's Jeep was a block away. We rode in silence to the hospital, got my hand bandaged to everyone's satisfaction, and went back to the gallery. Maggie dropped us off in the alley. I handed Mom my key. She unlocked, waved to Maggie, and led me upstairs to bed.

EIGHT

Ale I bring thee, thou oak-of-battle,
With strength and brightest honor;
'tis mixed with magic and mighty songs,
with goodly spells, wish-speeding runes.

I STEPPED OUT OF the bathroom in my sweats and clean wool socks, too tired to wash the stench of burning silk from my hair, to find my mother tossing the comforter over the fold-out couch. She held it horizontal in the air over the mattress; then it floated to rest, like the down inside it. She patted it into place, plumped the solitary pillow, and turned back the corner.

"Thanks, Mom," I said, sitting on the edge, waiting for the aspirin to take effect. Una stood in front of me and held out her hand.

"Let me see it," she said.

"It's fine, really." But she wouldn't take no for an answer. Reluctantly I held out my bandaged hand. Without the ice it had begun to ache. "Nothing to see."

She examined the gauze wrapping as if to check on the neatness of the job, perhaps to give the emergency room an evaluation later. Her sigh was audible but not relaxing.

"What I don't understand is why someone would harm that beautiful ship," she said. I shook my head. I hadn't the faintest idea myself.

"I would have thought it was an accident, all those torches around. Except for that snowboarder," I said. Una moved into the kitchen and began cleaning up, although nothing was dirty. "First Glasius, then Hank arrested. Now this. Do you think somebody's trying to tell us something?"

Una frowned, looking up from the counter she was wiping. Her gray hair was still neat. She had changed into a long white-

and-blue flannel nightgown with stand-up lace at the neckline. She might have been a fairy-tale godmother except for the lines of worry across her face. "Tell us what?"

I crossed my legs on the soft down comforter, settling in. It was late and I was tired, but I wouldn't be sleeping for some time if the burn kept hurting like this. "I keep thinking there's something else that went on that night. The night Glasius was killed." I paused. Una kept wiping, her eyes on the gold flecks in the cheap plastic laminate countertop. I pushed on. "Maybe we could go over that night again."

Una shrugged. "What's to go over?"

"Well, what did you and Hank and Glasius do after you left the Second Sun?"

"Before dinner? I told you. We went over to that bead shop you told us about. Glasius was intrigued with anything having to do with the runes and—"

"Wait a minute, it was his idea to go?"

"Not exactly, Alix. It was your idea."

"But he wanted to go?"

Una nodded. "He thought it would be interesting because the runes are so Norse, you know. He was some sort of expert on old Norse things, because of his research for the murals, I suppose. He didn't talk much to me about it. He told Hank, though."

"Where did you have this conversation?"

"In the gallery. Before we left. You mentioned the bead shop, and we talked for a moment, then we left. We walked over because it wasn't very far. I told you what happened when we got there. I looked at beads. That woman is a little too New Age for me."

"Mistress Isa?"

"Uh-hmm. That white skin and hair. She reminded me of one of those blind albino moles that lives underground and never sees the sun." Una shivered, twitching her shoulders.

"But Hank and Glasius watched the reading, didn't they?"

"Oh, yes. Glasius had her tell his fortune. Yes, I'm sure he did. I didn't watch, but afterward he told Hank what each of the runes that he had picked really meant."

"He didn't think her interpretation was right?"

"No, he laughed about it. Thought it was clever but ridiculous."

"Do you remember what runes he picked?"

Una shook her head. "I wasn't close enough to see. Oh, he and Hank were laughing about one of them later. It was something to do with her, that woman." Una stopped wiping and stared at the painted stars along the ceiling edge, trying to remember. "They called her a hag, a white witch. Does that make sense?"

"A hag? She's too pretty to be a hag, don't you think?"

"I guess, but that's what they said. Maybe hag was—I think it was part of the runes that she read to Glasius."

I moved around the sofa to the low bookcase that backed up to it, kneeling to find a mythology book that included a listing of the runes. Maggie had given me one a couple years before that had some of this modern interpretation of the runes in it, but I had never bothered to read most of it. It was a slender green volume on the bottom shelf: *Norse Myths Today*. I nestled back in the covers and used my gimpy left hand to hold open one corner while I flipped the pages with my right. About two-thirds of the way through the book, pictures of rune carvings on whalebone coffins and slabs of granite began to show up in the illustrations.

Runes are curious tall letters with no curved arms, the easier to chip into hard surfaces. With their rudimentary alphabet, each letter expressing a vocal sound, the Vikings made lasting memorials in wood, rock, and bone. The runes themselves came to be seen by common people as a source of great knowledge, since only a few knew their meanings. From knowledge it is a small leap to magic, to religion, to the gods.

"Do you see it?" Una said, hanging up the dishrag on the faucet and drying her hands.

"Let's see," I muttered, skimming through the runes, from Kano and Jera to Dagaz, then—"Hagalaz. Was that it?"

"Sounds familiar. But what does all this matter, Alix? What difference does a rune make? Glasius is dead. Hank is in jail."

The answer to that was, well, as opaque as the bandage on

my hand. I skipped through the meanings for Hagalaz in the little myth book. Hagalaz: Wasn't that one of the runes that Bjarne had picked for his reading? I thought she said it had something to do with the weather. Now I saw that she must have just made something up. Did she get some sort of weird vibes that day? And what of Glasius's fortune? Una moved out of the kitchen while I read.

"Why are you frowning like that? What does it say?" She sat next to me on the fold-out.

I shut the book. "It's a bunch of stupid mumbo-jumbo. That's what Bjarne said about it, and he's right."

"What does the book say, Alix?"

"Okay, I'll read it. But I don't believe it. Not for a minute." I opened the book again and found the page. Hagalaz or Hagal: A sudden disruption in routine or life's journey. A turn in the path. Can be full of negative and destructive power, especially when linked to other runes. An interruption or delay in your path. Illness or injury.

UNA WENT TO BED, and I tried to sleep too. If I slept on my left side, my ribs hurt; if I slept on my right side, my bandage dangled. I would drift into unconsciousness and scratch my face or push back my bangs, then wake up when the bandage swiped my forehead. I had dreams of fires at sea, of Vikings in fur coats plying icy oceans, of Merle standing with a giant ice phallus on board a longboat. Fire and ice. The white queen and her black helper. Contrasts, opposites, light and dark, heat and cold. Burning flesh and soft snowflakes.

I woke up tired.

FRESH WHITE SNOW in the square made the town a fairyland overnight. It must have begun snowing again after we'd gone to bed. I pulled on my boots about eight to shovel the steps leading down to the street. They extended beyond the boardwalk's overhang and had potential for dangerous slipperiness. Holding the shovel wasn't much fun with a burned hand, and I cursed and brooded over the torchbearer who had ruined the parade. What was the point in burning a thing of such beauty as Hank's longboat? The only thing I could think of was its connection to Hank and his troubles. Was it a message to Hank? A signal to those of us who carried on for him during his "isolation"? A signal meaning what, though? Stop participating in parades? Stop helping Hank?

The gallery floor needed mopping. Ugly, muddy stains from the reception and yesterday's wet, snowy weather dotted the wooden planks. One set of footprints, big and dirty, led right up to Glasius Dokken's murals. I filled the green plastic bucket with warm water and grabbed the mop. Half an hour later the majority of the dirt was gone. Another hour with clean water and some Murphy's Oil Soap, and it would have looked great. But my hand was really hurting by now. I dumped the water, stashed the mop, and squeezed out a damp rag to catch what I'd missed. Artie found me on my hands and knees, dabbing up some mud in the corner.

He poured himself coffee after sleepy, perfunctory greetings. I threw the rag back in the bucket and dried my hands.

"Do me, too, will you?" I said, nodding at my coffee cup. As Artie handed me the steaming coffee, he spied the bandage.

"Is it bad?" he asked, frowning.

I shook my head. It was clear this was going to be a near-constant refrain for a few days, and it was already boring. "Look, can you handle stuff this morning at least? I have some things to check out."

"About the fire?"

"Maybe. I don't think it'll be busy until later today. There's some freight to unpack, some ceramics back in my office. And the jewelry can be filled in again. We sold quite a bit yesterday."

I gave Artie a few more things to do to keep him busy during the slow morning hours, grabbed my coat and boots again, and was out the door. By now the sun had poked her reluctant head through the clouds, blinding passersby with the reflection off the snow. I pulled out my Ray-Bans, balanced them on the crooked nose, and trudged across the street. My ribs ached a little if I walked too fast, so I slowed as I reached the ice sculptures. I didn't have the concentration this morning to examine them. The thought of what Merle might be carving was too much to contemplate. I just hoped he changed his mind and pushed the whole issue into the nether chambers of my mind.

Despite blasted cold and nearly a foot of new snow, the sleigh rides for tourists, beginning on the south side of the square, went on as scheduled. They were a Christmas leftover. The old-fashioned sleigh, pulled by a big black horse complete with jingle bells and a bobbed tail, had been outfitted with a sign proclaiming "Nordic Nights: The Winter Fun Carnival." The horse looked cold, steam snorting from his nostrils and a light frost on his mane, as he waited for lucky, demented passengers on this cold Saturday morn. He made me think of Valkyrie, my own wild horse, pastured on Maggie's land near Wilson. She had been glad to see me the night Glasius was killed. Of course, I had the oats she liked that night. With this cold, I needed to get out there again today. Rubbing my horse's nose always cheered me up.

I looked at my watch. It was past nine o'clock. Bjarne was supposed to be racing at ten, and I had told him I'd go out and watch. The promise and other things I had planned for today tossed around in my mind, sorting themselves out. I'd made that promise before Glasius was killed, before the fire, before Hank was arrested. I picked up my feet, stepping over a huge plow pile onto the boardwalk toward the Wort Hotel. I would just have to miss the race. A wash of disappointment went over me. Bjarne was attractive, yes, and I liked his sly Norwegian laugh and muscular body and floppy blond hair. I sighed, passing a gift shop window filled with Indian pots and T-shirts and colored rocks. I hoped he would understand.

Room 219 of the Wort Hotel looked like any other door on the long hallway, except for its proximity to Isa Mardoll's hotel room next door. The yellow crime scene tape still decorated the door to Isa's room, but the police had gone, the door was locked. (Yes, I tried it, always hoping for the occasional miracle.) I paused in front of Room 219, listening. Hearing nothing, I rapped my knuckles loudly on the wooden door.

I didn't hear footsteps approaching the door, but finally a muffled voice said, "Yes?"

I cleared my throat and replied. "I was hoping to talk to you? If you have a moment?"

A long pause. The housekeeping cart went by, rattling, pushed by a pale, sad-looking woman who probably didn't make enough to keep her children from going hungry. I smiled at her, but she didn't look at me. I thought the occupant of Room 219 had gone away, but the voice returned: "What is this concerning, please?"

"About what happened next door. I was hoping—ah," I stumbled, trying not to sound like the police, who had no doubt already been here. "I'm a relative of the man who was arrested."

The door opened, the chain rattled in place. A dark face peered around the edge. I blinked at it, surprised. It was the face of the black man, Isa Mardoll's assistant.

"Hi," I said. "I'm Alix Thorssen. My stepfather is Hank Helgeson, who was arrested that night. Could we talk?"

The black man didn't say anything. He looked away at his room, then back at me, his dark eyes unreadable in the dim hallway light. He didn't shut the door, which I took as a positive sign.

"If you'd like, we can meet somewhere. Down in the coffee shop? Or at my gallery, the Second Sun? Anywhere you say." I smiled, trying to look as nonthreatening as possible. The man looked scared, timid. "It's Peter, isn't it?"

He looked at me, solemnly, then nodded almost imperceptibly.

"I came to Cosmic Connie's with some friends on Thursday, for a reading," I explained. "I remember you from there." I lowered my voice to a whisper. "Is Isa in there?"

Peter stepped back from the door and shut it suddenly. Damn. I had mentioned Isa like a dope. Here he was all ready to talk, and I blow it. I knocked lightly again, not expecting an answer this time.

"I just want to talk about that night. I want to help my stepfather if I can. Can you meet me down in the coffee shop?" I waited for an answer, hoping he was still by the door. The wood of the door's panels creaked slightly, as if he was leaning against it. "I'll be in the corner booth on the far right, if it's empty.

Otherwise the far left. Okay?'' I paused. ''Ten minutes,'' I said, feeling like I needed to give him the shoe-phone number in case he chose not to accept this mission. Oh, brother. I just hoped he would show up.

I padded slowly down the carpeted stairs into the Wort's warm, open lobby and bought a paper. The only one that was current was the *Casper Star-Tribune.* I carried it under my arm into the coffee shop and nodded to the hostess that I would take the corner booth. It was empty. She left a menu, poured me some bad coffee, and left me alone.

Opening the paper, I read the headlines without interest: Kosovo, oil prices, the cold weather. I brought myself up to date with Ann Landers and *Doonesbury,* read an editorial about funding for education, and had almost set the paper aside when a small headline on the front of the second section jumped out at me: Fire Mars Jackson Parade. My eyes were glued to the first paragraph when the black man slid into the booth across from me.

''Coffee?'' I asked nonchalantly, setting the paper aside. He shook his head, giving the room sideways glances. ''I'm glad you came.'' I smiled and took a sip of coffee.

He was the strong, silent type. Tall and thin with close-cropped hair, he wore a thin, blue V-necked sweater, the kind boys wore in the sixties, with a white T-shirt and black cotton pants. His hands were large and beautiful, his jawline prominent, and his skin like the glowing night sky. I fidgeted a little, made myself relax. He wasn't here for niceties, so I plunged in. ''I wanted to know if you knew what happened next door, in Isa's room, that night? Did you hear anything?''

He looked at me straight in the eye, perfectly still, his black eyes surrounded by vivid white. It was a dazzling moment that shook me with its gravity. ''I heard them,'' he said, his low, Caribbean voice rumbling even as he tried, unsuccessfully, to keep it to a whisper.

''Heard who?'' I whispered myself.

''The two men,'' he said. ''They came into the room and bumped into things. They talked. I heard them through the walls.''

"Glasius and Hank," I said, mostly to myself. "Then what?"

"They were looking for something. They open drawers and suitcases."

"You could hear this?" I asked. "Through the walls?"

He blinked. "They found something. Then they begin to talk loud. Argue."

"I see. They argued. Then what?"

"Then it stop. I hear door open and close. No more talking."

I sank back in the red vinyl booth, putting my hands on the laminate tabletop. So that was the way it was. "So the police talked to you?"

He nodded. "Yesterday."

"And you told them all this?" Another nod. "Did they say anything about you going to court on Monday and telling the judge what you've told me?" Nod. Right, of course. "Is there anything else? Did you hear or see anything else?"

He shook his head. He was finished.

"Where was Mistress Isa during all this?"

"She was out. She have something to do."

I raised my eyebrows. "Something? Do you know what?"

"She don't tell me." His face was impassive, his tone the same. But still there seemed to be a softening in his expression when he talked about her.

"Can you guess where she might have gone?"

He shook his head again.

"You work for Mistress Isa, don't you?" He nodded. "How did you two meet? You seem so different." Understatement Number 3,622.

"She come to Miami. On vacation. I was living there. We meet, have..." He waved his graceful hand back and forth between a spot on his chest over his heart and its invisible opposite. As if saying their hearts were connected. "We have some things we know the same. Some ways to feel the stones, the shells, that we can both do. That brings us together."

"You tell fortunes too?"

A slight smile crossed his full lips. "Reading the shells is not the same as fortune-telling. It is feeling the spirits, the winds, the sea, the sun and moon. These energies, and many secrets. Many ceremonies, drums.''

"But there is some similarity, things the same?''

"Yes, the runes as she tells them have many same meanings as the seashells the Palo Mayombe use. I am Yoruba, but I know the Palo Mayombe too.'' He glanced at me to see if I knew what he was talking about. I didn't.

"Yoruba? Is that in the Caribbean?''

He shook his head. "I am from Cuba, but my ancestors are from Africa. We are the Yoruba, we were slaves. We practice many rituals with shells, with coconut skins, for hundreds of years, in secret in Cuba.''

He hesitated, as if he wanted to tell me more but had been silent for so long. "Go on,'' I urged. "It's fascinating.''

"Some call it Santeria. The language we use, the Cubans call Lucumi. But it is really the language of the Yoruba from Nigeria. My people.'' Peter took a drink of water as if he hadn't had water in days, then set the glass back on the table. "Mistress Isa came to a Santero ceremony. That is where we meet. She likes to—'' He paused, biting his lower lip. "She is interested in Santeria.''

"How long have the two of you been working together?''

"One and one-half year,'' he said. "I must go now. She is waiting for me.''

"Wait, Peter, one last question. Was anything missing from the room? Did they find what they were looking for?''

His face dropped, very grave now. "They took them. They took the runes.''

NINE

A thurs rune for thee,
and three more I scratch:
lechery, loathing, and lust;
off I shall scratch them,
as on I did scratch them,
if of none there be need.

THE PAPER UNDER MY ARM, I put my head down into the cold and pushed across the square toward the county jail. I wondered briefly how much the county attorney knew about the stolen runes. Had Peter told them they were missing? Surely Mistress Isa had mentioned it. That would be one thing she would miss, since that was her current livelihood. Had she read fortunes yesterday, without the set? Peter indicated that she had another set. But not another one like those stolen.

I remembered admiring them at Cosmic Connie's. They were ornate with inlaid silver and turquoise, well-burnished wood grown dark and soft-edged from the oils of many hands. The box itself was remarkable: a sort of treasure chest with brass hinges and latches, also inlaid in a delicate scroll design in silver at the corners. Dinged and dented, it was obviously ancient. Peter had run his long fingers over its edges lovingly. The chest, Peter said, was gone too.

The light turned red at the corner of the town square. I peeked out of the collar of the down jacket to check for traffic and ran through the snow to the other side. My nose tingled, freezing. I had forgotten my hat. I reached the courthouse lobby, got directions to the jail, and gave my name and Hank's to the guard. He disappeared through a door as I settled in to finish reading the paper and thaw out.

FIRE MARS JACKSON PARADE

(Jackson, Wyo.) A fire marred the festive but freezing Nordic Nights parade last night in Jackson, a Teton County sheriff's deputy reported. Although a crime report has not been filed with the sheriff yet, the deputy said the incident is under investigation.

Bystanders at the scene on a side street near the Jackson town square said a float was burned. According to Chamber of Commerce director Gloria Worster, the float was a model of a Viking ship entered by Montana tourist Henry Helgeson. Helgeson was recently named in a murder investigation in another police matter. The model boat, Worster said, measured twelve feet long and was complete with a sail. The boat suffered fire damage and the sail was completely destroyed, she said.

Although the parade floats were not awarded prizes, Worster said the ship was one of the finest in the parade. "The details were exquisite," she said. "It's a crying shame."

The boat's owner, Henry Helgeson of Billings, Montana, is currently jailed awaiting a preliminary hearing in the stabbing death of another tourist, Glasius Dokken. Dokken was visiting Jackson for the Nordic Nights festival and was a well-known Norwegian artist. The Star-Tribune has learned that the Norwegian consul from Chicago will be in Jackson today investigating the "unfortunate death of one of Norway's most prominent citizens," according to a consul spokesman.

Chicago? The consul I talked to said he was from Billings. Apparently Glasius's death was causing some clamor at home. I had to get a copy of *USA Today* or a big-city paper. What did this consul think he was going to do? Bully the cops? Well, that was a local pastime I was familiar with. I could enjoy this if it weren't for my mother's anguish over her husband in jail.

The guard opened the door and poked his head out. "This way, please." He even held the door.

Hank did not look so good. The small interrogation room

where they put us (after patting me down) had fluorescent lights that made him look even greener than normal. He had dark circles under his eyes and slumped in his chair. He barely looked up as I entered.

"Your mother was just here," he said in a mumble. He wore the awful orange jumpsuit favored by jailers everywhere. He laid his hands in front of him on the scratched Masonite table as if examining his manicure.

"So she told you," I said. "About the fire."

He nodded. "I heard last night. There was a commotion here. Some deputies came back from the parade and told everybody. They didn't know it was my boat."

"I'm so sorry, Hank. It was beautiful, really."

He looked up, lips twitching as if he might cry. Five years in his garage, laboring over every authentic detail, up in smoke in five minutes. He glanced at the bandage on my hand. "Una told me what you did." He held my glance for a moment, the most thanks he could muster.

"It was nothing," I said.

He sighed deeply, hanging his head again. He was so still for a moment that I thought he had fallen asleep. I cleared my throat.

"Hank? I need to talk about the night Glasius died. Okay?"

He raised his head, looking up at the white sky out the tiny window near the ceiling.

I continued: "Were you looking for something? Did you and Glasius find something in Isa's room?"

His head whipped back toward me, a frown on his eyebrows. "Who told you that?"

"Her assistant, the big black guy."

"Who?" He shook his head. "I don't know any assistants."

"Isa's helper at the fortune-telling session? Wasn't he there?"

Hank shrugged. "Whoever he is, he's lying."

"You weren't looking for something in Isa's room?" His lips were pinched together now. "We know you were there, Hank. There's not much use denying it. I don't see how—"

"Stay out of it. You don't know anything." His voice was harsh and cut through me.

"How can I stay out of it, Hank? I burned my hand last night trying to save your ship, you know. Somebody torched it, Hank.

Somebody has it in for you, and that pisses me off. They're hurting people, including me. It's personal now.''

Hank looked at me, fear in his eyes. The stubbornness was still there but softened by the reality of the mess he was in, something he obviously preferred not to face. He dropped his eyes and hands to his lap.

I leaned forward, whispering now: "Listen to me, Hank. You've got to help yourself. I don't think you stabbed Glasius. Mom doesn't think you did. But the longer you keep your mouth shut about what you were really doing in that room, the greater the possibility that Una and I belong to an exclusive society with a membership of two."

He pushed his chair back, eyes still down. I leaned in more.

"Roscoe Penn is even losing interest, Hank. A man who doesn't try to save himself isn't much fun, even for America's Most Flamboyant. You've got to tell us why your fingerprints were all over that room. What were you doing there? What were you looking for, Hank?" I paused and gave him one last chance to tell me himself. The moment passed uneventfully. "Was it the set of runes?"

His head jerked up, mouth dropped.

"Peter, the black guy, told me. He's probably told the cops too. He said that gorgeous set of runes in the chest is gone."

"You can't tell anyone, Alix." He jumped up from his chair, the orange jumpsuit tugging at his round middle and billowing around his feet. "You can't, you mustn't."

"It's a little late for that, isn't it? Peter's probably told the police already," I said.

Hank paced back and forth, shaking his head. "No, no one has said anything about them. I don't think he has. Not that Isa woman either. That confirms what Glasius said. That they were stolen in the first place, so we might as well steal them back."

I sat back. "So you were there to steal the runes."

Hank waved his hand dismissively. "Reclaim, steal, whatever. They belonged to the Norwegian people, not to some white gypsy."

"Where are they from?"

"Glasius said he saw pictures of them in books, but they had been missing from his university in Oslo for years and years. Probably sold on the black market and made their way over to the U.S. somehow." Hank was agitated now, hands clenched, feeling the same injustice that Glasius must have felt that night in preparation for reclaiming the runes. That had a nice ring to it: reclaiming the runes. Much better than breaking and entering, burglary, or grand theft.

"What happened in the room?"

Hank stopped, put his hands on the back of the gray, institutional metal chair. "We went up to talk to her. That woman. Nobody answered our knock, so we let ourselves in. Remember that time we stayed at the Wort Hotel, Una and me? Well, I remembered how easy it was to jimmy those locks. Sure enough, it only took a minute with my credit card." He beamed, remembering, no doubt, the moment of victory over hardware. Hank was a big fan of television private eye shows, especially old ones like *The Rockford Files*. Now he was playing James Garner, only shorter, fatter, and balder. "We looked around, but we couldn't find the runes. We didn't find them."

I leaned into the table again, getting to the heart of it finally. "What happened to Glasius, Hank?"

"I opened the door, like I said." Hank frowned, rubbing his large forehead. "We looked around for a few minutes. It didn't look like the runes were there. Anyway, I was nervous and wanted to leave, so I left Glasius there. I expected him to come out, but he never did." Hank had a look of amazement on his face that in another time and place might have been called childlike wonder.

"Where did you go?"

"To the coffee shop. But then it closed at one o'clock, and they kicked me out. Glasius still hadn't come down. I hung around in the lobby for a few minutes, but that made me nervous. So I went home. Back to your apartment. Then—"

"Then?"

He looked sheepish. "I didn't go inside. I went back to look for Glasius. I didn't feel right just leaving him there, him being in a foreign country and all. I thought he might get in some trouble." I raised my eyebrows. *You got that right, mister.* "The door to the room was ajar, and I was positive I'd closed it. I pushed it open, just a little. And there he was. On the floor with that, that *thing* in his back.''

''That was when the police came?'' I asked. He nodded, hanging his head so low that all I could see was the top of his bald pate ringed by wisps of gray hair. My turn to rub my forehead and feel the bump on the bridge of my nose. ''Shit.''

Hank sat down again, resumed the slump.

''You've got to tell Roscoe Penn what you told me.'' He didn't answer. I stood up and walked behind my chair. ''Look, Hank, it's not going to matter what happens to those runes if you're in prison or get the death penalty. You can't help Glasius now.''

Hank looked up, fierce. ''You're wrong about that. Glasius is the only person I can help now.''

I shook my head. ''No, Hank. Help yourself.''

I CALLED ROSCOE Penn at home from the courthouse lobby. His butler or somebody said he was skiing but took the message to call me pronto or sooner. Everybody else has an answering machine, Roscoe Penn has a butler. I hung up, zipped up, and schlepped up the street to the Second Sun. It was noon already. Time to give Artie a lunch break.

My mother came through my office with a steaming bowl of soup for Artie as I opened the front door of the gallery, letting in a blast of freezing air. The weavings on the wall shivered in the cold breeze. I pulled off my pac boots and once again thanked the Canadians who had invented them. With their wool felt liners and impervious rubber bottoms, nothing felt better on the feet in winter. I picked them up by the fake fur collar, dumped them in the bathroom, and hung up my coat.

Una huddled by the jewelry case as Artie leaned over the bowl and sipped hot liquid. I caught my mother's eye, motioning her over to Paolo's sales desk. She looked better today, as if she had gotten a little more rest.

''I was just down at the jail,'' I said in a low voice. Artie didn't need to hear all the grisly details. ''Hank said you were there too.''

Una nodded. "He seems to be doing all right." She frowned and crossed her arms, then with effort changed her expression to something more hopeful.

"Stubborn old coot, huh?"

The frown returned, this time directed at me. She looked out the frosty windows at the ice sculptures. Again the low, incessant tapping of the carvers provided the day's backdrop.

"Well, he finally told me what he was doing in the hotel room," I said. Now I had her attention. "Did he tell you too?"

"No, he didn't tell me anything except not to worry." She harrumphed at that notion. "What did he say?"

"That he and Glasius broke into that room to look for a set of old runes that belonged to the university in Norway. They were going to repatriate them."

"Runes? You mean those fortune-telling ones?"

"Those inlaid ones. Glasius thought they were very old and wanted them back in the homeland."

Una rolled her eyes, set her mouth, crossed her arms again. "For that Glasius got killed?"

Was that it? Was he killed because he wanted the runes, or just because he broke into someone else's hotel room? That wasn't clear to me. But right now my hand was killing me. I followed my mother up the stairs, let her re-dress my hand with ointment and gauze, then gulped down three aspirin. I ate a peanut butter sandwich standing up at the sink after Una left to go to the garage and inspect the damage from last night. I told her to take a nap, she needed it. It was doubtful she'd take my advice on that. Napping was a sign of weakness in Norwegians, something practiced only by babies under duress. The rest of us have too many important and never-ending practical tasks awaiting.

LUCA SEGUNDO WAS staring at Glasius Dokken's murals, her head cocked and forehead furrowed, when I clumped back downstairs. I had changed my clothes into something more artistic for an afternoon in the gallery, finding a bright royal blue sweater on the top shelf of my closet that had been over-looked all winter. It was old, a present from Paolo years ago, and had bagged-out elbows, but it felt comfortable and upbeat. It looked presentable with the neatly pressed khakis (courtesy of Una) and certainly better than the jeans and sweatshirt I had mopped and shoveled in this morning. I poked my head out of my office door to see if Artie needed help, and saw Luca.

"Hey, *gringa*," she said, smiling as she spied me. "I want to show you something."

Luca had on more clothes than an Eskimo: long wool coat (red), muffler, hat, mittens, leather boots, sweaters (at least two), vest, wool pants, probably long johns too. She had spent the entire month of November holed up with mail-order catalogs, getting ready for her first real winter. Costa Rica hadn't prepared her for all this snow and cold.

But she was adaptable; I admired the way she plunged in, trying to get the jump on winter. It never worked, in my experience; winter always bit you back somehow. But it never hurt to be prepared. My father used to sing that every time he packed up his old station wagon for a month on the road selling lingerie and then hammers: "Be prepared, be prepared, the motto of the Boy Scouts." Then he'd throw a bottle of Jim Beam in the backseat and wink at me. My father was many things, but he was never a Boy Scout.

She spread the photographs, two packets full, out on Paolo's sales desk. I sat down behind it and began picking up the pictures one by one. As I looked at the shots of Gloria Worster in her fluffy boots and a couple of the marching band, Luca peeled off a few layers of clothing.

"Did you give these to that reporter?" I asked, curious about last night.

"Conrad? Yes, I had two sets made. Did you know it doesn't cost you very much more to do that?"

Everything about America was new and wonderful to Luca. It made her pretty great to be around; in fact it made you see the same old things with her fresh eyes. Even photo developing. "So, did you stay long?"

"Last night? No, just a half hour or so. You know I can't drink very much or I kill over." She laughed.

"*Keel* over," I corrected. "Like the keel on a boat. We don't want you killing, now do we? We've had quite enough of that."

She frowned, her black eyebrows jerking down. "There is one picture I want to show you." She picked up the other stack of photos and fingered through them. They looked like the ones of Hank's boat, its sail white as moonlight under her camera's flash. She handed me a photograph.

"This one. Look here." She pointed to a shadowy figure barely visible behind the boat. For this picture she must have stepped out into the street a little after the float passed. It showed the boat, sail unfurled, from the stem, with lines of onlookers on either side of the street. "This guy with the torch."

I squinted at the photo. The figure seemed to be holding a torch, or maybe it was the person behind him; it was impossible to say. His arm closest to the camera appeared to be down at his side. I say "him" with some ambivalence. The face of the person was obscured by the glow of the torch held near his head.

I frowned up at Luca. "Is this the only one that shows this guy?"

She spread out all the pictures of the boat on the desk. She had taken a lot of them, apparently enamored of the elegant sight. It did make a remarkable scene, the white-on-white of the sail and snow, the clean, sweeping lines of the lapped siding on the ship curving to the gilded prow. "This is the end of the pictures before I ran down the street after you," she said, pointing to the one with the figure next to the torch.

By the time she had gotten into position on the next block, where the boat was on fire, I was on top of the ship. What seemed to take hours actually took only seconds. In one picture I'm throttling the latch to the boom; in the next I've disappeared, flat on my back underneath the burning sail. I felt a sour place in the pit of my stomach grow as I looked at the pictures.

"He doesn't show up in any of these?" I scanned the fire pictures quickly, looking over the boat for the elusive figure. "No torches at all?"

"No, I don't see him," she said, coming around the desk to put her nose down on the pictures again. "I looked and looked. I guess he ran away."

Or it wasn't him at all. I looked at the lone photograph of the torchbearer. The figure wore a dark brown coat, bulky, with an indeterminate hat, perhaps a beret or some other head-hugging type. He or she was no taller or shorter than anyone else, it seemed, but then it was difficult to see anyone around him, because of the bleed of the glow of the torch.

"Maybe we could doctor this a little, come up with more of the face," I said. "Do you have the negative?"

"Oh, yes." She pulled the plastic sleeve of negatives from the paper envelope and handed it to me. "Conrad wanted them, but I refused."

"Good girl." I smiled at her. "Did he pay you for the pictures?"

"Oh, yes. I told him one hundred dollars for the fire shots. He said fifty. I said for fifty you can have just two. So he picked out two and paid me fifty. Did I do good?"

"Excellent. I'll take these over to a photographer I know. Maybe he can make something of it."

Luca pulled her hat back on. It was red and soft, framing her face. "Are you going skiing tomorrow?" She had recently taken up cross-country skiing and was anxious for me to accompany her on jaunts along the Snake River under the watchful eye of the Tetons. Before Christmas we had seen a herd of elk grazing there, much to Luca's delight.

"I'd love to," I said. "But with my mother here, and Hank's problems, well, I don't think I can swing it. And with my ribs and hands... Are you going?"

"If I can find someone to go with me," she said, giving me a playful squint. "Maybe that reporter, do you think?"

I laughed. "Con? Did you get a look at his waistline?"

She smiled, pulled on big black mittens. "You want to keep these photographs for some while?"

"If you don't mind, sure."

She agreed, already wrapping the black fuzzy muffler round and round, over her chin and mouth. Her goodbyes were cheerfully muffled as she pointed at the ice sculptures on her way out the door.

"What?" I said as she paused on the doorstep. I stepped

outside and closed the door behind me. Our heat bill was ridiculous.

Luca pulled down her scarf. "Have you seen the giant penis?"

BACK IN MY OFFICE I blew on my hands to warm them before I grabbed the old black rotary telephone. Heavy and solid and very, very slow, the rotary dial was ancient. This had been my father's telephone by his bed in the early sixties, the one he rarely used except to intercept late-night phone calls from my sister's many admirers. Rollie protected Melina, but he couldn't protect himself. His car flew off the narrow highway next to Flathead Lake one summer night and sank fifty feet into the frigid water. We never knew how it happened. It just did, and our lives were never the same again.

So now it was my turn to be old-fashioned and protective with the old phone. I had grown impatient, waiting for Merle to redesign his ice sculpture. The time had come for action.

"Gloria? Is Gloria there?" I asked a female voice that sounded enough like Gloria to be—

"My sister," Gloria said. "Visiting for the festivities. Oh, Alix, I'm so, so sorry, really, I am sick about that fire. It was terrible, terrible."

"Thanks, Gloria. I read what you said in the Casper paper. That was nice." She muttered some more exclamations in her southern syrup style. I held the phone out from my ear until she ran out of gas. "Listen, this is about the ice sculptures. I—"

She interrupted me: "Oh, my heavens, aren't they just the most fun you ever had with your mittens on? I was over there yesterday mornin', and I couldn't believe how pretty they were in the sun. How they sparkled—"

"Gloria. Listen for a second, please. There's a problem with one of the ice sculptures." I rattled on quickly so as to not give her an opening. "The guy's name is Merle something or other. He's a chef for the Rockefellers, wears a long duster and cowboy hat. He's carving something that I think you ought to take a look at."

"For the Rockefellers?" Gloria's voice got that hushed-in-the-presence-of-royalty sound. "The *real* Rockefellers?"

"The ones and onlies. The sculpture, Gloria, I want you to look at it and tell me what you think."

"Is there something wrong with it?"

"Let me put it this way. Everybody I've talked to has the same impression about what he's carving. And if he's carving what we think he's carving, we've got a problem."

"So? Spill it, hon. What is it?"

I sighed. I was hoping that if she went to look at Merle's monolith, she would see something different from the rest of us. Wishful thinking. "Well, Gloria, to most people it looks like a six-foot-tall phallic symbol." I decided not to mention details like the two large snowballs at the base.

"A phallic symbol?" Gloria gasped, quietly. Her voice dropped to a whisper. "You mean a big, icy dick?"

"Well, yeah." Such a sensitive soul. She harrumphed and gasped some more and told me she'd handle it. As I hoped. I hung up the heavy black receiver, put the telephone back on my desk, and rubbed my damaged hands together, still cold from standing outside with Luca.

Stepping into the gallery, I positioned myself in front of the heating vent near the plate-glass window. I looked through it at the foursome pausing to point at some pottery in the gallery, chatting for a second, then coming through the door, brisk and cold and jolly. I greeted them, staying where I was, getting warm in front of the vent.

"Looking for anything special?" I asked, even though I rarely posed so specific a question to art browsers: it was a waste of time. They murmured the usual reply, smiling back and moving off. They were two couples, both women blond, both men hunky.

Artie was showing jewelry again. The boy sold more jewelry than the day was long. Maybe he had a career going in jewelry. He should forget art. Nobody in their right mind would open an art gallery. The foursome gave Glasius's murals the quick once-over and exited. Quiet again.

The jewelry buyer, an older woman already dripping in gold,

found a pair of dangly silver earrings to her liking. Her old man got out his wallet, made the deal, led her out. Deep quiet. I swayed in front of the heat vent, almost drowsy with the warmth. I may have even closed my eyes. When the phone on Paolo's desk—a sleeker model, green but still rotary—rang next to me, the jolt brought me back to life.

"Alix! It's me," Luca said excitedly over the phone. "It's your mother—she, oh, dear, Alix. Come quickly. To the hospital!"

TEN

Of thy mother's words mindful thou be,
in thy heart let, darling, them dwell:
luck everlasting in life shall have,
the while my words thou heedest.

IN THE EMERGENCY ROOM, Luca paced in front of a pass-through window. The small waiting room was overpowered by a huge television set hanging in the corner, now showing soap opera tantrums. Luca seemed to jump six inches off the floor, her coat open and black muffler loose around her neck.

"I saw it. I was right there," she said. Her black hair hung in wisps across her cheeks and neck. Her eyes were wide.

"How is she? What happened?" I took Luca by the forearms.

"The truck went by and—blam! Hit her on the side. She fell down. I was across the street, over on, on—what is that street with the little restaurant I like?"

"Kelly? That's where the garage is."

"Yes, Kelly Street. I ran into that gas station and called the ambulance." Luca stopped, flushed and gasping for air.

"Wait here." I went through the door marked Emergency Personnel Only and came out the other side in the middle of a pod of rooms leading off a central desk that served as the hub and a place for doctors to write orders. I was just here last night getting my hand bandaged. I paused, and an ambulance jock came through, stethoscope and various wires dangling from his neck.

"Help you?" he asked amiably, eyeing my bandaged hand professionally.

"Una Helgeson. Where is she?"

"Family?" I nodded. "Let's find her," he said.

He poked his head into two rooms before we found her behind

a drape in the trauma section of the emergency room. A doctor and nurse hovered over her. I waited as the EMT whispered to the doctor and took a look at my mother. He stepped back out of the draped area and whispered to me, "He'll be out in a minute to talk to you. Can you take a seat outside and—"

"No. I'm waiting here. What's going on? Is she hurt?"

He had a kind face, tanned, and a skier's body, long and lean. "She's pretty shaken up. They're still assessing her injuries. But it looks like she was lucky." The automatic doors opened at the end of the big room lit with high-powered fluorescents and cluttered with movable drapes on stands. The EMT straightened. "You can wait here. Keep it quiet, though, okay?"

As he moved away to help the next patient, I thought about just barging in to see Una. But the thought of seeing pain on her face, an unusual and unwelcome prospect, kept me hanging back. She would never forgive me for seeing her without her guard up. My stomach was in knots. I'd had time only to throw on my clogs and grab the down jacket. I slipped off the coat in the warm room and felt the wet spots on my socks. Luca's face peered through the wire-glass window from the waiting room. I went back, spoke to her briefly, and took up my vigil.

It took ten or fifteen minutes for the doctor to finally turn toward me and smile. He introduced himself as Dr. Anderson. He was gray-haired, short, with blue eyes. "Your mother is doing fine. Apparently a vehicle clipped her as she walked down the street. She slid on the ice a bit; that may have saved her getting worse injuries."

"What injuries does she have?" I said, my voice nearly disappearing. Dr. Anderson took my arm and led me back into the enclosure.

Una lay with her eyes closed as the nurse continued to wrap something around her arm. She looked pale and fragile, her hair a mess, her slacks smeared with snow and dirt. Her shirt was gone, and a green paper drape covered her chest.

I swallowed hard. "Mom?"

Her eyes fluttered open. She attempted a smile, but just then the nurse did something to her arm.

"What's wrong with her arm?" I asked the doctor.

"A fracture. It's not bad, but she'll have it in a cast for a while. She must have tried to catch herself as she fell. She twisted her ankle, too. Luckily that's not broken."

I saw that her shoes and socks were off, and one ankle appeared blue going to purple. They hadn't wrapped it yet. I looked sharply at the doctor again. "That's it? Nothing else?"

"We want to keep her in the hospital overnight. She fell pretty hard, and at her age—"

"I heard that," Una piped up, her voice mock-stern. She winced then, as if the loudness of her own voice hurt her head.

"Quiet, Mom," I said, much relieved that she still had her sense of humor. "Does it hurt?"

The doctor answered. "We've given her some medication for pain. She's going to feel it a bit later, all the bumps and aches. But she'll be all right. We want to watch her overnight, as I said. Make sure nothing else crops up."

I cooed a few more assurances to my mother and let the doctor lead me away. It was clear she was floating on an anesthesia cloud and didn't need me to tell her it would all be better soon. Maybe it would even be worse after the drugs wore off. I fought battling emotions of anger at whoever had done this thing, and relief that it hadn't been worse. She was hit by a truck! Jesus Mary, she could have been killed. The voices in my head pounded so that I hardly heard the doctor asking me about my hand. He seemed to want to redo the bandage. I rubbed my forehead with my other hand and let him go at it.

"The thing about burns is, they need air, but they need to stay clean," Dr. Anderson was saying. "I thought I remembered you from last night. That was quite a little fire you put out."

"Yeah." I blinked, looking back at the slice of Una's feet I could see through the drapes. The doctor unwrapped the gauze, cleaned the burn (ouch, that hurt), and re-dressed it. Several times a day, he told me. Keep it clean. Yes, sir, I told him. Because it's so fun, I sure will.

"Now try to stay out of trouble," Dr. Anderson said amiably. "I don't want to see any more of your family in here for a long, long time." He opened the door to the waiting room. Luca sprang from her chair. I thanked the doctor and promised to be back this evening to see Una.

Luca searched my face. I began: "She's all right, but sh—''

"She's okay? *Gracias Dios.*" Luca sagged like a deflating balloon. "I was so worried I thought I was going to burst. I am thinking about Paolo and your hand and I am sick, you know? Sick." She put a hand on her stomach.

I linked my arm through hers and walked toward the door. "Me too. But it's just her arm and one ankle. I'll come back tonight and see her."

We walked out into the afternoon sunlight peeking under the high clouds. To the west the mountains loomed white and massive, crowned with the golden glow of the sun slipping away. I felt the shock of Una's accident slipping into something else, a sick worry that ate away at my stomach like Luca's.

"My car's over here," I said, guiding her toward the right. As if she couldn't see the Saab Sister half on the sidewalk, engine still sputtering and burping. The old beater, spewing fumes: I loved this car. It stayed running when you didn't want it to, and died when you needed it. Luca stopped by the front fender, looked at me, and laughed.

"You do this in Argentina, no more car!" she said, throwing up her hands as if the car would disappear in a poof. We got in, and I backed Sis off the curb gently. We headed west, into the setting sun, pulling down our visors.

"I'm thinking about Argentina today." Luca looked at me, rubbing her mittened hands together. "This is how it begins there. Little things."

"What begins?" I asked, steering around a mangy dog that had taken up position in the middle of the street next to what looked like a decomposing porcupine.

"The intimidation of a family. Someone is arrested. Something they love is burned or destroyed. They are hurt, but not so badly they die. But they have pain."

I looked at her profile, her clear, iced-coffee skin and black hair pulled off her face, disappearing into the red hat. "Why are they intimidated?"

Luca shrugged. "The usual reasons. Political, family rivals, money. You don't have any enemies, Alix?"

"Can't think of any right offhand," I said, frowning partly because of the sun in my eyes. "You think someone is trying to intimidate my family?"

"I don't know. I just wondered, because in Argentina things happen like this. First little things. Then, if you are not careful, if you do not pay attention, something big."

"Something big?"

Luca looked out the window at the Tetons, turning pink in the afterglow, a vision of winter's beauty, stark, picturesque, and heartbreaking.

"Big," she said quietly. "Like someone is killed."

DROPPING LUCA OFF at her house, formerly her brother's bungalow, made me remember my little studio in the back. I ducked down the alley, swearing at myself for indulging my fancy at a time like this, and parked beside the former garage. The Saab was half in the alley, but traffic back here was light; not even the garbage was collected back here anymore. I unlocked the padlock on the door and stepped into the coldest air I'd felt since—well, since last week.

The tiny studio was cheery despite the cold. Its yellow walls had been a snap decision at the hardware store. From there it was easy to progress to other brights: orange trim-work on the two windows, green curlicues on the beams overhead, a blue ceiling. Can't seem to get away from blue ceilings, no matter how hard I try. Blue should be up there, high in the sky, so it is.

The woodstove was cold as a tomb. I bundled up some old newspaper, laid on a few splits, and lit it up. Woodstoves, although labor intensive because they are always needing hands-on fuel and careful tending, touch something basic in me. The warmth from a woodstove is like no other, except maybe mother's warmth. The intensely personal heat from the beating of a mother's heart: maybe that was why I'd gotten a bright red enamel stove. It had been so long since my mother held me to her breast, the woodstove would have to suffice.

My mother. In the hospital with a broken arm, a battered leg. In pain. Should I be there, hovering? Should I be trying to get the truth out of her husband? Should I be at the gallery tending to tourists? Should I, should I...

Sighing, I sat down in the one chair, a battered castoff with wobbly legs, faded red velvet upholstery, and curved wood arms. The heat was meager but building. Why was I here? I didn't want to look at my paintings. Please. They were just therapy for Paolo's passing. They had served their purpose but weren't going to see the light of day anywhere, anytime. I couldn't even bring myself to look at the stack under a drape in the corner.

The fire had caught the logs, a cheery golden glow. Closing the door to the woodstove, cracking the damper, I turned to the worktable. It was clean, empty of paints and brushes, which I had taken home to keep from freezing. The oval palette was leaning against the orange window frame, smeared with color but resting. As the air warmed, the peculiar odors of the art studio trickled up my nose: the pungent oils, the piney solvents. The smells were comforting if nothing else. For a moment I closed my eyes and was reminded of Paolo, in his first gallery in the Village. Where we met. How exciting those times were, and how far away. He was gone now, and I had to trudge forward without him.

I reached for the telephone and surprised myself by knowing the number by heart. Carl answered on the first ring.

"Hey," I said. "Thanks for the flowers. You have the day off?"

"Not really. I just traded with another guy so I could take the afternoon off. I couldn't take a whole day today."

I hesitated. He didn't sound as down as he had, but a complete attitude recovery hadn't taken place either. "It's not going well?"

"Oh, it's all right. It's me. I can't figure out why I'm here. Do I really want to fly helicopters?"

"Do you?"

"I don't know. Some days I do, some days they scare me shitless."

Carl scared? I tried to remember another man who admitted

as much to me. "A healthy respect for helicopters seems to me to be a very smart line of thinking." I cleared my throat. "Hey, some stuff's been going on here I need to talk to you about."

"Yeah?" His voice was sharp, alert for once.

I filled him in quickly about the fire last night, made light of my burned hand (but did mention it, in an attempt to overcome some of my dysfunctionally stoic Norsky qualities), and then told him about Una's accident.

"What did the officer say at the scene?" he asked, police to the end.

"What officer? Oh, I didn't talk to anybody."

"Did they take a report? Was it a hit-and-run?"

"I was so worried about Mom, I didn't ask."

"Well, ask. It makes a difference, doesn't it? Was she intentionally run down, or was somebody just careless on the ice? Did they stop and help her or leave her lying in the gutter?"

A shudder went through me. "God, Carl."

"If you're going to find out what's going on, you have to ask, Alix." He took a deep breath, his voice softened. "Are you all right?"

"I don't know." I felt a wave of nausea flow over me and recognized it as fear. "My hand is okay. But Mom and Hank—"

"Goddamn it," he spouted, startling me with his anger. "I have another four weeks here. You know I'd come, Alix."

"No, no, don't come, Carl. I just needed to talk about it, get some perspective on it." Whatever it is. "Do you think something's going on?"

"Hell, yes. I'd be suspicious. Hank is in the can for a murder he says he didn't do, his boat's torched, his wife is run down. *Possibly* run down," he added for my sake. "What's this about? Do you have any idea?"

"I think it has to do with a set of runes. They're Norwegian, very old. I think Hank stole them from the lady's room where the artist was killed. Anyway, they say they're missing."

"Who says?"

"The lady, she's a fortune-teller. And her assistant."

"Are they telling the truth?"

"How the hell do I know? I don't really believe Hank right

now. He's still covering for something or somebody, maybe himself. My brother calls him the Swedish meatball. He's got an iron grip on some things and pretty slippery on a lot of others."

Carl sighed. Something creaked—bedsprings. I imagined him lying there in camouflage pants, no shirt (because of the desert heat), black hair buzzed to an air force clip, mustache trimmed neatly, muscles rippling. I kicked the damper of the woodstove closed with my foot. It was getting hot in here.

"I wish I was closer," he said quietly.

"Yeah, me too. I'll call you in the morning, okay?"

"I'm flying in the morning. I'll catch you later on." We said goodbye. Sometimes I wonder whether talking to Carl is good or bad for my perspective. And I had no idea where his head was at. I shut down the stove and stepped back out into the snowy alley, the moisture on my cheeks freezing instantly. Hell, at least it was warm where he was.

A DOZEN TINKLING bells rang as I pushed open the door at Cosmic Connie's. The smell of incense, that old standby patchouli, lay heavy in the air. The lighting was low: gooseneck lamps over the bead counters, a fan with lights with purple paper shades, a rose-colored fringed lamp by a plump, overstuffed chair. That's where I found Connie herself, curled up with her feet under her, sipping tea. The only sound was recorded flute music, eerie and soft.

Five o'clock and dark outside, but the stores stayed open until seven at least in the winter. This should be a busy time, après-ski, but Connie's place was, to put it mildly, dead.

Smiling, I nodded at the proprietress as I shut the door behind me. She set down her teacup on a small side table draped with a batik cloth. "Alix! So good to see you." Her voice seemed forced, insincere. I noticed her teeth suddenly, outlined darkly as if they were rotting, or perhaps had rotted and been replaced. I wondered how I had missed them before.

"Connie." She didn't get up, and I felt disinclined to approach her throne, so I stood awkwardly in the center of the room. "No fortune-telling tonight?"

She sighed and twisted a strand of her lavender hair through her fingers. "Mistress Isa canceled on me. Can you believe it? I had twenty people in here at four o'clock, and I had to send them all away mad." She stood up suddenly and fumbled around for her sandals. She wore a long, flowing dress today, white with tie-dyed spots of green and yellow. Her socks were pink. She would blend in well with my studio, I thought.

"So I'll have to disappoint you too. But you aren't alone," she said, frowning and flinging back her waist-length hair. I wondered idly if she'd followed up on her obvious attraction to Bjarne and how it had gone. She didn't seem his type at all. I blinked, looked at my clogs. I had no reason to wonder, or even care, about Bjarne's social life. Did I?

I cleared my throat. "Do you know where Mistress Isa is? It's very important that I talk to her."

"Sorry." Connie snorted in disgust. "We are not talking. No, ma'am. We are not communicating in any way, shape, or form. She left me in the lurch, and for all I know she's on her way back to Minnesota by now."

"Oh, I see." I stuck my hands in my pockets and admired the mural on the back wall with its swirling planets. "She's from Minnesota, is she? Whereabouts?"

"St. Paul, I think. Is that where you're from?"

"No, but I have relatives in Minnesota. Home of Nordic purity, you know."

Cosmic Connie picked up a chartreuse feather duster and flicked it here and there, over the glass cases and windowsills. "Yeah, well, she thought she was some fount of purity, I guess. Too good to do what she promised. Bitch," she added, half under her breath.

"Do you have an address for her back in St. Paul? In case I want to get in touch?"

Connie went to the cash register and began pawing through a desk drawer underneath it. It took her ten patient minutes to come up with a scrap of a magazine page with a tiny ad offering the services of Mistress Isa, at a post office box in St. Paul, with a telephone number. I thanked Connie, wished her luck, and left.

On the way back to the gallery I stopped in at the Wort Hotel just to double-check. As I suspected, Isa had checked out, as had Peter Black. That was Peter's last name, the clerk told me without my even asking. Isa Mardoll and Peter Black: two phony names if I ever heard one. She was one long, cold item, and he was without a doubt black. The clerk had no idea about their plans, but saw them loading their suitcases into a battered station wagon.

BUSINESS AT THE Second Sun was only mildly better than at the bead shop. Two groups of customers browsed aimlessly, talking loudly. Artie had had a good afternoon, though, selling three large framed prints. I had begun clearing the register, sure that the day was finished, when a woman brought over a sweet black-and-white raku pot to the counter. She wanted it wrapped and shipped. We took her money, told her we'd take care of it, and closed the gallery.

"Where did you take off to and never come back from, missy?" he said, hands on hips and a mocking smile on his elfin face. "I've been, like, swamped here, girlfriend."

I filled him in about my mother's accident. He gave me a big hug and was mortified that he'd admonished me even in jest. "I'm so sorry, Alix. Is there anything I can do?"

"Work tomorrow? Please?" I said, wrapping the pot in tissue and setting it in a box filled with excelsior.

Sunday was Artie's only day off, and I knew he relished it. He paused before answering, but put on a smile at last. "Sure thing. No prob, Bob."

"I'll give you a week off, well, half a week off, later on. I promise, Artie."

"It's a deal. Hey, some guy came by and checked out Glasius's murals. Said he was from the Norwegian consulate or something?"

"What did he want from us?"

"Wanted to talk to you. But he's sticking around till Monday, he said. He can't get anything done tonight or tomorrow, so he'll call Monday morning."

I nodded. "Are you sure it's okay about tomorrow?"

He waved it off. In the past we would just close up if things outside got hectic or if we wanted to go skiing on Sunday. Now, though, especially while the shop was busy, I couldn't afford to do that. I'd learned that a locked door once means fewer customers many times over down the road. If you want 'em to buy, you gotta be open, Paolo used to say, and only now did I listen to his faraway voice. Paolo who taught me so much, everything but how to keep him with me.

Artie snapped tape on the box, stuck a mailing label on it, and grabbed his ski jacket, a fancy East Coast Gore-Tex job that probably would have cost him a week's wages if his parents hadn't given it to him. I didn't begrudge him anything, though; Artie was a find. I've never been as lucky with help, and probably never would again. I waved him off from my office as I settled in by the telephone.

The photographer's name—the one I wanted to doctor that shot of the torch chucker—was Joel Lear. He was a struggling wildlife photographer, not as famous as Tom Mangelsen, who had a huge gallery in town, but getting there. To keep solvent Joel did custom work for other people.

Joel answered the phone in his darkroom and said my timing was good. He had the chemicals juiced. I promised to bring the negative right over. Before I left, I made the mistake of running up the stairs to change into my jeans and wool sweater again. The phone rang. I thought it might be the hospital, so I picked it up.

"So there you are, sitting around at home on a Saturday night again," Maggie whined, her voice droll, no doubt a beer in her hand.

"Not exactly." I was still zipping up my pants, the phone wedged under my chin. I decided not to burden her just yet with the story of my mother's accident.

"So you've got a date?"

"Not exactly," I repeated.

"You're getting cryptic on me, Thorssen. What are you hiding? A new guy? Somebody cute? Don't tell me, you've got a date with Bjarne with the hair and the cute little ass, right? Tell me, or I'll have to whip you with a wet noodle. Is it Bjarne?"

"Take a breath, Maggie," I told her. "I've got to go see my

mom. She's in the hospital. She got sideswiped by a truck and broke her arm.'' So much for later.

"Oh, shit. Is there a hex on your family or what? Is she okay?"

"She's okay, I think. Do you want to go visit her tonight with me?"

"Sure. Of course. I mean, I was going to try to get something lined up with Carter and Bjarne for us, but that's—"

"—dumb,'' I finished.

"I didn't see you at the race this morning."

"I couldn't make it. How'd it go?"

Maggie sighed. "Bjarne won his race. You should have been there. Carter was busy doing whatever a race official does with his little stopwatch and flags and stuff. I didn't get to talk to him much. I don't know about him and me, we can't seem to get it together."

"He's just busy, Maggie. Wait until Nordic Nights is over. He'll have time for you. Who wouldn't? A gorgeous, sexy gal like you."

"Oh, I knew there was a reason I called you.'' She started to giggle. "I have to tell you what I did last night. This is so funny.'' I pulled on the down jacket, yanked the pac boots over my jean bottoms, and laced them.

"Maggie? Can you tell me later? I'm just running out the door with Luca's photos. I'm going to get one of them blown up."

"Oh, God, sure, I'll tell you when you pick me up to go to the hospital.'' I loved Maggie's take-charge assumptions. They did make things simpler. "What time, hon?"

"Eight, okay?"

"Let me see, I have to file my nails. Yup, that'll do. See ya then."

I was out the door, clutching the negative in its plastic case, hoping the chemicals were still juiced at Joel's.

ELEVEN

What welcome word rewards thy toil?
Tell while aloft thy long tidings:
sitting, one oft his errand forgets,
and lying, tells lies altogether.

THE IMAGE floated up through the developer slowly, as if emerging from a fog. The darkroom was eerie, blood red light with strange magenta shadows. Joel had curly black hair and, tonight, a red face. He had gotten contacts since I saw him last, and he looked more grown-up, more worldly. Maybe even a little gray in his hair.

Joel worked the face of the person by the torch, and we hovered over the developer tray and watched that area intently to see if anything would show up. He sloshed the chemicals back and forth, then rubbed the face with his thumb.

"Hmmm. That place is burned out from the torch. We'll get a few lines, but not what you would call true definition. Sorry." He picked up the corner of the paper and let it drip, stuck it in the fixer. I stared at it, the fumes Roto-Rooting up my nose, eyes blinking. "Nothing?" I asked, glancing up at the red lightbulb.

"Hang on a sec," Joel sit, bouncing on the balls of his tennis-shoed feet as he pulled the print out of the fixer, washed it, and hung it up on a clothesline. He turned on real lights as the red bulb went out. "Okay, now take a look."

The eight-by-ten print showed the stern of the boat on the snowy street, the sail a wide swath of golden white billowing under the streetlight. The trailer's wheels gave the boat the look of a squatty lizard instead of a sleek, oceangoing vessel, but still the illusion with the sail was nearly complete. The mast cut the square of silk into neat halves. To the right, on the boardwalk, onlookers stood in the shadows. On the left, a few hardy souls stood in the gutter next to a pile of snow. I looked closer. There was the baggy jacket and black-patched pants of the snowboarder who had told us about the torch flying over his head.

And there was the torch. But who was holding it? A cluster of people melted into each other around the torch: the bulky brown coat might now be fur, maybe. The beret now seemed to belong to someone else. Another person was short and almost hidden. All three had their faces obliterated by the bright glow of the torch. None had arms visibly holding it.

"Not too clear, huh?" Joel said.

"Well, you tried." I looked at Joel, disappointed. I had hopes of this photo nailing somebody, or at least giving us a lead. "Can I have this? At least I can give it to my stepfather to show him how nice the boat looks. I mean, looked."

"Sure, but you want me to dry it? I can drop it off tomorrow." Joel nodded toward a big silver dryer. I told him fine, no rush, and shuffled off into the night.

Maggie and I finished the Mexican food I brought over in ten minutes, each of us wolfing down a bean burrito with extra guacamole. We hardly sat down at the table. We were on our way to the hospital when she remembered the story she wanted to tell me.

"It doesn't seem so funny now, for some reason," Maggie said. "Now I feel kinda depressed because your mother is lying in the hospital, hurt, your stepfather's in jail, your hand is burned, and we don't have dates and it's Saturday night and I heard there's a great band at the Stagecoach."

"Just tell me the story," I said. We were almost to the hospital, driving out Broadway in the direction of the entrance to the Elk Refuge. The night was clear and cold with a million stars. The moon wasn't up yet, lazy bum. But without him we could see stars and galaxies and swirling masses of cosmic gas and dust city dwellers couldn't imagine.

"Doesn't this heap have any heat?" Maggie said, wrapping her blanket coat tight around her knees. She knew very well the Saab Sister didn't have any heat, except when she felt like it, which wasn't tonight. My pac boots were cozy, though; Maggie was wearing light hiking boots that offered little insulation.

"Okay, here's the story," she began. "After the fire and taking you to the emergency room last night, I couldn't sleep. There were still quite a few people roaming around downtown, so I decided to walk over to get a cup of coffee at that new place. You know the one."

"The one where all the ski instructors hang out?"

Maggie laughed. "Yeah, but they were gone. I got a decaf latte, to go, and drank about half of it inside. Nobody interesting showed up, so I decided to walk home drinking the rest. I cut through the square to look at the ice sculptures, especially that naughty one."

"Wait, I took care of that, Maggie." I pulled the Saab into a space in the parking lot between a Jeep and an RV. "I'm tired of hearing about Merle's phallus, really."

"Well, you have to hear about it one more time," Maggie said, slamming her door as she got out. "Because this is the funny part, and now I feel better because I'm telling it. I walked up to that big cock and thought to myself, I wonder what it tastes like. So I took a big drink of that latte and stuck out my tongue and gave it a big ol' lick."

I opened the main door to the hospital for Maggie and waved her through. "So? What did it taste like?"

She chuckled. "My tongue stuck."

"To Merle's phallus?"

She was trying to hold down her laughter and nod. "There I was, in all my glory, with"—she leaned close to me and whispered—"my tongue stuck on the world's largest dick!"

I tried not to laugh as I asked the admitting clerk for Mom's room number. As we walked down the hallway, I grabbed Maggie's arm to keep her from falling over with laughter.

"So what did you do?" I asked, reading numbers next to doors.

"Only thing I could do. Poured the rest of my latte over my tongue. That did the trick. But there is an ugly brown stain on the side of that—what's the nice word you use?"

"Phallus."

"Yeah, that phallus has got a latte stain."

THE LIGHT WAS dimmed in Una's room. I realized I didn't have flowers or even a card. Guilt washed over me. The windowsills and tables were barren of gifts. No balloons, no green plants, no tacky ceramics. I turned quickly to Maggie as we stood in the doorway and whispered, "Would you go buy some flowers? I'll pay. The gift shop may still be open." I shooed her off and eased into the room. The television was on without the sound.

"Mom?" My voice was just above a whisper but seemed way too loud. "Mom, it's Alix."

Her right hand gripped the remote control. Her thumb twitched on it as her eyes fluttered open. It took her a minute to realize I was in the room. She smiled, switched off the television, and turned on the overhead lights, all with just her thumb.

"Wow, you've mastered the gadgets already," I said, sitting on the edge of the upholstered chair next to her bed. The room was hospital basic, soothing creams, greens, and beiges. Una punched another button and raised the head of her bed. She smiled proudly as it stopped.

"You betcha." Her voice was strong but sleepy. My father always said, You betcha. The sound of the old phrase caused a little flare-up under my sternum. I asked her about the pain, her ankle, her wrist. She assured me the doctors were taking good care of her, that I needn't worry, that everything was fine.

"I'm calling Erik. He'll want to talk to you," I said, standing to get the phone.

"No, no, no," she protested. "It's late. We don't need to worry him."

"He'll be mad if I don't call him about this," I said. He would also be mad if I made him speak to Una when neither one of them was ready. I sat back down in the chair. Mom sighed. "What happened? Do you remember?"

She closed her eyes. I thought she had fallen asleep, but she began talking, eyes shut. "I went to check on the boat. Things were really a mess, and I wanted to clean it up, make it look as best as it could for Hank. It was all I could do for him. I just kept thinking that." She swallowed hard, blinked up at the ceiling once, then shut her eyes again.

"It took a long time, three, four hours. I got hungry, so I

walked down the street to that little restaurant that serves tacos. When I got back, I opened the garage doors. They're heavy, you know, much heavier than new metal ones.'' The old garage doors opened in the middle, swinging to either side, and were made of wood. ''I pushed one open, then the other. Then I stood for a second to catch my breath. The garage was dark. Then there was a truck. A pickup with its lights on. It came at me, and all I had time to do was jump a little to one side.''

I rolled my eyes, privately. ''Did the police ask you about all this?''

''Uh-huh, they just left.'' She seemed to sink a little into the pillows and sheets, shrinking in fatigue.

''I can get the rest from them. That is, if you're tired?''

She sighed, breathing lightly, and opened her eyes. ''I'm fine, dear. How's your hand?''

''It's okay. The doctor who saw you in the ER put a new bandage on it for me.''

''That was nice, wasn't it? Everyone is so nice here.'' She gave a light smile. No complaints, no bother, no fuss.

''Did you recognize the driver of the truck?''

''I didn't see him. The police wanted to know about the pickup truck too, and I told them it was blue or green, that's all I remember.''

''Why would somebody be in the garage? Was the boat damaged some more?''

She shook her head. ''I don't know.'' She clamped her lips together in a way I had seen before. I let the pause grow while I observed her now-alert eyes, darting to the corners of the room.

''Mom?''

''Hmmm?''

''Is there something you're not telling me?''

Another sigh. ''I'm just worried about the boat. I hope the police locked up the garage again. My purse is in there. And—''

''And what?''

''Some of Hank's things.'' She turned to me abruptly. ''Would you go over and fetch our things? I know you're busy, but if you wouldn't mind?''

''Of course, Mom. Your purse and what else?''

"Hank had a box of things under the seat of the pickup. Nothing expensive, but it needs to be locked up. You'll find it there, wrapped up and in a cardboard box."

Maggie knocked on the door and stepped inside with a vase full of red roses. Una was all smiles. Maggie kissed her cheek, signed her cast, and set up the roses where she could see them: right under the TV set. After a few minutes of cheerful banter that both buoyed and fatigued Una, from the look on her face, Maggie and I slipped out. Call her, Mom asked, when we found her purse. As we left, Una dimmed the lights and flicked the television back on to *Homicide*.

"She seems okay, don't you think?" Maggie said, striding more easily down the carpeted hallway in her light boots than I was in heavy ones. Her blanket coat flapped around her ankles.

"She sure enjoyed seeing you," I said.

Maggie smiled, her spirits recovered, it seemed, from the degradation of a dateless Saturday night. Nothing like a Good Samaritan whirl to give you a shine. We stepped into the freezing night, ducking our ears into collars. In the car I said, "Want to check out the scene of the crime? She wants me to pick up some stuff at the garage."

"No time like the present." Maggie checked her watch. "We could still go out to the Stagecoach and catch that band."

I debated. My fatigue had blurred into a low-grade overall ache, the kind that enjoys being dulled by beer and smoky pool halls. Yet I knew I should keep my mind clear for the Hex, the Family Problem. I swung the Saab around the corner near the town square, up toward Kelly Street and the garage. The still, white yards with rusting wire fences and piles of firewood heaped in front lawns yawned and settled down both sides of the street.

Maggie sighed. "Oh, come on, quit being so—so—"

"Norwegian?"

"So serious, that's what I meant. You're not going to save the world this one fine night, Miss Joan of Arc. And it is one fine, fine night."

"Fine and frozen solid. And we're going to be if we don't get inside soon."

"I bet it's plenty warm at the Stagecoach."

I hazarded a look at her eager face with the flashing black eyes and cupid lips. "It won't take long at the garage, I guess."

"Yee-haaaaw!" Maggie hollered, slapping her thigh silently with a mittened hand.

THE GARAGE I had found for Hank to store and work on his boat sat far back from the street past a tiny, vacant cottage that was rumored to house a family of raccoons. The cottage and garage were owned by a lawyer friend of mine who was sitting on the property until he had enough money to tear down the mess and start over. In the meantime the garage gave him a little income. It was huge, probably built in the forties for grain trucks, and looked more like a barn with its faded tomato siding and peeling white trim. The doors were fifteen feet high and eight feet wide each; no wonder Una had such a time opening them.

As she had suspected, the garage's padlock dangled, unengaged. Una hadn't locked up before trotting down the street for a taco, so the cops hadn't bothered either. Maybe there hadn't been any cops on the scene at all. That would be typical for Charlie Frye's team.

I slipped the padlock in my pocket. Maggie and I each took a door; they groaned open. We stood in the dark doorway, blinking.

"Where's the light?" Maggie asked. I tried to remember, patting down the side walls for a switch. Then it came to me that you had to walk all the way to the back of the building, to a workbench. I stumbled forward, arms out, straining to spot masts and prows and oars protruding from the blackness. I found the side of the boat and patted it blindly toward the other end. A minute later I found the switch. Fluorescents, a bank of three hanging from the high roof, buzzed and flickered.

"Oh, jeez, this is depressing," Maggie said, surveying the damage. The boat was singed, blackened all across the gunwales and the top. Not a single oar remained intact; the stubs that were left were half burned. The gilded prow had blistered and blackened. The mast was still upright; Artie had taken a chance that it would fit through the garage door.

The boom with charred bits of silk sat on the dirt floor of the garage next to the trailer. Ready for the junk pile. I bent down and felt the burned boom. It was completely black, with long striations where the fire had penetrated beneath the surface. Structurally unsound, I guessed. Too bad; it was an exceptionally straight and sturdy piece of pine, lodgepole maybe. Not what the Vikings would have used. Something stronger, harder, like ash or maple or even oak, to withstand the rigors of the high seas.

I stood up and sighed. "Let's get out of here. Una said her purse was around here somewhere. Can you look for it? It's brown vinyl, lots of pouches."

Maggie spun around, checking the workbench, the boat, as I opened the door of the pickup. Under the seat—Hank's things. Tools, I figured. Tools Una couldn't remember the name of, so she called them "things." In a cardboard box.

The bench seat of the old Ford pickup had been a pale green once. Strips of vinyl curled up around the dented seating areas, left and right. More left, on the driver's side, naturally. Hank had owned this truck since it was new, Una told me once. And it hadn't been new for some time.

The mats looked freshly swept. I stuck my hand under the driver's side of the seat, felt only springs. Slamming the door, I stepped around the other side, repeated the hand sweep. Nothing. I stuck my head inside, down where the mud smell was strong, and looked under the seat. On the passenger's side there were candy wrappers, pennies, a mitten, a french fry. On the driver's side—nothing. Just a clean place where something like a cardboard box had once sat.

I closed the door. Curious. I scanned the pickup's bed, hauled myself up on the bumper of the truck to look inside the boat.

"I found it. Appears to be all here. There's thirty-two dollars in her wallet," Maggie said below me.

"Good." I jumped down. "I can't find the box she wanted. She said it was under the seat, but it's not."

We both looked every place in the truck and garage we could find for the next five minutes. The garage was mostly empty. A few cupboards below the workbench constituted storage. A mousetrap, a rusty coffee can, and a stiff paintbrush rested together there peacefully, gathering dust. The glove compartment of the pickup held insurance cards, scraper, and registration.

"Do you think we should look in the hull of the boat? Would Hank have stashed it in there?" I wondered aloud.

"Yuck. That boat is filthy now with all that charred stuff. I am not getting up there and mucking around." Maggie looked at me hard. "You're not, are you?"

"No. Not tonight. Not for a bunch of tools that probably aren't worth much anyway." We hit the lights, jammed the padlock back on the doors, and took off on snow-packed streets in the dead of night for beer, secondhand smoke, and loud music.

ONCE, WHEN I first moved to Jackson, I made the typical flatlander's mistake (although technically I am from Montana and not a true flatlander) and agreed to ski down Teton Pass. The precipitous drop of the mountainside from the pass to the valley floor, some twenty-five hundred feet, draws the adventurous and the foolhardy in spades. The top of the mountain pass accesses numerous routes to the east and west, back to Wilson on the east, or to Idaho on the west, either way high mountain powder, waist-deep and untracked if you're early and lucky. You can go up, around, or down: of course, eventually you have to go down. My small group included some experienced backcountry skiers, of which I was not one. I knew how to cross-country ski but had never delighted in the pleasure of going fifty miles an hour straight down the mountain on a couple of wobbly boards that aimed for every crevasse and snowbank and tree on the whole damn hillside.

All of this would be irrelevant if I hadn't made a big mistake. *Another* big mistake, besides actually agreeing to this exercise in humiliation. That was, I wore jeans. No long underwear, no plastic or Gore-Tex or even rip-stop nylon. Just jeans and a pullover anorak and a turtleneck. Maybe long socks. By the time I reached the Stagecoach Bar in Wilson, my teeth were chattering and I was dripping, sloppy, a ridiculously sopping excuse for an outdoorswoman.

Thus it was that every time I walked into the Stagecoach Bar,

I felt that same clammy mortification I felt that Sunday afternoon long ago. Even without a soggy rear end and a trail of melted snow, even without a towel wrapped around my waist courtesy of the bartender (he also gave me a plastic bag for my jeans). Some moments are indelible.

Just like that day, all eyes of the male persuasion turned toward me and Maggie as we emerged from the clean air into the blue haze of the Stagecoach. We maneuvered around the pool tables, blinked into the blue gloom for a table, and ended up joining a lonely cowboy at a four-top. The band either hadn't started yet or was taking a break. Two electric guitars and a saxophone were propped on stands along with a drum set on the low, black-painted plywood box they called a stage.

We ordered beers. Maggie asked the cowboy about the band. He shrugged, noncommittal, looked away. A gleam sparkled in Maggie's eye; she liked nothing if not a challenge. As she rearranged her chair, threw off her coat to showcase her goods, and dabbed her puckered lips daintily, I excused myself to call Una.

The pay phone was by the toilets. I never understood this. Was relieving yourself somehow related to the telephone?

"I didn't wake you, did I?"

Una purred a little. I had wakened her.

"I'm sorry, I just wanted to tell you we found your purse. The money's still in it. Seems okay."

"That's good, honey." Her voice was watery, muffled.

"No sign of that box, though."

"Hmm?"

"The box under the seat—it wasn't there."

"Under the pickup seat, the driver's side? You looked?"

"Several times. Sorry. I'll go back and look again tomorrow if you want." She sounded awake now, even anxious. "Was it something valuable?"

"Oh, Alix," she whispered. "Hank will be so angry. Was it gone, really?"

"Mom? What was in the box?"

A commotion began across the bar, next to the pool tables. The bartender straightened up, pushed back his long hair like he was going on a date. The Stagecoach's owner came rushing from the back room. A charge of electricity went through the languid beer slackers.

"Mom? Are you there?"

"Yes, I'm here." She sighed long and hard. "I need to talk to you about that box. I was hoping I wouldn't have to, that Hank would forget about it, send it away somewhere. But now…"

"So talk to me." The noise level rose with hearty laughter and a chorus of whispers.

"Not now," she said finally. "I'm so tired, and they've given me some pain medication. My head feels like a balloon ready to fly away. I can't think about this right now."

We agreed I would come by first thing in the morning, and we'd talk then. What could possibly be in the box? I wondered, my head down, plowing out through the bar again. Apparently not tools. Hank hadn't lied to me and really stolen that set of runes from Isa Mardoll, had he? Something else? A gun? People do keep guns under the seats of their pickups, either that or in the gun rack. But Hank? Even if he didn't have a permit or used it in a— Ish, that could be sticky. If he used it in the murder. But, wait, Glasius had been stabbed with a—

Oooof.

"Excuse me." Running into the man had interrupted my thoughts. There was a crowd of people through the pool tables, stopping play completely. Three or four guys held cues in their hands, annoyed.

"No problem. Are you all right?" the man said, turning toward me. He smiled, a handsome guy with a lot of wrinkles, very tan. Black leather jacket, nice. His voice sounded familiar. I gave him a polite smile, edged around some New York types with pale skin and red lipstick and pointy shoes. Then around a very short man with a tiny ponytail hanging over his turtleneck. When I got to my seat, Maggie was bright red herself.

"Do you know who that is? You bumped right into him. What did he say? What does he *smell* like?" Her hands were gripping my arm, her face inches from mine.

"Who?" I looked around her at the group of tourists again. I thought they were tourists. They didn't look like locals.

"That is—" She strained to control the volume of her hiss. "That is Harrison Ford!"

"Yeah?" I could see him talking to the shrimpy guy. "So it is." No wonder his voice sounded familiar.

"God, I hope he smiles. I *love* his smile." Maggie sank back in her chair, blissed out.

"Is that other guy the one who played the short robot? What was his name? R2D2?"

Maggie stood up, pulled down her cream-colored sweater tight over her not-that-impressive chest, and straightened her jeans. "I'm going to bump into him now." She stepped around me. "I saw how you did it. Head down like you're thinking about something important. Then"—she smacked her hands together—"right into him. I'm going to get a good whiff."

I sat back and took a drink of Teton Ale as Maggie wound through the group on her way to her pseudo bathroom visit. The cowboy and I exchanged looks. He wore a purple silk bandanna wrapped around his Adam's apple and was draining his third Pabst Blue Ribbon. I wondered if Maggie had gotten any conversation out of him.

She came barreling out of the rest room like a heifer in heat, her head down, hands in her pockets. All the better to get full body contact. She twisted by three tables, avoiding them at the last moment, her long black hair falling over her shoulder. She didn't slow as she plowed right into one of the New York women, a very pale, emaciated type with black arching eyebrows and blond-streaked hair. The woman yelped. Maggie sprang back, hand over her mouth.

The pale woman was cursing violently. R2D2 was bent over her injured foot, massaging it. Maggie's eyes swung wildly from the damaged foot to Harrison Ford, who stood at the edge of the chaos, smiling wryly. The insurance agent in Maggie bubbled to the surface at last, and she bent down by the woman, now seated in a chair, and apologized. At that the woman began to slap Maggie on the shoulders with both hands and had to be restrained by R2D2. By this time the cowboy and I were laughing so hard we almost fell off our chairs.

"Maggie? Are you all right?" I kneeled down next to her. She sat flat on the floor now, her legs splayed. The floor was thick with mud, beer, peanut shells, and cigarette butts. "Did she hurt you?"

Maggie blinked up at me, and I winked. "Let me help you up." I grabbed her arm, swung her upright, and slapped her fanny a few times. "Now. Let's take inventory." I turned her toward me and did a systems check like I was a doctor or somebody. I ignored the New Yorker, who sat behind me, muttering things like, "Clumsy bitch."

When we were done with that, Maggie had rallied. She bypassed the irrational one and spoke to R2D2, who was at her side. "I'm terribly sorry about all this. If you need anything, don't hesitate to call me." She stuck out her hand to the little man. He had intelligent eyes and a cynical mouth. Hollywood, I decided. Harrison Ford's producer or director or somebody.

"My name is Alix Thorssen," Maggie said, smiling at Harrison, at the woman, at R2D2 as she stepped away. "I'm in the book."

TWELVE

Long is a night, longer are two—
how shall I thole three?
Shorter to me a month oft seemed,
than part of this night of pining.

Two HOURS LATER we fell out the door into the bitter cold. Our lungs starved for air, our heads stuffed with beer, music ringing in our ears, we tumbled into the Saab Sister. The headlights were two bright spots on the faded red paint of the Stagecoach's siding. I looked at Maggie, burst out laughing, still hearing her stomp her feet on the dance floor after the cowboy had dipped her backward. She had thrown back her hair and shouted, with apologies to Sheryl Crow: "This ain't no disco! This ain't no cowboy country club! This here's Jackson Hole!"

She chuckled now, put her head against the low seat, and closed her eyes.

"What the hell were you thinking, girl?" I said, not unkindly, for we had already hashed this out over ale and cowboy jitter-bug.

Maggie threw her hands up in the air, held them there, and splayed her fingers outward before dropping them. She never opened her eyes. She had told me inside that she didn't want them finding out she was in insurance because everybody knows that insurance agents carry big umbrella policies for liability and that makes them lawsuit magnets. Well, sure, I thought: Make me a lawsuit magnet instead.

"They're not going to sue you, Alix. Didn't you see her out there trying to dance? She's just a crybaby. A hundred people saw her dancing after the so-called incident."

Maggie's voice fell to a husky whisper. She muttered on for a little bit about Harrison Ford, trying to decide which of his movies was her favorite, confessing she was so glad he finally found the one-armed man. Then I drove her home, found my alley parking spot untouched and unoccupied, and stomped up the back stairs to my empty apartment.

The moon had come up while we danced in the Stagecoach, rising over the valley, lighting up white-spangled fir trees with moonglow. Out the north window of my apartment I could see the edge of the bluff that separated the town from the peaks of the Tetons, sheltering us from the view of grandeur. Why was it that an ugly, hardscrabble mesa covered with sagebrush seemed so beautiful tonight? Snow clung to it in artistic swirls lit by lunar shine. Black dots of sage speckled across it. If I had a view of the Grand Teton out my north window, I would feel truly blessed, maybe the way a movie star feels when everything he ever dreamed of is his for the asking, when money and power bring more privilege than any man needs. But I have an extraordinary view nonetheless. A view it takes special eyes to appreciate. Anyone can appreciate the Grand Teton.

Last year I was dying for a new view. Maybe a little cabin at the base of the mountains, a garden, a dog. Especially a fabulous view, as if having a view made a difference in your life. Maybe it did, I don't know. But I had my thinking rearranged. Now I think your view comes from inside somewhere, where you plan the kind of person you'll be and the kind of life you want. Last year, losing someone so close to me, had done that for me.

I put on the old sweats for bed. They were freshly laundered by Una, soft and comfortable, reassuring. Una, in a drug-induced sleep in a sterile hospital bed. Hank, on a lumpy jail mattress with no sheets. Did they give them sheets? Poor Hank.

In bed the moon shone in brightly through the square-facing window. I pulled back the shutters and let it light up the blue-and-white quilt on my bed. I slept in the bed alone, for the first time in over a week. I stretched out my arms across the double bed, my feet down to the end of the blankets. The cool sheets against my toes felt grand, the pillows soft and familiar. My own bed, alone.

It shouldn't feel so good. But it did.

I LOOKED THROUGH the cracked door of Una's hospital room the next morning at ten, a white sack of muffins from the Bunnery under my coat. My body had insisted, because of exhaustion and the comfort of my own bed, that I sleep until nine-fifteen. I had only enough time to shower and grab a coffee to go, along with the muffins. If only those blackened sacks under my eyes proved I'd had a good night's sleep. The sun streamed into Una's windows, a blinding reflection off the white snow that blanketed the town. Past the white lawn, sunlight glared off windshields and chrome in the parking lot. I pushed open the door and poked my head in. "Mom?"

"Yes? Come in, come in," she called, sounding cheery. She smiled broadly at seeing me, accepted a chocolate-cream-cheese muffin, and sat up as I plumped her pillows. We dispatched the niceties and bit into our muffins. By that time my curiosity about what Hank had squirreled away in the pickup was brimming over. My mother, on the other hand, seemed to have forgotten our conversation completely. Maybe she was half asleep and didn't remember me calling. Finally, I had to ask.

Her face clouded. "Yes, I remember. I've been up since six thinking about it." She sighed. "He didn't want anyone to know. He was afraid of this. I scoffed, I thought who would want it, let alone steal it? I couldn't fathom it, not in a million years. And here it's happened."

"What's happened? What was stolen?"

"Remember last summer, when we went on that archaeological dig at Fort Union?"

I nodded; how could I forget? I saw the slides of that trip just this week.

"Something happened," she continued. "Something happened at that dig that was quite unexpected." She sat back on her pillows, her hands still in her lap. "I was really bored with it all, the digging with a teaspoon, the tiny squares marked off with string. At first it's exciting, but then it is so tedious they have to get a new batch of volunteers every week, or they'd all be batty. It was Friday, our last day, except Hank wanted to stay over and help on Saturday. I had plans to go see Marquis what's-his-name's house on the Missouri River, Teddy Roosevelt's friend? Anyway, Hank was digging away with one of the archaeologists from the National Park. I wandered off.

"I walked about a half mile down the river. You know where Fort Union is, where the Yellowstone and the Missouri come together? In North Dakota but in spitting distance of the Montana line."

I nodded, hoping this story was going somewhere.

Una continued: "Anyway, I'm walking along, enjoying the sunshine, minding my own business. I sat down under an old cottonwood tree, very shady, nice. I see that there are lots of interesting rocks, flat and round or square. I'd been looking for some rocks as we traveled around, for my patio and my garden. We always picked up a few.

"I found this one that was very smooth and seemed perfect. It was stuck half in the ground. So I walked back, and on Hank's break I took him back there. We dug it out of the ground and turned it over. Hank saw it first." Una opened her eyes. "Sometimes I wish I'd never found that rock."

"What was on it?"

"That writing. Runes, like we were talking about. Old Norse lettering."

"Runes? Carved on the rock?"

"That's right. At first I thought it was just scratches, weeds, roots, worm tracks or something. But Hank was right. They were letters, carved into the stone. It was a slab, like the Ten Commandments."

I frowned at my coffee. "Did he have it translated?"

"Partially. He thinks it's authentic."

"Authentic what?"

Una looked away, out the window, squinting into the light. "He thinks it's from the Viking days."

I blinked up at her, uncomprehending. "What?"

Una pressed her lips together and nodded, now looking me in the eye. She didn't believe it either, but she wouldn't say anything against Hank. Not now while he's in a heap of trouble.

"I see," I muttered. "Viking-era runestone. Uh-huh." I sipped my coffee. "Does it have a date on it?"

"Of sorts. They didn't use exactly the same calendar, he says.

He says he needs more experts to look at it. But ones he can trust not to blab about it prematurely.''

"And verify that it is what he thinks it is," I added.

"Right."

"That makes sense." For Hank, that was right up there on top of the sense-o-meter. "What makes him think it's that old? We're talking about a thousand years ago, give or take a century."

"It mentions King Magnus. Hank says it was King Magnus who sent out the expedition that ended up carving the rock found at Kensington."

"In Minnesota? That big stone?" She nodded. Hank had been talking about the Kensington Stone so much for the last year, I was even starting to believe in it. "What else does it say?"

"Not much. Hank thinks it was written by the last survivors of that party. Maybe they were captured by Indians. That's what Hank thinks."

"How big is it?"

Una raised her broken arm and the good one, about twelve inches apart. "About eight inches wide, an inch or two thick. Not big, really. Not much room for a long inscription."

I stood up and stared out at the blinding morning. My head immediately felt like it had been skewered. A Viking runestone, for Pete's sake. And yet a man was dead, a man was accused of murder, and my mother had been run down by a truck.

"Did Glasius Dokken know about this stone?" I asked.

Una nodded. "Hank told him that afternoon. He showed him the stone, and Dokken was able to read some of it, not much. Some of it was faint, hardly readable at all."

"Who else knew?"

"No one," Una said, her eyes wide. "He told no one."

"What about experts?"

"Oh, yes, two experts. One he sent a letter to. He lives in Sweden. The other one is a professor in Wisconsin who studies Old Norse."

"What did they say?"

"We still haven't heard from the man in Sweden. At a museum, he is. The professor was very excited. He thinks it proves that the Kensington Stone is real. With all the new information about the Kensington, this really confirms that Vikings were here first."

I sat down again, crumpled up my muffin cup, and threw it in the trash. "That's important to Hank, isn't it? Proving that the Vikings were first."

She cocked her head. "Sure, it is." Frowning, she continued: "But not so important he would lie or put Glasius in danger or—"

"Or what?"

"Or kill Glasius. He would not kill someone over that stone. I know him, Alix. He wouldn't."

"I know that, Mom."

She checked me out. "All right."

"But somebody did. And somebody seems to have run you down after stealing this rock carving. Have you named it? Or do we just call it The Rock?"

"Hank calls it the Viking Vindicator, but that's too long, don't you think?" I smiled. She added, "So I call it the Union Rock."

"That's good. Nice and short," I said.

She settled back in the pillows, pleased. "I thought so."

"How about Union Rune-ion?" She looked at me, puzzled. "Just kidding. What's the name of this professor?"

"Breda. Harvey Breda, University of Wisconsin. Are you going to call him?" Una said brightly. The effect of the stone was to make people eager and alert, if nothing else.

"Should I?"

"Oh, yes. By all means. He can tell you all about it, Alix."

I held the door open, one last muffin in the sack. Una didn't want it, too tempting, she said. I asked, "Have you talked to Hank? About the accident, I mean."

Una cast down her eyes. Her hair looked freshly shampooed, fluffy and coiffed. For an injured person she looked damn good. "No, I should have called him, but I didn't want him to worry. He will be worried when I don't come see him today. They want to keep me one more night. Now they want more X rays of my ankle."

"Do they think it's broken?"

"I'm not sure. You know doctors. They never tell you what you really want to know."

"I'll go see Hank. Okay?"

Una nodded, smiling at me gratefully. "Tell him I love him, will you?"

I LEFT UNA tripping through the usual Sunday television fare, fishing shows, talking heads, infomercials, right-wing fundamentalists. Whoever her doctor was, I wanted to kiss him. Keeping Una another day was a stroke of genius. I could see us now, hobbling up and down the steep, narrow steps to my apartment. Knowing she was well cared for and resting easy meant a lot to me.

Going to see Hank again, though, did not ring my chimes. And I certainly wasn't going to convey my mother's love. Part of me flipped, twisting, as she said she loved him. I had never heard her say that. It was unusual for Una to express love in such an offhand manner. She rarely, for instance, told me she loved me. Maybe I should get myself arrested.

I drove home, made a pot of coffee, and put in a call to Professor Harvey Breda at the University of Wisconsin. He was ice fishing, his wife said, but would call back this evening if he could. I explained a little about who I was, without giving out too much information about Hank. Then I called Erik. My brother would be sleeping late, but he had a two-year-old at home. Willie answered, after some knocking of the phone to the floor: "Hello?"

"It's Aunt Alix, Willie. How are you?"

Silence. He didn't remember me from last summer. That was probably good, since I was practically catatonic when he was here.

"Willie?"

"Huh?"

"Is your Daddy there?"

"Sleepin'."

"Can you wake him up? I have to talk to him."

Clunk. Phone falls to the floor again. Patter of little feet. Minutes pass. Then more minutes. I consider hanging up.

"Hello? Yeah. Who's this?"

"Erik, it's your sis. Did I wake you?" I grinned.

"No, you didn't wake me. I'm still asleep, can't you tell?"

"Got any good jokes for me?"

He groaned. "Too early, X. You wouldn't believe how hard it is to round up a hundred octogenarians and get their clubs and rides and dinners sorted out. I have a killer headache." He cleared his throat and rustled bedsheets. "What's happening? What time is it? Where am I?"

"It's past ten. Listen, Erik, Mom's in the hospital. Nothing serious, just a broken arm and a twisted ankle."

"Shit, did she fall?"

"She got sideswiped by a pickup truck." He cursed a few times to show he cared. I continued: "Do you know anything about Vikings in the New World? You know, before Columbus?"

"Well, sure. They were here. There are foundations of buildings in Newfoundland, with nails and stuff from the Old World."

"What about coming inland? Has anything ever been proven?"

"Oh, you mean like the rock carvings? They found that one in Minnesota—the Kensington—a hundred years ago and thought it was a hoax. Then they thought it wasn't a hoax, that there had been explorers later, after the Vikings killed themselves off. Late Middle Ages."

"So they think it could have happened?"

"It's doubtful. There was something new about it recently. Can't remember what. It's controversial. Some historians think it could have happened. What's this about?"

I told him the short version. More groaning, more cursing.

"You've got to be kidding. Hank thinks he found a runestone?"

"Actually Mom found it."

"And now it's missing, they think somebody stole it? Whatever for?"

"I guess the only reason would be because they think it's significant, authentic, whatever. To be the discoverer of the Viking Vindicator."

Erik sighed, then cursed. This was Erik's usual state when dealing with the family. If he hadn't been such a Viking buff, I wouldn't even have told him about it. "Let me do some checking, find out who the top guys in the field are now."

"Hank called this Breda, at Wisconsin."

"Never heard of him but, well, I'll call you back."

We hung up. The sound of melted snow dripping off the eaves was punctuated by falling icicles. The sun brightened my apartment, but only indirectly; I had no south windows. I looked out my west window toward the square, curious if the ice carvers were still at work. One man hunched over a large sculpture, but there was no sign of Merle. The thermometer said it was twenty degrees. Still cold—but with sunshine beating down, things were going to melt. The streets already had the transparent look of slush. Today at four I had to judge the ice carving. If the weather held.

The phone rang in the kitchen. The voice was soft and accented. It was Bjarne, wondering why I hadn't made it to the race yesterday. It took a second to put my mind in reverse.

"Sorry. I, ah—" So much had happened in the last twenty-four hours I hardly knew where to start. "You know about the fire, don't you?"

"Oh, yes. That was terrible for your father."

"Stepfather. Yes, it was awful. And he's still in jail, so I felt a little guilty going out, even to watch you race."

"A true Norwegian sentiment, let me tell you. Better to sulk around the house." His voice was teasing, sweet. "Now, you come today."

"Today? But—"

"No buts. I race at one o'clock today, and you must come. I strained a muscle in my calf yesterday. Remember what my fortune said?"

"Something like…when you need the power, it will be there?"

"Yes, if the need be great enough. Well, it is great, but I

don't want to rely on Thor of the runes. I want a Thorssen there too.''

''I've never been a good-luck piece before. What would I have to do?''

''Oh, give me a kiss, that's all. Just a simple kiss.''

''For luck?'' I breathed, fingering the edge of the kitchen counter like it was a newfound instrument of success.

''For luck. You'll come?''

''Oh, Bjarne. I wish I could. It's just I have too much to do today. I really can't. But I'll wish you luck from afar, okay?''

A pause. Was he pissed? ''I wish you'd come,'' he said at last, his voice low, disappointed.

''Sorry, Bjarne. Good luck.'' I hung up the phone, sighed loudly, and eased my chin down to my hands with my elbows propped up on the counter. He certainly did want me, that Lycra-legged Romeo. *Just a simple kiss.* Mmmm. I could taste it.

A swallow of coffee. That helped. Because I had to go visit the jail again, not one of my favorite places. But I told my mother I would. A last slug of coffee for courage. And maybe for luck too.

For luck, Bjarne. For luck.

THIRTEEN

Wise was the lady,
had her wits about her,
full well understood she
what in stealth they whispered.

SUNDAY AT THE Teton County Jail was visiting time, a time to make amends to the brother you turned in for selling cocaine out of the bedroom, a time to cry over the uncle who couldn't stop drinking and driving, a time to beg for mercy and forgiveness. I didn't want to do any of these things with Henry Helgeson. But the group in the waiting room seemed ready, if not willing or able: nervous, teary wives, thin, drawn girlfriends with tattoos, a mother staring numbly at the beige wall.

When my name was called, I followed the woman officer to a small interrogation room where Hank sat in a standard metal chair. He didn't look as bad as my imagination had pictured him: still pink cheeks, still plump, still bright eyes unbeaten by the mounting legal machinery against him.

I sat down. The officer shut the door and remained in the small room, breathing down my neck. I glanced back at her to register my complaint against privacy, but she kept her eyes on Hank and her hand on her gun.

"Mom can't come today, Hank," I began. His head began to bob up and down philosophically. "Did you hear?"

"I don't blame her," he started. "It's a burden, I—"

"Someone sideswiped her with a truck, Hank. Listen." I moved closer. "She's got a sprained ankle and a broken arm, but she's okay." He looked so bereft that I patted his arm. "She's all right," I whispered.

"Sideswiped her?"

"While she was down at the old garage, cleaning up the boat.

She was going back inside, and a pickup truck came out and almost ran her down.''

Behind his glasses, Hank's eyes fixed on my face and began to blink, his second chin quivering. ''A truck was in the garage? Not my truck?''

I shook my head. ''Another truck.'' I fixed him with a cocked-head look. ''Una had to tell me about it, Hank. She had no choice. Because, well, the rock is gone.''

He stood up, still blinking like mad. He took two steps around his chair, headed for the corner, and was there in two more steps. He clamped his hands together behind his back until his knuckles turned white.

''What rock?''

''Hank, she told me. All about it. I want to help find it, if I can, but I need your help. Maybe this whole mess you're in is about the rock. Somehow,'' I added softly.

He refused to turn around. ''I have no idea what you're talking about. No idea at all.''

''The Viking Vindicator. The one Una found at the Fort Union dig. With the runes? The rock possibly proving that a Viking troop came through these parts a hundred or more years before Columbus—''

''Possibly?!'' he shouted, spinning. His eyes caught the woman officer, and he paled. ''You are sworn to secrecy, woman! Nothing said in this room shall leave it! Nothing!'' He gripped his chair back as spittle shot from his mouth. ''And that goes for you too!'' He waggled a finger at me.

I sat back as he struggled with his emotions. He took a gulp of air as the redness seeped down off his jowls into his neck.

He plopped into his chair, lips tight. I put an elbow on the table. ''I need to know who you talked to about the rock, Hank. Who might have known.''

He crossed his arms and looked at the wall.

''Hank, please, I think I can run this down for you, maybe get it back.''

He harrumphed. No fury, no threats. Just a harrumph.

''Talk to me, Hank.''

As the pause stretched, my own stubbornness set in. I refused to beg him to help himself. I had offered, I had cajoled, but I would not pry information out of a stubborn cuss like Hank Helgeson.

I stood up. "I'm going now. Una is at St. John's, if they let you call. Consider my offer for her sake."

The whole frustrating business with my stepfather had taken less than an hour. I stood in the sunshine outside the county courthouse, where the sidewalk had turned into a small river of melting snow. As the runoff swirled around my pac boots (where my feet were now slow-cooking), I stared at my watch. In five minutes Bjarne would start his race. If I hurried, I could at least catch the end of it. Splashing and jumping puddles, I reached the Saab Sister with the sun on my shoulders, eager to leave the dreary hopelessness of the jail behind.

THE TETONS GLITTERED in the sun, their pine-cradled slopes giving way to alternating granite cliffs and glacial snowfields above the sagebrush plains of the valley. The red gondola bobbed up the cables, carrying sardined skiers to the peak of the ski area, where, from the looks of it, they would be fighting their way through a cloud.

Teton Village, all parking lot and chalets, held little wonder for me anymore. Oh, there were memories: the March day we all skied in black garbage bags in the rain, my friend the ski patroller who was hit by lightning while we cowered in the cafeteria, hoping everyone was off the mountain, the days of powder so fine and rarefied that it was hardly necessary to ever ski again.

I paused in the back of the parking lot and stared up at the slopes. I had skied one day this season: New Year's Day. Maggie had dragged me up with the promise of champagne in her bota bag. She was good on the promise, but the champagne made me queasy, and I quit early.

I took a deep breath of mountain air and began walking across the parking lot. The air smelled more of exhaust fumes and wood smoke than pine forests. The lot was full of cars and puddles, and it took ten minutes to negotiate the huge area and walk across to the Nordic race.

The crowd bellowed as I approached, walking gingerly through the slush. This weather couldn't be good for racing. It would slow the course with wet spots. I looked up from watching my footing to see what they were bellowing about; in the distance a skier charged out of the trees and began the last stretch of the race. The crowd had gathered on the finish line, surrounding the timers with wet wool and fur collars and more boots than a Canadian trading post.

A cloud passed over the sun as the lone figure, still too far away to identify, moved toward us. His diagonal stride chopped the air, arms swinging with long red poles. Then behind him from the trees another figure burst into view, skating to catch up in electric blue Lycra. The first man, in black, jerked his head back as if he had heard his approacher, then redoubled his efforts. They were both moving fast yet had a quarter mile at least to go before they crossed the finish line.

Now another skier shot out of the pines. At this distance they all looked alike, but something about the third man—the thatch of blond hair? Each had muscular thighs, lean, strong shoulders, perfect builds. The woman next to me in the crowd turned to a friend: "Isn't that the Norwegian? Mmmm, tasty." I gave her a look. She was perky, young, and wearing a fur-lined purple suede jacket.

Pushing through the large crowd, I tried to see the racers. The man in black, in the lead, was being seriously challenged by the guy in blue. The people began to cheer for him, shouting, "Go! Go! Catch him! Faster—he's right behind you!" They were a hundred yards away when Bjarne made his superhuman try at winning. He came out of nowhere, in third place, in an orange-and-red-swirled Lycra bodysuit, his face beet red. Most were watching the other two, and his move was so sudden that a combined groan and gasp went up from the crowd.

The man in black put his head down and plowed for the finish. Electric Blue was on his left, crowding in for the kill. Bjarne was as red-hot as his Lycra on the right, striding long and hard, knocking into the leader's poles with his own. The crowd was wild, cheering, hollering, our throats sore from shouting, the excitement building. A few more yards—

Then in a heap of color and clatter of hollow wood and fiberglass, the racer in blue fell, tangled, twenty feet shy of the finish line. We all sucked in air in disbelief that he had faltered so close to his goal as the other two stretched and leaned and made it over the line. The man in black held his lead, but Bjarne was close behind. He was second! And missed winning by a hair. A swelling of pride filled my chest, and a stupid grin stuck to my face. I knew him! Yeah, Bjarne, that bighearted challenger, I knew him. Wow.

I stuck my hands in my pockets. All around me people hugged each other or clapped their hands and cheered some more. The man in blue was helped, cursing, to his feet by the medical crew and checked over for injuries as they whisked him out of the path. More skiers were coming now, a pack of four all trying to break free of each other, all hoping for that last burst of speed that would propel them beyond what they thought they could do.

Craning my neck, I spotted Bjarne bent over, hands on knees. Gasping or barfing. I wondered about that pulled muscle he'd mentioned. Maybe the heat of competition made you forget all the pain, forget everything but winning. Bjarne was some competitor. I could understand why he was favored for the next Olympic team. He had reached deep into his guts and found another ounce of courage, another ounce of determination. That made him a world-class racer.

The flock of four was approaching the finish line now, still packed tightly, as if there were security in numbers. The man with a slight lead—only half a stride—now pushed harder. But that made the man next to him push, and the other and the other.

The crowd yelled at them: "Do it, now! Go for it! Harder, harder!"

"Courage!" I hollered over the din.

The fabulous foursome finished together, unable to break their pattern. They would have different times, but they would be thought of as the boys who couldn't break out, who lacked some last iota of strength to be different, to win. Yet they had done their best. They had tried. At least they hadn't fallen down on the finish line. That guy would be chastising himself for a while.

As I looked again in Bjarne's direction, I couldn't see him at first. Odd, in that fluorescent outfit, but there were many brightly frocked skiers around by now. Then a flash of neon orange and red peeked through the crowd across the finish line from where I stood. Bjarne had his skis off now, his gloves in a heap at his feet. A woman threw her arms around him. She had a long navy coat with a hood, so I couldn't see her face. They embraced briefly; his face disappeared into her hood. A well-wisher, I thought. He is such a sweet guy, so warm.

Then he made the smallest motion. Just a flick of his hand across her cheek or lips. A smile on his face and a touch of her cheek. So intimate. He knows her. No, more than that. They are lovers.

A chill went through me, and my feet wouldn't move. *They are lovers.* How could I be sure? But I knew; there are just some things a woman knows. Practice with Paolo had sharpened my man-observation skills, and a cheek caress was one of the most intimate things a man could do in public. People kiss all the time, and it's meaningless. They hug, hold hands, shake hands. But a caress of the cheek was right up there with fingering your lover's forelock. It meant something.

I backed out of the crowd, my head down so Bjarne wouldn't see me. When I had turned and walked ten yards, I saw her, coat flapping against tall black boots. Who did she think she was—Dr. Zhivago's lover?

I clenched my teeth. My God, I was jealous. This was ridiculous. She headed for the parking lot. I was just going the same way, I told myself, picking up my heavy boots. Trying to hurry was impossible with these things. I swore silently, making an oath to buy something more streamlined. It wasn't hard keeping the woman in sight in the lot filled with rental cars and muddy pickup trucks and every color Explorer known to Ford. Her head bobbed along in the hood, one hand holding up a corner of her coat from puddles.

She ducked around a camper and didn't come out the other side. I kept walking in a line parallel to hers, about twelve car widths down the rows. She must have gotten in her car. I paused beside a silver Toyota with a bumper sticker that read, "Democracy Is Not a Spectator Sport,'' and pretended to be looking for my keys. I practiced this a lot in my everyday life, and it didn't take much to make it look sincere.

A station wagon bumped down the row behind my back. I took a furtive glance and ducked. The driver was intent on missing the potholes filled with muddy water. Next to him sat the woman, her hood down and her platinum hair pulled into a bun at the nape of her neck.

The rusted tan station wagon had Minnesota plates. It was driven by Peter Black.

FIFTEEN MINUTES LATER I turned at the Pearl Street light next to the grocery store and pointed the Saab Sister in the direction of the station wagon. Traffic wasn't too heavy, but huge lakes had formed in low spots, and rivers gushed down the gutters. Ahead the station wagon turned right on a side street. Two blocks back I swished through a puddle, slowing so as not to spray the pedestrians, then hurried to turn where they had.

So Peter and Isa hadn't left town. Peter said he was supposed to testify at Hank's hearing on Monday. Was there another reason?

I passed a small trailer park full of crowded, rusty mobile homes, then two cottages with funky linoleum siding, then the Squirrel's Nest Motel. ''Cheep and Cleen,'' the fading red sign proclaimed. And full of nuts. There was the station wagon, empty.

The Saab crept past the motel. Fifteen rooms facing the street, ten down, five up. I kept going and turned around at the dead end next to the mountain. As I passed the Squirrel's Nest again, I saw Peter in the parking lot, carrying a bag into the room. Isa stood in black boots, jeans, and a creamy white turtleneck sweater, holding the door open. She patted his back as he went through, and she shut the door.

As I pulled back onto Pearl Street, west toward Teton Village again, I wondered about Isa and Peter. Was he just her assistant, a helpful, thoughtful, loyal bearer of boxes and runes? Had they been staying in the same motel room since the fiasco at the

Wort? Were finances tight, or were they lying low at the Squirrel's Nest?

So many questions without answers. Such a fascinating couple, the White Queen of the Runes and her black Peter.

But now I had a skier to talk to.

FOURTEEN

Choose a shield for shelter,
a ship for speed,
a sword for keenness,
a girl for kissing.

THE EDELWEISS had Warren Miller's ski movies on the big-screen televisions, and as usual much beer drinking was taking place. By the time I arrived back at Teton Village, it was almost three and the après-ski crowd had begun to fill the chalet-style bar that sat at the bottom of the ski runs, next to the tram building. The warm wood paneling and large windows made the Edelweiss much more than a saloon, though, and a convivial spirit of well-exercised muscles and vacation leisure filled the place.

Bjarne had changed into civvies, the first pair of jeans I'd seen him in, cowboy boots, and a red fleece pullover. He stood at the bar, his damp forelock dropping over his forehead as Carter Reineking clapped him on the back. They were laughing, both red in the face, as I tapped Bjarne on the shoulder. I couldn't help smiling at the happiness on the skier's face.

"Alix, you came!" He set his mug down on the bar and hugged me hard, picking my feet off the floor and spinning me around. How could you not like this guy? I thought, pushing away as he set me on the floor again. "Did you see it? I knew there was some Thorssen luck on me today."

"I saw the end," I said. "You almost caught him."

"If only I had a kiss from you at the start," he said, pulling me close. "Then I would have made it all the way." He kissed me hard and quick, making the color rise to my face as tables of skiers around us stared.

"With that leg it's a damn miracle you came in second,"

Carter put in, leaning his back against the bar. "God, it's good to have the races done." He took a long gulp of beer, then peered at me. "How's Maggie? I need to—"

I waited for him to finish, but he let the thought slip away. "Yes, you need to call her," I said.

Bjarne bounced on his toes, grabbing my hand, then winced. "This leg is killing me, all right. But I'm so glad you came."

He looked like he might kiss me again, so I ordered a beer from the bartender. When it came, I waited for a pause in the victory celebration before drawing Bjarne aside.

"I guess the runes were right about when you needed power, and all that," I said. Bjarne smiled, sipped beer. "Did you need another consultation with Mistress Isa for luck?"

He frowned and shook his head. "What are you talking about?"

"I saw her at the finish of the race. She gave you a kiss."

Bjarne squinted into my face, too close, then smiled. His voice was low, an intimate whisper. "Are you jealous? Could that be, my sweet?" He moved closer until I could feel the heat coming off him, masculine and dense. "I could fix that, I could."

This time the kiss was much longer. My head filled with non-sense and snow flurries that wouldn't clear as long as his lips touched mine. I gasped for air, and the spell was broken. Bjarne ran his hand through his hair, turned toward the bar, and took a long drink of beer. I stood motionless, stunned. All around us the prattle of chitchat rose again in my ears, the squeals, guffaws, low rumbles of conversation, until when I swallowed at last, I was back in the Edelweiss, here, now.

Carter said something, nudged me. He was pointing at the TV screen, where a pink-haired skier was doing a somersault off a cliff. A collective groan crossed the room, then faded as the skier sank into deep powder, emerging victorious.

I looked at Bjarne. He glanced at me, nervous, then away.

"But what about Isa?" I croaked. My voice sounded like someone else's, someone who couldn't stop obsessing when it was obvious the earth had shifted under her feet.

"I haven't seen her since she read my fortune," he said. "I don't know what you mean."

"The woman in the hooded coat? Navy blue. You kissed her after the race."

He shook his head. "I didn't recognize her. Was that her?" He turned back to me, touching my hair with his fingertips. "I have to go soak this leg. Come back to my room with me, yes?"

I closed my eyes for a second, feeling his hand on my cheek. He rubbed his thumb on my lower lip, then gave me a quick kiss and moved his lips to my ear. "Come back to my room, my sweet."

"I—I can't. The, um, ice sculpture judging starts in half an hour. I have—"

He hadn't moved his lips, his cheek warm against mine. "Let someone else do it. I need you, my sweet. Come celebrate the races with me. I will be all alone in my room without you."

My body was on fire. I thought about his room, so dingy and depressing. And yet it didn't feel that way. It beckoned me, *he* beckoned me. His heat could melt me: me, an icicle dripping from his warmth. I felt myself draining, drawing down, down into his heat.

I stepped back quickly. He set his beer mug on the bar and took my hand. I let him pull me through the crowd, all the time telling myself I was crazy, I was nuts, I had to be back in town. And all the time not listening to myself.

Bjarne unlocked a room in the adjoining hotel. It was strewn with literature about the Nordic ski races, a desk pulled out into the room. The bed was covered with sign-up sheets, ribbons, badges, numbers. Bjarne swept a hand across the bedspread, sending it all onto the floor in a heap.

I felt dizzy. I leaned against the wall by the bed as he came up to me, took my hand. "Wait a minute," I squeaked as he kissed me hard. Pressing me against the wall, his hands pulled out my shirttail and felt cold against my burning skin. Oh, shit, this was too much. I kissed him hard, then gasped for air.

"Wait, wait, I—"

He silenced me again, finding the zipper on my pants. As they drooped to my knees, as I felt him hard against me, as my mind slipped a gear and let instincts take over, voices came in the direction of the hallway. I kept one ear on them; all else was engaged. Bjarne pulled back my hair and kissed my neck.

Carter Reineking opened the door, still talking. I jumped an inch. Bjarne looked at his friend, then at my khakis on the floor, and stepped between us. I bent over, cursing with my eyes closed, and pulled up my pants.

A young woman with a cardboard box full of badges and numbers peeked around Carter's shoulder. Carter himself smiled benevolently.

"Excuse us." He smirked.

"We were just leaving," Bjarne said, reaching behind him to grab my hand as I stuck my shirttail in under my sweater. My face felt hot and red. At least I didn't know the woman, I thought. Bjarne pulled me past them, out into the overheated hallway. Carter closed the door behind us, shaking his head.

"Come, we'll go to my place," Bjarne said, his breath still short. He moved closer to me as I walked down the hall, trying to stop me. I pushed him gently. "Alix, come on."

I couldn't talk. I was embarrassed and flushed and feeling light-headed and very, very alive. I wished I could tell him that. He pleaded with me down the stairs to the parking lot, all the way to my car. I kissed him quickly as I got in the Saab. I rolled down the window, listening to him still trying to cajole me as I drove away, winter air on my face.

Fresh air, fresh, cold air. That was what I needed. Maybe a faceful of wet snow. Even a slushy mud puddle.

Something to bring me to my senses.

MAGGIE WAS WAITING in the gallery when I dragged myself through the back door, yanking off the pac boots on the mat and breathing heavily. The drive back from Teton Village had been adequate to cool my jets, but the pit of my stomach might never be the same. I wasn't exactly sorry about what had happened, but I wasn't exactly proud either. I couldn't remember any man *ever* talking to me that way, and Bjarne's words kept running over and over in my mind. But as much as I was attracted to him—hell, I'd probably have to tattoo his name on my ass before this was over—as much as I wanted him, there was something about him I couldn't quite put my finger on.

"There you are," Maggie said, smirking in the doorway to my office, arms crossed.

"Am I late?"

"Does the bear shit in the woods?"

That only raised a half-smile on my lips. I dumped my backpack on my office chair and stared at the pile of pink messages that Artie had placed on my desk. I couldn't bring myself to read them, so staring would have to do.

"What's the matter? Is it your mom?" Maggie touched my shoulder.

"No, no. It's just, um, this festival. There is way too much going on. Next year I'm out." I heaved another sigh and looked around the floor for my clogs.

"Tired? I shouldn't have taken you out dancing last night. But it sure was fun, huh?"

I looked up at Maggie's smiling face at last: tanned, happy, glittering eyes, mischievous eyebrows, shining hair. I smiled. "It was a lot of fun, Mags. I wouldn't have missed it. I've just got a lot on my mind right now."

"Well, the drag queen hasn't arrived yet. She's supposed to meet us here for the judging, right?"

"Yeah." I poked my head out my office door, past Maggie, and saw a flash of purple satin on the boardwalk. "Here she comes."

Gloria Worster, the Chamber of Commerce drag queen—a white-bread-and-mustard gal masquerading as a flat-chested Dolly Parton—gave Artie a big howdy as she sashayed into the gallery. The violet satin shirt had rows of white fringe and pearl buttons, her skintight black jeans tucked inside red and white cowboy boots that really should have been wearing those cute pointy galoshes today. Gloria had done something new with her hair, more Dolly-ish, bigger and blonder.

"Let's do it," I said, grabbing a yellow legal pad and a pen from my desk drawer. I still had my down coat on, even though the weather was now mid-thirties. It had been too warm at the ski races in the sun, but now the mountains had the town in their shadow. The day was almost done.

"Hey, Gloria," I said, nodding unenthusiastically at the Chamber of Commerce exec. "Are you ready?"

"Sure thing." Gloria and Maggie were not legendary pals. No doubt Maggie's remarks about Gloria's snazzy wardrobe had gotten back to her. Something about the set of Gloria's jaw when she nodded to Maggie told me this was true.

"A couple of the sculptors called me today, Alix. Even though I told them this was really your gig," Gloria said pointedly. "They told me they couldn't get ahold of you."

The pile of pink messages seemed bigger suddenly. "I've been busy. What did they want?"

She put her red-polished nails on her hips. "I think they want to have one more day. They couldn't do much today because of the thaw, you know?" She was snapping her gum, honest to God. "So I told them to call that Dieter guy who set up all the chefs."

I peered out the front window. Some of the sculptures had huge golf umbrellas shading them; others were draped with canvas to keep the sun off. I saw Dieter Moritz on the far side of the square, talking to a sculptor in coveralls.

"Well, let's go talk to Dieter, then," Maggie said, plowing toward the door.

"There's no use all of us going. The street's a mess." I looked at Gloria's boots, then at Maggie's feet. She wore her low-top hiking shoes. "I've got my pac boots right here. You guys wait here."

DIETER'S FOREHEAD WAS beaded with sweat. He confirmed, unhappily, that four sculptors had asked for extra time because of the weather. Suggesting that it was partially my fault because I had relayed (and thus reinforced) the weather prediction for a thaw, he had to agree with the sculptors. Cold weather is best. Warm weather is death to ice sculpting. So it was agreed. A twenty-four-hour delay. A prayer to Skadi for her mountain-cold weather.

With a sigh of relief, I trudged back to the gallery, vowing never to wear the stupid, heavy pac boots again as long as I live. Or until the next blizzard. I informed Maggie and Gloria of the decision and made appointments with them for four tomorrow. Gloria breezed off, all of us watching her well-defined swagger on the boardwalk as she waved a toodle-oo to passersby.

Just before Maggie and I slipped off upstairs, I looked back at Artie with his elbows on the counter, chin in palms, a wistful look in his eyes. "How's it going?"

"Okay," he said. "A couple good sales."

I nodded. "Give it half an hour, then go home." I made a silent pledge to give him a day off later in the week, come hell or high water. If I didn't, he was likely to quit on me. And that was the last thing I needed.

MAGGIE PRONOUNCED HERSELF beat and flopped onto the sofa upstairs. I headed for the kitchen, thinking of a snack. Maybe some of that cheese was left from the reception. Now it seemed like food left over from a wake, nibbled on mournfully for weeks. I was just grateful it wasn't tuna noodle casserole with potato chip topping.

As I stuck my head into the fridge, Maggie yelled: "Light's blinking on your answering machine."

"Probably my mother." I found the cheese, only slightly dried out, and hacked off the bad stuff with a large knife on the cutting board. "You want to hit it?"

Unable to contain her curiosity, beat or not, Maggie leaped to action. In a second, clicks and beeps, and the mechanical voice of my answering machine (I called him Sigmund; he sounded a lot like my conscience) proclaimed robotically: "You have three new messages. First message left today at two-oh-seven-p.m." The voice of my mother came on. "Alix, this is your mother. Hank called, he was worried. I wish you'd let me tell him about the stone, but I *do* understand. I just wish…oh, honey, I wish all this hadn't happened, you know? I wish I'd never found that stupid stone. I——" She growled a little, which was her way of being annoyed and sad. "Call me later," she finished.

"What stone? What's she talking about?" Maggie piped up

between Sigmund's pronouncements. I waved her off, mouth full of cheese.

"Alix, this is Bjarne." Maggie raised her eyebrows at the throaty, low tone of his voice. "I just wanted to talk to you again. No, that's not true. I want to see you again. Can I come by tonight? I hope you're not busy, because I have a bottle of wine and this time we will really celebrate. No more interruptions, I promise. Okay? I'll call you later, sweetheart." He gave me the number of his motel and whispered goodbye.

Maggie was fanning herself with both hands. "Sweetheart?" she asked pointedly. I felt myself redden, then grinned back at her as the last message began.

"Alix, this is Earl Simms. We met last night at the Stagecoach over in Wilson? Listen, I want to apologize again for my friend Lucinda. She really overreacted. I was hoping you'd let us make it up to you. There's a cocktail party tonight"—Maggie stepped right up to the machine on the kitchen counter like she was trying to eat the words—"at a neighbor of Harrison's. It's a fund-raiser for something, wolves or clean air or something. Anyway, can you come? Bring your friend too, if you want. About seven-thirty." He gave an address in Moose, in the ritzy part where you couldn't see the houses from the winding lanes. Then he just about begged me—or rather Maggie—to come.

Sigmund signed off. Maggie was holding her sides like she might burst, a dumbstruck smile on her face.

"He is hot for you, girl," I said across the counter from her. "Too bad he's a foot too short."

Maggie threw her arms wide. "I *like* short guys. In fact, I just realized short guys turn me on!"

"Short, rich guys with movie star friends."

"Well, I never considered that." She twirled around the sofa like a woman in love in a romance movie.

"So when are you going to tell him your real name?"

She pulled her black hair up, twisting it and prancing a bit like she was Cinderella off to the ball to meet Prince Charming. "Oh, later. It's just a cocktail party. We can pretend for one measly cocktail party, can't we? You *are* coming, Alix."

"If Alix Thorssen is coming, why do I have to?"

She let her hair drop. "I can't go into a big celebrity party by myself. Are you crazy?"

I busied myself with cheese. The way I was feeling, it wouldn't be good to stay home and wait for Bjarne. I had no faith in my ability to act rationally around him. "So am I Maggie Barlow tonight? Or can I be anyone I want?"

Maggie rushed around the counter and hugged me. "You can be anybody you want except yourself. Just for tonight, please?"

"I've always had a secret fantasy where I'm an insurance agent."

Maggie stuck out her tongue at me. "Nobody ever wants to talk to me at parties anyway. Don't tell them you're in insurance. I never do."

"Now that's settled, the big question remains: What are you going to wear?"

Maggie threw up her hands. "Oh, God, I have to think about this. Something arty, maybe floaty and bright, purple or blue. Yellow! Do you ever wear yellow?"

"Nope."

"Oh, who cares what you wear? You don't dress like an art dealer."

"I don't?"

"Of course not. You aren't trying to make an impression with your clothes. Now, Paolo, he dressed like an art dealer. Those silk shirts and flannel slacks that hugged his gorgeous bod...those peasant blouses he used to wear? Where did he get those? Never in my life have I seen a man who oozed machismo in a peasant blouse like Paolo." She paused and looked up at me. "Oh, shit. I'm sorry. I thought—"

She hugged me again, and I realized a hard spot in my chest had formed when she spoke about Paolo. It even hardened around the spot of desire for Bjarne that remained. I took a deep breath and tried to ease it away.

"It's okay," I said, stepping back. "It's time to let him go. I never thought it would be so hard."

Maggie slapped herself in the forehead. "What about Bjarne? He wanted to come over tonight. And here I made you promise to go to the party with me." She paced out into the living room.

"I'll just not go. Forget it. What was I thinking, passing myself off as you with a bunch of movie stars?"

I walked over and took her hand, made her stop pacing. "I don't think I want Bjarne to come over. He's going home in a couple days, and I'll never see him again. I *want* to go to the cocktail party."

"You're sure?" she asked. I nodded. "Okay, what are we going to wear?"

FIFTEEN

All hail to the givers!
A guest hath come
say where shall he sit?
In haste is he to the hall who cometh,
to find a place by the fire.

THE SUB SANDWICH dripped into the napkin in my lap as I idled past the Squirrel's Nest Motel in the Saab Sister. It was five o'clock, and I was starved, biting into the fat meatball sandwich as if I hadn't eaten in days. The light was fading, a purple twilight etching the high clouds as the color drained from the sky. I turned the steering wheel awkwardly with one hand as meatball juices plopped onto my jeans. Pointed back toward Pearl Street now, I slowed to a stop across from the motel.

Not a stakeout, no, I told myself. Just some place to eat a meatball sandwich and look at the view. The fading pink paint of the Squirrel's Nest made a decorative contrast to the tall pine trees sticking up from the pile of snow near their parking lot. I munched and tried not to think about how to act like Maggie tonight. That wouldn't be too difficult and might even provide a small diversion from the tumult and heartache of this weekend. I wondered idly if Gloria would even propose having Nordic Nights next year. Certainly I wouldn't be inviting any Norwegian artists into town again.

The dead-end street was quiet. The rusting station wagon sat listing in one of the parking lot's many potholes. Isa and Peter would have to come out for dinner. Or at least Peter would go fetch something. That was my hope, to corner him and get some information. Isa didn't look like the type open to prying. But based on Peter's willingness to meet me in the Wort's coffee shop, I could at least expect him to be civil.

At five-thirty I had finished my meatball sandwich and used four napkins to clean up. Gathering all my trash in the white paper bag supplied, I exited the Saab and pulled my down jacket together. The warmth of the day had gone, the first stars popping out overhead. The street had melted off in the sunshine, but a thin layer of water had frozen in the chill. I picked my way over the ice in my clogs, wishing I hadn't sworn off the clunky but functional boots. The Squirrel's Nest didn't shovel their sidewalk, I noticed as I almost landed on my better side more than once.

My destination was a garbage can on the corner of Pearl Street. When I got there, I ducked into Mama Inez, where a public phone hung on the wall near the kitchen. Somehow in my short life I had come to know where every public phone in Jackson was. I borrowed the cashier's phone book, found the Squirrel's Nest number, dialed, and asked for Peter Black's room.

Unfortunately, Isa answered the telephone. I started, improvising: "This is the manager. Do you need any extra towels?" I sputtered in a vaguely Oriental accent that was absolutely politically incorrect.

"No, I do not," Miss Mardoll declared.

"Ah, yes, fine," I said. "Is your automobile a Dodge station wagon, beige in color?"

Breathing on the line. "Yes." Irritated.

"We are beginning to use the snowplow on the parking lot," I went on, Charlie Chanlike, wincing at the improbable nature of it all. "If you would be so kind as to move your automobile to the street now for an hour or so?"

"Right now?"

"If you would be so kind?"

Annoyed sigh. "All right." She hung up.

Head down, I plodded through frozen slush back down the street toward the Squirrel's Nest. As I approached the motel, Peter emerged from Room 16, jacketless, and jumped into the station wagon. Slipping on the icy mess of the lot (which was essentially unplowable at this point), the wagon spun out on the incline to the street. After a minute of false starts Peter piloted the car over the sidewalk, against the curb where I walked slowly. As he stepped out of the car into the street, I stopped and faced him.

"Peter? Is that you?"

He blinked into the dim lights of the motel. Beside us "Cheep and Cleen" flickered in green neon. He looked at the motel door, then back at me.

"Alix Thorssen, remember?" He blinked, looking scared. I walked closer, around the front of the car to the street side. "How are you?"

"Okay," he said quietly, taking a step back.

"Can we talk for just a second? I know Isa's probably waiting, but—"

"She *is* waiting."

"I saw her today," I said, ignoring his retreat. "Out at the ski area. Did she come out to watch Bjarne race? That's why I was there." I paused for confirmation in his eyes. Forward movement on this one-sided conversation was paramount. "I saw you too, driving the car. I thought you left town—but then, you have to testify tomorrow, don't you? You are going to testify at my stepfather's hearing, aren't you, Peter?"

He nodded. "I have to go."

"Is Isa going to see Bjarne tonight?"

He shook his head. "What are you talking about?"

"I just thought maybe they had, you know, a thing going."

That got his interest. He frowned. "A thing?"

"Lovers."

Peter's eyes grew huge, the green neon glow of the sign gleaming off his dark skin. He spun suddenly and took two steps away and stopped. His fists at his sides clenched angrily. I could see his shoulders shake slightly under the thin black turtleneck he wore. He turned back toward me, intensity tightening his face.

"Stupid girl. Don't you see? How could anything be plainer to you?" He jerked his head toward the motel room, then looked at his feet in black motorcycle boots, then back finally at me.

"*I* am Isa's lover."

A small smile crept onto my lips as I watched him walk briskly back to Room 11. Not only had I discovered that Bjarne was telling me the truth, or at least enough of the truth, but I had forced Peter to reveal the nature of his feelings for Isa. I wasn't completely sure Isa felt the same way. She seemed like the kind of woman who used men to suit her purposes, and the way she ordered Peter around, made him chauffeur and wait on her, wasn't exactly like a woman in love. But what did I know? Maybe it was an act for the public. Maybe in private she waited on *him*. I thought about her haughty airs, the harsh white hair, the set of her crimson mouth. No, I don't think she did any waiting on anyone, in private or public.

MAGGIE DROVE HER old Wagoneer with fake wood side panels through the sage-studded snowfields toward Grand Teton National Park, singing along with Loudon Wainwright's "I Wish I Was a Lesbian (and Not a Hetero)" at the top of her lungs. Between joining her and Loudon on the chorus, I wondered briefly about the wisdom of wearing her clothes as well as her name to this party. It was possible I would know some people, even though it wasn't my usual crowd. I sold art to some of these nouveaux riches now and then. And Maggie was known to have insured a number of them too. But she was oblivious to these worries, so I let it slide that she had on my sister's ancient blue wool blazer and my clogs. How many black-haired Thorssens there were in the world, I couldn't be sure. Tonight, at least, there was one.

The house in question, a mere cottage—a shack, said Maggie—loomed in the darkness behind a sweet grove of bare-limbed aspens flanked with towering spruces laden with crusty snow. According to our meager information, the million-dollar log home belonged to the scion of a railroading fortune who had his sights on a Hollywood career. Right now he had little else to do with his time but manage the foundation that gave away daddy's money, and give parties for causes that attracted the "right" people.

His name was Michael James Fairchild III, husband of Reenie, of whom I had heard a few stories around town for her personal diet and fitness plan that created fabulous bods and took only six hours a day and several thousand dollars a week to apply to you, glorious you. The Third, or Jim, met us at the door, a trim and attractive man of forty, tan, relaxed, and vacant of face. He wore his Wyoming outfit: an Abercrombie & Fitch fishing shirt with incongruous leather pants. His smile was automatic and impersonal when he realized we were nobody. Maggie practiced our first switched introductions on him and winked at me as we eased into the crowd.

Almost immediately R2D2—aka Earl Simms—spotted Maggie and trotted over. He gave her the Hollywood air kiss and shook my hand. I guess you have to meet twice for the air kiss. He had warm eyes and hands, and smelled like oranges, some new citrus cologne. He was still very short, but his hair was absent the itsy-bitsy ponytail, so he looked more grown-up.

Earl didn't seem to mind, or even notice, that Maggie and I had a good six inches on him when he took both of our arms and led us to the bar. Ordering up a gin and tonic for me and white wine for Maggie, Earl began to give us the lay of the land.

"You met Jimmy, right? And Reenie? Oh, I should say James and Irene, what they call themselves now. I knew Jimmy back in prep school when he was a ninety-eight-pound weakling who used to get pounded on every night by the football players."

"Which one is Reenie?" Maggie asked.

Earl pointed out a reed-thin woman chattering and waving her hands at a white-jacketed server with an empty silver tray in his hands. Reenie had overstreaked hair and seemed to have taken the "never-too-rich-or-too-thin" maxim to heart. I looked over the crowd of men and women, dressed in various hides and pelts and silks, checking each other out over their wineglasses. Women pointed at each other's shoes, discussed them animatedly. Men clapped each other on the back and guffawed bravely. Small talk. Cocktail parties. I felt a yawn grow deep in my throat, and only a splash of gin squelched it.

Another server came out of the kitchen with a large tray of intricately wrapped canapés. He set them down on the table and scooped up the empty one. I realized with a shock that it was Merle Tennepin of Phallus Phame. Making a step toward him, I wondered if it was bad form to hobnob with the help at one of these society functions. What were we raising money for again? Clean air, wolves, black-footed ferrets? I took another look around for a clue and found none.

Patting Maggie on the arm as I edged away, I found Merle in the kitchen with a staff of six, madly rolling, cleaning, pouring, and shouting. At the doorway I paused, taking in the size of the room. At one end a restaurant-style kitchen gleamed and hummed with activity, its long, antique table covered with trays ready to go out. Seven people fit easily into the confines of the work area. On the other end of the room, connected by broad, heavy timbers that soared up to a high peak, was a sitting area including three sofas, five armchairs, assorted tables, a chess set on a game table, river-rock fireplace ablaze.

The kitchen of this house was as big as my apartment.

When I recovered from that, Merle was frowning at me from under his white chef's hat. He looked ready to bite, so I bit first.

"Merle, hi, remember me from the ice carving competition? Alix Thorssen." I said my name before I remembered I was someone else. Ah, hell. I stuck out my hand. He stared at it and went on stirring a big bowl of something.

"I guess this was why you needed more time on your carving." He shrugged. "I'm pretty curious to know what it's going to be. And I'm not the only one."

"The carving's done. The rest will be finished tomorrow." He set the bowl aside and wiped his hands on his apron. "And for your information, I didn't ask for the extension. That was someone else."

"Okay," I said, suddenly very interested in the art over the fireplace. What was I doing chatting with this asshole?

"You know, Miss Thorssen, I have heard of contestants sucking up to judges, but I have never heard of it the other way round." He picked up another large silver tray and disappeared out the doorway.

I set down my glass on a wood table, hoping immediately for a water stain. My stomach churned, and I realized I needed to eat something. Maybe I could hang out in the kitchen with the staff for the rest of the night, eat rich canapés, and trade barbs with Mr. Personality Chef. Now, there was a plan.

A woman server with kind blue eyes stepped up to my elbow

as I frowned at the fire. "Try these," she said, handing me a plate of warm crepes and a fork. "They've got rum in them. They keep all of us back here sane."

I thanked her and accepted the plate. "I guess I better go back to the party before, you know."

She nodded and went back to work. I sighed, popped a mouthful of huckleberry-rum crepe in my mouth, and headed back into the milling crowd. It seemed to have gotten larger. I checked my watch—eight-thirty. We'd been here only half an hour. How long would Maggie want to stay?

The next forty-five minutes passed slowly for me. I had another plate of crepes, two shrimp rolls, some sushi, a glass of fume blanc, carrot and celery sticks, more sushi. One can never eat too much sushi, can one? I smiled at people but struck up no conversations, preferring to blend into the wallpaper. Well, the walls were log, massive ones, the furniture oh-so-correct in the grand lodge manner, the large room easily containing the fifty or sixty guests. No one talked to me, a fact I found more curious than hurtful. Everyone was too self-absorbed to bother. No one asked me about the bandage on my hand, even though I had a story all ready about a stapler accident. I didn't even get hit on, which might have been because of Maggie's yellow sweater or the sushi juice on my chin. I prefer to think it was the sweater.

Commotions attended the entrances of several guests. First Harrison Ford came in (I recognized him this time) with one of his children, then Roscoe Penn blew in, dolled up in knee-high snakeskin and an Indian blanket jacket. For peace of mind, I stayed away from him. He probably wouldn't talk to me anyway, at a party like this.

Then the fun started. Reenie clapped her hands and announced the evening's entertainment. First Merle brought out a small ice carving he'd made in honor of the cause du jour. It turned out we were raising money for wilderness areas. The ice depicted a forest of pine trees with tiny bears and moose and elk embedded in the icy wonderland. Merle had colored the animals with food coloring or something so that they stood out among the white trees. He even included a tiny green tent and two wee back-packers. Coexisting with nature, I guess.

The bidding on the ice carving, a symbolic gesture for the wilderness itself, began at five thousand dollars. It rose steadily, with no help from me, to thirty-five thousand. At that point Reenie stopped the bidding and said she would be glad to take everyone's final bid (or just a little bit more, ha-ha-ha, it's for a fabulous cause) in the form of a personal check made out to the Rocky Mountain Wilderness Alliance and dropped on the silver tray that was just now being circulated by dear James. How subtle, how coy.

The second part of the entertainment began as I exited a lux-urious guest bathroom tricked up in granite and bent willow. There had been a bit of a wait before the woman ahead of me got her face rearranged and squirted another bottle of Poison on her cleavage. She paused as she came out, allowing me the honor of her odor and a dear sliver of smile. My stay was much quicker, long enough to wipe the sushi juice off and freshen the lipstick. As I came out I too paused, but because of what I saw.

Framed against drawn curtains stood Mistress Isa, White Queen of the Runes, and her pal Peter. Isa wore a floor-length cream wool robe tonight, trimmed in fur, over her habitual tur-tleneck and slacks. Already she had the runes out on a blue velvet tablecloth in front of her and was examining them for a young woman. About half the party attended this demonstration idly, drinks in hand, while the other half talked and ignored the whole thing. I positioned myself between the two groups, close enough to see, but not so close as to be seen. I tried to find Maggie and Earl but couldn't spot them in the crowd.

Isa smoothed the sides of her platinum hair with both hands, eyes closed, conjuring up the spirits in the runes. The young woman whispered to her boyfriend and giggled. Somebody in the back yelled, "I think you're levitating, Muff!" Muffy gig-gled again. Isa frowned, an angry stare at the disbelievers.

"The runes are ancient ties with the world, a cord that draws us nearer Mother Earth and the bonds we refuse to acknowledge in our everyday lives," she lectured, challenging us to put aside our frivolous ways. "The runes tell stories of war, death, and destruction, of heartache and life beyond the body, of spiritual paths that take us out of mean pursuits that pollute our bodies.'' She looked sharply at the cocktail glasses and wineglasses in everyone's hands. More than a few dropped their glasses lower. "The runes illuminate our inner souls, release energy and creative fevers, foretell events. With the runes you can be anyone, go anywhere, do anything.''

Now she had them. The attentive crowd was still, silent, ready for Isa to unlock the secrets of power, money, and success. James, who had been chatting with the movie star, moved away to listen to Isa, along with several others. Isa smiled benignly and began the reading.

The first rune Isa held up for the group to see was Tyr, the upward-facing arrow, ancient symbol of war. Mistress Isa eyed Muffy, a slender brunette with preppie lawyer written all over her, and declared that some legal action was imminent for her. The woman smiled knowingly and flung back her shoulder-length hair. Isa placed the rune back on the tablecloth and picked up the next one.

"Raido," she said loudly, holding up an R-shaped rune. "Some think Raido is symbolic for riding, for the knights who avenge the lady's honor on horseback. This is closer to the truth—for Raido is the rightness inside of us. Our responsibility to honor, to justice. Combined with Tyr, Raido tells us that your legal problems will be resolved favorably, with honor and honesty.''

The lawyer whispered something to her boyfriend, and both laughed. Probably calculating their take from the lawsuit they were involved in. I glanced at Big Roscoe, rocking back on the heels of his boots, thumbs in his belt loops, giddy. The lawyer probably worked for him.

When I looked back, Peter had spotted me, his dark eyes darting immediately away after the brief acknowledgment. So much for concealment. Isa finished the reading with an eloquent speech about Mannaz, the entwined *M* that stands for mankind, all earth's folk. Cooperation with peers, Isa counseled, in the legal affairs to follow. A plea bargain, or out-of-court settlement,

I guessed she meant. Or not pushing so hard for the corner office.

The runes were swept back into the box held by Peter. He waved his long, slender fingers over the facedown runes in preparation for another reading. I blinked and rattled the ice in my glass. Time for a refresher.

Maggie and Earl sat behind the bar on a sofa, talking. I asked the bartender for tonic and a lime and snagged another shrimp roll on the way to break up the cozy tête-a-tête. It was ten o'clock, and I felt I had done my duty. I wouldn't have minded talking to Peter again, but with Isa so close by, that seemed impossible. I was ready to bag it.

I sank into an armchair next to a soaring red sandstone fireplace with half a tree trunk for a mantelpiece. Maggie looked up, surprised to see me. Earl's feet barely touched the floor, but side by side on the couch they looked the same height. No wonder they were sitting.

"Hi, you two," I said around my shrimp roll. "See who's here?"

"What?" Maggie frowned, then looked over her shoulder. "Oh, yeah, that woman from the bead shop. She gets around, doesn't she?"

"Going to get your fortune read, Earl?" I asked.

He smiled at me, a little annoyance around the mouth. "I guess I'll pass tonight. Go ahead, though, it sounds like a lot of fun."

The conversation died about then, at least between me and them. Maggie was having too much fun to get the hint from my sudden appearance. Their voices lowered again to intimate whispers. I communed with the fire for half an hour, wishing I had a fireplace at home half as beautiful as this one. I thought about my little woodstove in my art shack, about Carl so warm and tanned in midwinter despite his confusion over helicopters. I thought about Bjarne too, his sweet breath in my ear. It was a pleasant reverie, and when I saw Peter take long strides toward the kitchen, box of runes in his arms, black sleeves flapping, I had to rouse myself to jump up and follow him.

At the door to the kitchen I paused, hoping he hadn't taken

the back door. He was sitting on a red plaid sofa, his black head lowered over the box of runes. I walked quickly over, sat down next to him.

"Evenin', Peter," I said. "We meet again. Must be some kind of cosmic destiny."

Peter looked up briefly but said nothing. He was straightening the runes, replacing them in some kind of order. Their smooth wood edges glowed in the soft firelight; the silver twinkled as he turned them over.

"A beautiful set. Is it old?"

"Very old." Peter's voice was low, clipped. "Please go away from me. I do not wish to speak to you."

"Is this the set that Hank supposedly stole from Isa's room?"

Peter's hands faltered as he reached to close the lid on the elegant dark trunk. He didn't look at me, and I could only guess that Isa had coached him about questions. His manner was so studied, his answers so rote. He latched the brass clasps on the trunk and stood up, careful to keep the box horizontal. He gave me a dismissive side glance.

"Can't we talk, Peter? I thought we had—"

"Goodbye." He disappeared out the kitchen door, which led to a parking area sparsely lit by pole lanterns. Beyond the Mercedeses and Range Rovers a fancified barn hulked in the moonlight. The tall figure of the assistant blended into the shadows until the dome light of the station wagon popped on. He placed the box gently on the backseat, fixing it somehow—with a blanket?—then slipped behind the wheel. The light went off, plunging the lot into darkness again.

I half expected Isa to be right behind him; they seemed almost joined at the hip. But there she was, visible through the door to the great room, mingling, laughing, throwing her head back in such a studied way, her perfect white hair, her pale white skin, her flowing white robe, all of her so, so much like a caricature of a real person, I wanted to pinch her to find out if she was made of sugar. Maybe throw a bucket of water on her and see if she melted.

I watched her awhile, then looked through the glass, fogged by my breath, at Peter. Were those the so-called stolen runes?

How many other sets could Isa have that Glasius might want? Peter had said they were very old before he remembered he had accused someone of stealing them. Was it a mistake, or was it a different set? I kicked myself for not making him talk. I could go out to his station wagon right now, force him to spill his guts. I didn't think it would help somehow. She had him programmed now; maybe she had seen me talking to him at the motel.

Not for the first time their relationship struck me as odd. How long would Isa make him sit out there? Sure, it got warm today, but the temperature must be near zero now. Just a little nippier than balmy Florida, or Cuba for that matter. He is her lover, huh? So he says.

SIXTEEN

Better burden bearest thou no wise
than shrewd head on thy shoulders;
in good stead will it stand among stranger folk
and shield when unsheltered thou art.

MAGGIE DROPPED me off in the alley. She hadn't had much comment about my seeing the old set of runes, catching Peter in a lie. She hadn't even raptured about finally getting to meet Harrison Ford.

"So, is it true that you should never meet your heroes, then?" I asked, pausing with my hand on the door handle, unwilling to step into the chill quite yet.

"Hmm?" She rubbed her mittened hands on the steering wheel of the Wagoneer. "You mean Harrison? I guess. Now when I watch his movies it won't quite be the same. I'd rather remember him as Han Solo, you know?" She turned to me, eyebrows scrunched together. "That Earl turned out to be a scumbag," she said flatly.

"Oh." So that was it. "Sorry."

"Single Girl Rule Number Seven: Any guy who wants you to blow him in the guest bath on the first date doesn't have much potential." I gave a half-laugh; it isn't really that funny, if it happens to you. Maggie tapped the steering wheel. "Listen, I'll bring back your stuff in the morning, okay? I can't believe I made you switch and all, just for me and my stupid ideas. I feel like a jerk now, I'm—"

"Forget it, Maggie. It was no sweat to be you for one party. It was fun." I put my hand on her arm to reassure her. "Besides, I saw Mistress Isa and Peter again. And their runes."

Maggie blinked. "And?"

"And—I don't know what. Why were Glasius and Hank in

her room? If they were there to steal runes, why was Glasius killed? I think they know.''

I LEFT MAGGIE with a promise to watch *Blade Runner* with her very soon. The back stairs were cold, but my apartment was quiet and peaceful and warm. After hanging up my down jacket—we did switch our coats back—I called the hospital and talked to Una for a minute. She was resting comfortably but most eager to get out of the "sick hotel" tomorrow. Hank's hearing was at ten, so I would pick her up on the way.

After I hung up, I punched the message button on the answering machine and heard Sigmund's voice again, then a message from the professor in Wisconsin. He sounded very excited, in a professorial kind of way. I stood by my bedroom window that overlooked the square, turned the volume up a little on the machine. The draped sculptures, the umbrellas dusted with frost, and the still, white snow made an eerie landscape, a surreal wasteland.

"Miss Thorssen, I have sent you a fax, but let me tell you this discovery has potential to be a very important finding. Of course, I need to inspect the stone itself, but the language, the script on the stone, is very similar to the Kensington Stone, in ways that would be difficult for anyone but the most sophisticated forger to accomplish—and he'd have to be an expert in medieval languages. There is the mixture of Norwegian and Swedish, very subtle, but the kind of thing that would happen with both Swedes and Norwegians on a long voyage such as this. The Latin ending is just like the Kensington, which we know is from a time when Christians had only been influencing the region for a few short centuries."

He took a breath. "The soonest I can get away here is Friday. I've made a reservation on a flight that gets in at ten-thirty in the evening, your time. Well, we'll talk later."

Professor Breda hung up, not quite done with his excitement and sounding a little frustrated to be talking to an insensitive machine. I ran downstairs to get the fax, trying to decide at the same time if I should call him tonight to tell him there were a few glitches in his plan, namely the rock was stolen and Hank was in jail and Una in the hospital. But it was after eleven, and later in Wisconsin, so I ripped the paper off the fax machine and stared at his symbol-by-symbol interpretation.

It was short, sweet, and to the point. "2 (left of) King Magnus Vinland (exploration) captive weak. AV(e) M(aria)." The professor had added comments about the Norwegian versus Swedish parts, the similar grammar and spelling to the Kensington Stone. And the Latin, Christian ending. I wandered out into the darkened gallery, clutching the slick fax, trying to make the runic symbols say more, be more. It seemed like so little to go to prison for, so little to be run over by a truck for. Just a hunk of rock with squiggles on—

The crack of the shot rang out a split second before the plate glass on the front window of the gallery took the bullet. I instinctively hit the wood floor, banging my knees as my socks slipped out behind me on the way down. The second shot went through the weakened glass, continuing over my head into the back wall. Army-crawling toward the front of the building, I plastered my body against the short wall below the plate glass and covered my face. Thirty seconds, forty-five. The rush in my ears, the adrenaline pumping my blood around my body, made the silence seem electric. How long should I wait? Every second seemed hours.

I moved a little, took my hands away from my face. Was he done? Up on my elbow, I raised my head an inch, then two. The third shot erased my growing assurance that it was over. I shrank back to fetal position, feeling the shower of tiny slivers of glass. Only when the sirens began did I loosen a little from my curl. Imagine my surprise when they passed right by and faded away into the night.

After half an hour of cold, cramped fear I scrunched over to my office, by way of the edges of the room, and closed the door that joins the gallery proper. Shivering, pissed off, and sore all over, I stood up and turned on the light to make a personal assessment. Aside from a bruised knee and a lot of dirt, I was fine. I peeked out at the window. A bull's-eye, with two minor shots, radiated right under the arch of lettering that spelled out Second Sun Gallery in gold. It looked like target practice, but I tend to take things like this personally. The boardwalk was deserted on both this side of the street and the other. The shadows around the draped sculptures were deep and dark, the pines thick with snow. No one to be seen, not even a car moving around the square.

Cautiously waiting another fifteen minutes, watching for movement outside, listening, I found a large piece of cardboard in the storeroom and grabbed the duct tape. Unwilling to stand up, exposed in front of the window, I taped the edges back in the office, scooted around the walls, then used the broom handle to push the cardboard up against the broken window. It wasn't pretty, but it would help until morning. When the coast would hopefully be clear.

Back in my apartment I sank onto the sofa and wiped the sweat off my forehead and upper lip. I felt the exhaustion of post-anxiety, and also the elation of survival. I closed my eyes for a moment and took three deep breaths to relax, then decided a glass of wine was called for. I drank the wine quickly, took a hot shower, and crawled into bed, hoping for sleep.

The ceiling cracks hadn't changed since my last sleepless night. I should have called the police, I knew. But it was so late, and that would only make it later. What could they do for me tonight? Give me some unnecessary advice about standing in front of windows? Ask me who my enemies were? Tell me that random vandalism wasn't personal and to quit thinking somebody disliked my business, hairdo, politics, body odor, family—

My family. What had Luca said? They warn you with little things, like breaking your arm or burning your property; then, if you don't listen, they move on to dangerous stuff. But what was I supposed to listen to? Who was warning me, and against what?

Somebody must think I know a lot more than I do.

SNOW COATED the Justice Court steps, making Una's progress torturous, even on my arm. The sky was coated like a milky tongue. We'd gotten two or three inches overnight, and the chill, familiar and bracing, was back.

Una's ankle was taped now, the swelling down. It still hurt

like the devil, she assured me on the way out of the hospital.
Her doctor told her to keep off it for at least a week. And here
we were, trying to walk up snowy steps and around slick boardwalks. So much for obeying orders. Her arm was in one of those
fancy plastic casts that don't weigh much so you forget your
arm's broken. A bright blue sling wrapped around her neck held
the arm close to her body. The fact that the bad arm and the
bad leg were both on her left side made the hobbling go even
slower.

I got her situated in the courtroom with a half hour to spare
before the hearing; the courtroom was filling up. Danny Bartholomew waved at me, his reporter's notebook flipped open.
Next to him sat a man with an open sketchbook, filling in the
outlines of the witness stand. I nodded at Danny but didn't want
to talk to him right now. He'd be calling me later, no doubt, for
details.

I wandered out into the lobby of the courthouse, looking for
Penn. The reporter Luca had befriended passed by me, glower-
ing. Right after him, a veritable parade of local personalities
streamed in: Cosmic Connie resplendent in tie-dye, Charlie Frye,
police chief, two members of the town council, the night clerk
at the Wort, Luca, who paused to squeeze my arm, Isa Mardoll,
and Peter Black. I saw these last two as I turned around at the
drinking fountain. She in white, he in black, they ducked into
the courtroom. I was ready to follow them when Roscoe Penn
came out from the side door of the lobby and walked toward
me.

"Roscoe, good, I have to talk to you." I took his arm to stop
him from entering the courtroom.

"Later, please. I have a hearing right now; I'm needed in
court." He looked annoyed, glancing at his watch.

"I know, Roscoe—my stepfather, remember? Listen, I found
something out. Glasius Dokken and Hank, my stepfather,
were—"

"Is this necessary?" Roscoe pulled his arm away.

"Yes. You have to ask him this on the stand. It's important."

"Thirty seconds." He was timing me, the bastard, on his Ro-
lex.

"Hank Helgeson, your client, is my stepfather. He and the Norwegian were looking for an antique set of runes. They're little pieces of wood with letters inscribed on them. Glasius thought they were stolen. He went to Isa Mardoll's room to get them. But, according to Hank, they didn't find them and left empty-handed. I was told by Peter Black that they were stolen, but then I saw them myself last night, in Peter's possession."

Roscoe smoothed back his gray mane. "That's it?"

"It establishes why his fingerprints were there."

"They could also be there because he killed Glasius Dokken in the act."

"Roscoe! In the act of what?!"

"Of stealing these, these—"

"Runes."

"These runes. But, oh, I see what you mean. He wasn't stealing them from Glasius."

"No. Maybe Isa Mardoll killed Glasius to keep him from stealing her property. I don't know."

"Interesting. And who is this Isa person?"

I let out an exasperated sigh. It was 9:53. "It was her hotel room!"

"Right, right." He puffed out his chest. "Time's up." He had a jacket like a Navajo rug on today, with bright red boots that Gloria would probably sell her mother for. As we stepped into the courtroom, I had trouble taking my eyes off them; they shone like hot peppers on his feet. I turned away for a moment, making an effort to keep the door from slamming shut but really wanting to give Roscoe Penn a head start down the aisle. A girl can't be too careful about her reputation.

As IF A SWITCH had been turned on inside him, Roscoe Penn morphed from a fuzzy-brained Hollywood cowboy into a sharp-tongued orator with razor reflexes and a nose for blood. He cajoled, he sweet-talked, he sliced, he diced. Outside the courtroom he was only half alive; here he was filled up with the legal juices that fired on every piston, zero to sixty in ten seconds. He was a high-performance vehicle, and here was the racetrack. Judge Juliette was more in a mood for his pyrotechnics today, and he cruised and purred through the night clerk at the Wort Hotel, making him stammer and question his identification of Hank Helgeson. Hank sat slumped in orange again, a picture of mental fatigue. No wonder the clerk didn't recognize him. The prosecutor put the policeman who had first arrived on the murder scene on the stand, then the evidence man who told about the fingerprints in the room, matched to Hank, Glasius, and Isa. Then he moved on to other incidental witnesses—the coffee shop waitress, a customer in the lobby, the guy who owns an all-night convenience store down the street from the Wort Hotel. Peter took the stand, and nobody brought up the runes, not even Roscoe Penn. I began to squirm. Peter gave his testimony as if by rote: he heard the two men talking, searching, only one man leaving. Roscoe tried to punch holes in Peter's story, but it held water pretty well.

But first Hank Helgeson had to take the stand and explain himself. Una held her breath, waiting for him to continue with the stubborn act and make them all suffer. She was ready to suffer, having spent two days in the hospital worrying about him. God forbid she should worry in vain. Norwegians are always ready to suffer, it suits them so.

I was holding my breath too, I realized. Peter's testimony had been damaging. It put Glasius and another man in the room, and Glasius definitely did not leave. Hank moved slowly to the witness stand. The air in the courtroom stilled, pencils stalled on paper.

The DA, Mr. Robbins, wasn't a flashy guy, but he had obviously spent the weekend rounding up witnesses to make his case. He wasn't about to let things slip away now. Slender with slicked-back brown hair, he wore a navy blue suit and red tie. He approached Hank on the stand, saying his name very loudly, jerking Hank to attention.

"We're all interested in your response to the question put before you last Friday. The question you decided at that time you couldn't answer. Are you ready now, Mr. Helgeson?" Robbins stood in front of the witness stand, his hands clasped behind his back. Hank didn't answer, just hung his head, dejected. "Mr. Helgeson?"

"Yessir?" Hank's voice was weak.

"Speak up, please, Mr. Helgeson," Judge Juliet said.

"Were you in the hotel room, number 221 at the Wort Hotel, on the evening of January nineteenth?" Robbins asked.

Hank looked up at my mother and me in the first row. I gave him a stern look and small nod. He looked at the judge as if assessing her humor this morning, then back at his questioner. Finally he said, "Yessir."

A rustle went through the courtroom. The judge allowed herself a small smile. I let out my breath and swallowed. He was going to cooperate. Una squeezed my hand.

"Can you please tell this court what you were doing there?"

Hank squirmed in his seat and sat back. His voice was flat. "Mr. Dokken wanted to get back something he said belonged to him. Or to his country."

Robbins spun around, gave his assistant a frown. This was news to them, apparently. "And what was that?"

"A set of runes." Hank peered into the prosecutor's face now, enjoying the sense of power this new information gave him. "You know what runes are?"

Robbins straightened. "I ask the questions here." He cleared his throat. "Can you tell the court what these runes are?"

"Small pieces of wood with inlaid silver. A set of old Norse letters from the Viking days. Glasius says they were that old, almost a thousand years."

"Let's back up a minute, Mr. Helgeson. You and Mr. Dokken broke into this hotel room together? Entered without a key or permission?"

Hank shrugged and hung his head again. "It's easy."

The judge looked dismayed. "Answer the question, please, Mr. Helgeson."

He looked up at Robbins then. "Yes."

"So you broke into Miss Mardoll's room. Then what?"

"We looked for the runes. But we couldn't find them. They weren't there."

"Was anyone else in the room with you?"

"Just Glasius."

"Miss Mardoll was not there?"

"No, sir."

"All right. Then what happened?"

"I got nervous, and I left."

"And Mr. Dokken stayed behind?"

"Yessir. I went down to the coffee shop to wait for him." His eyes picked out the waitress who had testified to serving him. "Then it closed down, so I left the hotel and walked back to my daughter's apartment. But I decided to go back because I didn't feel right leaving Glasius there by himself. When I got back to the Wort, the door to Room 221 was open, just a little. I knew I'd closed it." Hank paused, took a breath. "I pushed it open. I was scared now, it was so late."

When Hank didn't continue, Robbins prompted him. "And what did you see in the room, Mr. Helgeson?"

Hank breathed out, hard. "Glasius. Lying on his face. With that ice pick in his back."

"It was at this point that Sergeant Ashford came into the room?"

Hank nodded, then said yes.

"Mr. Helgeson, did you kill Glasius Dokken?"

Hank jerked his head up, alarmed. "No sir, I did not."

"Isn't it true that you would have liked those runes for yourself? That you in fact have been researching runes for the last six months, hoping you could get your hands on a set of your own?"

"No, where'd you—"

"Mr. Helgeson," Robbins thundered, "isn't it true that in an argument with Mr. Dokken over that very set of runes you were both looking for, you stabbed Mr. Dokken and stole the runes for yourself?"

"No sirree, I did not!" Hank was red in the face.

"Isn't it true that in September of last year and several times since, you have consulted a Professor Harvey Breda, a world-renowned expert on Norse runes at the University of Wisconsin?"

"Yes, but—"

"Did you not tell your neighbor, Mrs. Ethel Tillot, that you felt like you were, and I quote, 'eating, sleeping, and breathing runes'?"

"Well, that was—"

"Did you say that to her, Mr. Helgeson?"

"I guess so. Yes."

"Would you say you had an obsession with old Norse runes and that you would do anything to get your hands on them?"

"No! I mean, sure I'm interested in them and everything, they're my heritage, but I wouldn't do *anything*—"

"Wouldn't you have killed to get those runes, Mr. Helgeson?"

"No sir. No sir. I wouldn't kill anybody. I never touched him. You gotta believe me, Your Honor!" Hank turned to the judge, pleading with eyes and voice.

Roscoe Penn did his flamboyant best, but the damage was done. Pleading, puppy-dog eyes or not, Henry Helgeson did not make a good impression on the judge. But she delayed making her decision on the spot, leaving us all up in the air for at least one more day. Penn stayed upbeat, reassuring my mother that he had an "in" with Judge Juliette Foss. Una didn't look as if she believed it.

MY MOTHER AND I had a cup of tomato soup together in my apartment as I smoothed out the fax from Professor Breda on the coffee table. It was noon and gloomy outside, as gloomy as inside. I could hear Artie downstairs, so I knew at least the gallery was open. I wondered what he thought about the window. I hadn't had the energy or the nerve to tell my mother about the incident yet. I had called Maggie first thing this morning to get an appraiser over for an estimate on a new window. Damn. Two new windows in a year. At least my insurance agent was my best friend. And I did lend her my persona on occasion.

Almost as soon as I set the telephone on the coffee table so Una could reach it easily from the sofa, it rang. She set down her bowl and spoon and answered it as I put my own bowl in the sink and wiped my mouth on the dish towel. She said hello, then just listened, her jaw jutting out. She held the phone out toward me without a word.

"For me? Who is it?"

She shook her head. Bjarne probably, and she couldn't understand him. I took the receiver.

"X, is that you?"

"Hi, Erik." I gave Mom a look, but she refused to meet my eye, staring at something over the sofa back, then adjusting the pillows under her ankle. "Find out anything?"

"Yeah, I checked out the experts. There's one at the British Museum in London who's supposed to be the best. Jane Ann Nightingale. About this Breda at Wisconsin—"

"He faxed me his interpretation. He seems to think it could be the real thing."

"Hmm. He's got a pretty good rep, but he is the grandson of one of the first scientists who examined the Kensington. He's not exactly unbiased. I don't think this rock is anything to get excited about, Alix. It's a hoax, just like the Kensington."

"You think the Kensington is a hoax? I thought you said some scholars believed it might be real."

"Some scholars. But the vast majority of the scientific community thinks it's just a well-done prank. That's probably what this other one is too. Maybe it's a hundred years old, not seven hundred, not a thousand."

"Anything else?"

"Hank still in the can?"

"Yeah, the hearing was this morning. The judge hasn't made her decision yet on actually binding him over for trial. Maybe this afternoon, Roscoe says."

"Roscoe Penn? Well, this is serious." He paused. "Mom's out of the hospital, I see."

"Yeah. On the couch with her foot up."

"She's okay?"

"Well enough. I've got my eye on her."

"I'd have you give her my love, but I know how that would be received."

"I'll do my best. Call me tonight, okay?"

I hung up the phone and found a blanket and the remote control for my mother. Situating the oyster cracker box where she could grab it, I asked her if she was comfortable. Her answer, affirmative, was clipped. I would wait awhile before bringing up Erik's name.

I paused at the door at the sound of her voice. "He doesn't believe in the rock, does he? You believe it's real, don't you? After what Professor Breda said?"

I turned, frowning. "Well, I don't know, Mom."

She looked at me, jaw tight, eyes hot, holding me in her sights until she had interpreted my disbelief and had time to become infuriated with another of her children. Then she turned away, flicking on the television to the noon news.

THE GALLERY was busy, for a Monday: relief. I didn't have to think about Una solemnly alone with grief and pain, cycling endlessly through the soap operas. Artie bombarded me with questions about the window, right in front of Luca. What could I say? I lied and told them I found it that way early this morning and taped up the cardboard. Had I called the police to report it? he wanted to know. When I hemmed and hawed Artie marched right over to the phone and dialed up the cops himself.

Bundled up for the long winter's night, Luca unwrapped her black scarf and cocked her head at me. "What is it? You were here when this happened, no?"

I rolled my eyes.

"You hear it? Boom and bang?"

I was saved from answering by the sight of two distinguished-looking gentlemen in gray suits and wing tips turning into the door. The cold wind caught their coiffed hair, setting it up on end like a boyish prank, then it settled to their touch as they stepped inside.

The younger, and shorter, of the two looked at me quizzically. "Miss Thorssen? Harry Jorgensen from the Norwegian Consulate. May I present Helmar Ruud of the consulate office in Chicago."

We shook hands. Both men spoke excellent English; Harry was apparently an American, albeit of Norwegian descent, like myself. Helmar was the real thing, with an accent not quite as thick as Glasius's. The pause that crept up on us made me feel sad suddenly. Glasius had come here with such high hopes, such an enthusiasm for his work. He was so darn cute. And here were his murals, so exquisite, so fine. The last of his works.

"Well," said Harry, "so these are the murals, Helmar. Have you seen them?" He led the consul away. Helmar admired the depiction of the Viking ship. It was during his examination of the rigging on the ship that the bullet hole was discovered. Centered between the mainsail and the jib, the hole appeared to be a second moon in the distance until one pressed one's nose against the canvas. Helmar was astonished, Harry was pissed off. Me? I tried to explain about the gunshots. Vandalism, I said. Probably took potshots at several businesses. Artie, off the phone now, concurred. The policeman he just talked to had alluded to windows shot out all over town last night. Even as the two men calmed down, I wondered about that explanation. It was no drive-by. Not with three shots meticulously aimed at the same spot in the glass. No, somebody meant it, and meant it good.

The Chicago consul was talking: "I would take them back on my next trip, but that won't be until summer, I'm afraid."

"Would you consider going, Miss Thorssen?" Harry Jorgensen asked, blue eyes flashing.

"To Oslo?"

Helmar clapped Harry on the shoulder. "Excellent idea. You know how to ship large paintings by air, do you not?"

"Yes, but—"

"Haven't you always wanted to go to Norway, Alix?" Artie chimed in. Luca smiled and patted and encouraged me. What could I say? My stepfather facing a murder trial and my mother an invalid? Naw. I told them I'd do it if they were flexible about the time. No problem, they said. They went away happy, despite my breach of security and the small problem of a round hole in fine art.

Luca ran off for a late lunch with Conrad Baker. Probably pumping her for information about Hank Helgeson. I opened my mouth to warn her but changed my mind. What did she know about my stepfather? Only what she learned the night Glasius died, at her dinner party. Let her talk. It didn't matter now.

"How's the hand?" Artie asked, leaning over the glass jewelry counter.

"What? Oh, good, thanks." I had almost forgotten about my burned hand, that's how much it had improved. I had rewrapped it last night after my shower, re-gooed it with ointment. "What's happening today, Artie?"

He laughed. "You're kidding, right? Well, it's the end of the Weekend from Hell. We've had fires, gunshots, stabbings, and lewd ice carvings."

I smiled and gave a half-baked laugh. If he only knew. Theft, lust; what did we have left, gluttony? The thought made me hungry. I dug around in my desk drawers for a sack of candy left over from Christmas and poured it into one of the pottery bowls we were supposed to be selling. Artie and I silently unwrapped fancy chocolate truffles and devoured them. As we crumpled up the shiny purple wrappers, I, for one, felt a whole lot better.

I went back to my desk to begin to plow through the stack of messages that had built up. Second down on the heap was Danny Bartholomew at the *Jackson Hole News*. He had called right after the hearing. I put in the call. After last summer I felt a debt, a bond, to Danny. Everyone else could wait.

He was in a hurry. "I'm just going out the door but, oh, hell, wait a second." Rustling of paper. "Okay. Do you have any more details about the night of Dokken's murder? What he ate for dinner? What kind of socks he wore? I'm desperate here."

"Well, I can tell you what we all ate for dinner at Luca's. Paolo's mother's recipe of black beans with chilies and cinnamon over rice. And I can't tell you a thing about his socks."

"Okay, somebody called him a curmudgeon. Comment?"

"What's that mean, grumpy? He was very sweet, Danny. My mother and Hank liked him instantly. About his paintings he was very particular, a perfectionist. Have you seen them?"

"Very briefly. Viking stuff?"

"A depiction of some of the old sagas—um, there's a big sailing ship."

"Like the one that burned? That was your stepfather's, right?"

"Yeah. A terrible thing." I paused. "I need to talk to you

about all this stuff, Danny. There's been some—I don't know. I'm kind of worried."

"About what? No, don't tell me now. I've got to go to this press conference, of all things. You know that *white* fortune-teller, Mardoll?"

"Isa? What's she doing?"

"Having a press conference. Boss thinks it's something about the murder, since it happened in her room. I don't know what to think, but I have to go." He paused. "I suppose I should ask you to come, since it might relate to your stepfather."

"I suppose you should."

"This got me in dutch last time."

"Danny! This is different. Don't ask me if you think I'm going to get you in trouble. I've got an invalid mother to take care of, you know."

So he told me: Isa Mardoll was having a press conference, starting immediately, at the Chamber of Commerce conference room. I'd have to talk to Gloria about that decision later. Right now I grabbed my coat, kissed Artie goodbye, and ran.

SEVENTEEN

Heed my words now, for I know them both:
mainsworn are men to women;
We speak most fair when most false our thoughts,
for that wiles the wariest wits.

DANNY WAS IN the throng when I arrived, straining his short neck to see over television cameras and other tall photographers. His ratty fleece-lined jean jacket lay on the brown, industrial carpeting in the airy conference room. This was where the Nordic Nights committee had met all fall, but it had been transformed today. The long table had been pushed to one end and turned, draped with a dark blue cloth. Behind it stood Isa Mardoll in all her white glory. As I examined one more creamy outfit, visions of her dry-cleaning bill danced in my head.

"Quite a turnout," Danny mused, clicking his ballpoint. Isa had gathered a crowd on short notice. I had to hand it to her.

"What's the deal, has she said?" I asked. Isa had her head down, talking privately to another woman.

"They've been waiting for this camera crew that just showed up," Danny said, pulling on his black beard. "Looks like CNN."

"Really?" I had a hard time believing CNN would be interested in fortune-telling. I nudged him. "Here she goes."

The other woman turned toward the reporters and cameras as the TV lights went on, harsh and glaring. Dark-haired with bright red lipstick, she didn't even blink. But when she opened her mouth to speak, I realized she was the woman—Lucinda, had Earl called her?—who had cursed out Maggie for stepping on her foot. Her hair was in a French twist today, very chic.

"Ladies and gents, my name is Lucinda Wooley. I'm a news producer for CNN. Thank you for coming. I'm not here to make a statement, only to introduce a friend of mine who has come across something so truly unique that it is a once-in-a-lifetime event.''

The runes, I thought. She's going to give them back to Norway. What a gracious thing, and good PR.

Lucinda looked at an index card cradled into her palm. ''Isa Mardoll is a resident of St. Paul, Minnesota. She studied medieval literature at Carleton College and worked toward her Ph.D. at Stanford. She has taught old Norse and Norwegian literature and studied with many experts in the field. She can both read and write old Norse, which comes in handy sometimes.'' Lucinda paused and gave Isa a small smile. ''I'll say no more. Let me introduce Isa Mardoll, who can tell you her story herself.''

Isa moved a step forward. The blue pendant around her neck twinkled. Her features were washed out by the lights; Lucinda should have mentioned more mascara.

''Six months ago, last summer,'' she began slowly, making eye contact with everyone just as if they were an audience at her readings, ''I came across something truly remarkable. Unique, as Lucinda says. Well, almost unique, as you'll see. But first, I must start at the beginning.

''In the north of Minnesota there are many lakes. Land of Ten Thousand Lakes, I'm sure you've heard that. Potholes left by retreating glaciers, chunks of ice left to melt and dig their own nests in the earth. I have a special spot there I go to every summer, a cabin by a small, insignificant lake. Just a pond, ringed with birch trees and pines, a favorite landing spot of Canadian geese, great blue herons, and kingfishers.

''Every day when I am staying at my cabin, I walk. Sometimes just around the small lake on the deer paths. Other times I strike out for a rise, a bluff. Every day, without fail, rain or shine. But one day was very different from all the rest. One walk truly changed my life.''

My curiosity reaching the breaking point and her supercilious voice grating on me, I couldn't resist rolling my eyes at Danny. He crossed his at me and chewed on his pen harder.

''On this particular day I had decided to walk to some Indian mounds that were about five miles away. It was a long walk, ten miles total, and I had never attempted it before. But I felt strong, and strangely powerful. Purposeful, as if I had a mission. It turned out my premonition was correct.

"The Indian mounds are not very interesting themselves because they are, after all, simply large mounds of earth overgrown with forest now. These had been excavated many years before. I reached them at about eleven o'clock in the morning and sat down to rest. I had brought along food and water and began to eat an apple from my pack.

"As I sat under a beech tree, I felt at peace in this burial place, despite the fact that the bones had been disturbed by archaeologists. At least, at first I did. I let myself be still and listen carefully to the earth. Yes, there was peace there. The Indians had lived hard but well, and buried their dead with dignity.

"Then I felt something else. A kind of agony, almost like a scream coming up from the land. I shook it off and stood up, and laughed at myself. I don't believe in evil spirits, I told myself. I must have a vivid imagination." Isa paused, touching her chest with long, graceful fingers, taking a deep breath. Where was Peter? I wondered. He was usually her shadow, and yet he was nowhere to be found in the full room.

"I paced around the mounds. There are three of them in this spot, each about fifteen feet high, thirty or forty feet across, and rounded. I thought about climbing to the top of one but decided it would be disrespectful. I came back to the beech tree and listened to its leaves rustle in the wind. Still the feeling persisted, that something terrible had happened here. So I moved closer to the scrapes made by the archaeologists, the hole in one side of the closest mound.

"It had weathered badly over the years. Rain and snow had washed away the earth, caving in parts of the hole. It might have once been ten or fifteen feet deep, but now only about six feet of it was open, the rest filled with debris. An old cottonwood tree had grown next to it, then died, leaving just the leafless trunk, limbs broken by the wind.

"I stood at the entrance of the decrepit excavation, the sun on my shoulders. But did I feel warmth? No, I did not," Isa told us, her eyes closed, remembering that oh-so-fateful day. The woman should seriously consider acting, I mused.

"I looked into the darkness and saw only dirt, rocks, and roots. Then I stepped closer, against my will. I truly felt a chill from this mound, this gaping cave in its side. But something wanted to be seen, and I guess no one else had been this way for a long, long time. Because, as I moved closer, I saw this rock sticking out from the edges of the cave wall, near an obvious cave-in.

"The rock had a carved look to it, square corners. I touched it carefully with one finger, rubbing at the dirt that clung to it. Something was scratched on it. I began to dig. It took a long time, because I had to be careful. But finally, nearly two and a half hours later, I had unearthed the stone."

"Fuck."

Danny stared at me, frowning. I hadn't realized I had spoken aloud, in a voice higher than a whisper yet. But I didn't have time to curse again, as Isa continued.

Lucinda had bent down and brought up from under the table an object wrapped in black velvet fabric. Isa now carefully unwrapped the velvet, spreading it wide on the tablecloth, and lifted the stone so that the reporters could see it.

"This is that stone. You can see, barely, the carvings on it, but they are no doubt meaningless to you unless you read old Norse. I have had this stone authenticated by three of the top scholars in the field of Scandinavian history and antiquities. You will hear from one of them today. Before he speaks, however, let me just summarize what he will verify to you.

"We believe that this stone, carved with ancient runes, old Norse lettering, is proof that an expedition of Viking sailors reached the New World in the fourteenth century. This is the second such stone found on this continent, the first being the Kensington Stone found in Minnesota a hundred years ago. We believe that this stone was left by the same party, perhaps as they knew they were dying, captive to Indians."

"What does it say?" a reporter impertinently asked.

Isa blinked, emerging from her narrative. "Let me introduce

Professor Hjelmseth from the University of Northern Minnesota. Professor?''

A middle-aged man stepped out of the crowd, nodding to Isa as she laid the rock back and stepped aside. He was tweedy and long-haired, gray, but had an attractive face and might be somewhat buff under all that wool. He pulled out wire-rims and squatted next to the rock so his face was right up against it.

"You ask what it says. Let me do a word-by-word translation. Old Norse lettering is a primitive form of our English/Germanic alphabet, based on the same vocal sounds. This is an evolution of Old Norse, not the same version as the Vikings used. So here goes: Two men remain from Magnus Vinland. Captive. Tired. Then there is a typical Latin prayer, abbreviated as AVM, or Ave Maria."

From there the professor launched into a lecture about the King Magnus expedition, that Vinland was what the Vikings called North America, how the expedition had recently been learned of in old documents from the post-Viking period, how no mention is ever made again of the expedition, so it is likely that all the men perished. He summarized the information on the Kensington Stone as well for the reporters, who were looking a little restless by now, used as they were to politicians who at least understood the concept of the sound bite.

"The Kensington Stone has had its many detractors over the years. But also many believers. It was exhibited at the Smithsonian Museum and studied in depth. No one has ever come up with anything definitive on it, condemning it absolutely as a fraud or proving that it is absolutely authentic. Until now."

He stood up, picking up the small tablet carefully. "This stone, which Miss Mardoll found and has called the Isa Runestone, proves that the expedition described in the Kensington Stone was true. These men survived, only to die in captivity later. Ladies and gentlemen, now: the bottom line."

He paused. Maybe he did understand sound bites. "Viking explorers reached the New World more than a hundred years before Columbus. They traveled and saw the continent in a way that Columbus never attempted. The Vikings were here first."

I SANK ONTO a park bench without bothering to brush the snow off it and lowered my head into my hands. The square was bustling with last-minute chiselers and carvers, but I couldn't focus on them. The tapping irritated me. I covered my ears with my gloved hands and stifled a scream.

That woman, her easy guile, her astounding nerve, her lying, her cheating! I could hardly fathom what she had done, and so calmly, so neatly. Experts even. CNN, for godsake. A preemptive strike with guns so big that even a return shot would glance off, maybe even boomerang back to harm the sender.

Not a good sign, thinking about firepower. Not in the mood I was in. No, I had to concentrate on what I would tell my mother. And Hank. Maybe he wouldn't hear about it for a few days, or at least we'd think of some easy way to break it to him. Did they let him watch television in there? I hoped not.

But Una. I trudged back to the gallery, crestfallen and angry at the same time. The overcast skies hung, waiting, for a sign from Skadi the snow goddess to let up already. Enough snow for one day. A little sunshine would cheer us up. Skadi, buried deep in her snow castle in the sky, wouldn't hear of it.

Una, buried deep in the comforter watching Oprah, didn't want to hear of it, but I gave her no choice. I was gentle, sparing in the details. In other words, I cut to the chase. The rock had surfaced, someone else was claiming ownership, and getting it back wasn't going to be easy, or perhaps even possible.

She took it well. Those stoic genes are good for something. I suppose in her mind it was already gone, stolen, disappeared for good. She worried about Hank, and we agreed to wait to tell him until we knew more. What more we needed to know, I wasn't sure, but it made both of us feel relief not to have to spring this on him in his circumstances, which were none too pleasant anyway.

The phone rang as I was talking to Una. She let me pick it up as she was wringing out a tissue and Oprah was blathering on about her new fitness book. It was Artie; someone was waiting for me downstairs.

At the door, a thought. I turned back to my mother. "How

did she know about it?'' Una frowned up at me. ''How did Isa know about the stone? Did Glasius mention it at the reading?''

''I—I don't know. I don't see why he would have.'' She rubbed the tissue on her nose again. ''Why, Hank hadn't even told him about it by then, had he? No, no, he didn't tell him until afterward, at the funny bar.''

''At the Six Point? When did you go there again?''

''After the reception.''

MY BLACK JEANS, dressy for the hearing, sort of, were now wet in the seat and dirty from running to the Chamber office and walking back with Danny. He had had a million questions, and I wasn't sure where to start, if at all. I had to tell him one thing, though, and that was to hold the story. He'd be glad he did, I told him. She's a fortune-teller, I reminded him. Have there ever been better con men than fortune-tellers?

I pulled my blazer lower over my snowmelt ass as I lurched through my office into the gallery. The Norwegians were who I expected, back to discuss Glasius's murals again. But I was only half right. Right country, wrong guys.

Bjarne had one elbow on the jewelry counter, chatting with Artie. The gallery was otherwise empty, the midafternoon slump. I stumbled a little when I saw that blond thatch of hair, those dimples, remembering yesterday a little too well. He saw me, pushed off the counter, and smiled.

''Why didn't you call me last night?'' he scolded after a friendly hug. ''I had to drink that wine all by myself. And just thinking about you was nice and all, but I really had other plans.''

Artie was rapt, watching Bjarne finger my hair. I grabbed the skier's hand and pulled him back into my office. He spun into my chair and tried to drag me onto his lap.

''Bjarne, please. This is where I work,'' I said, unable to think of anything more intelligent to say. He looked good today, as always: jeans, blue fleece pullover, hiking boots, white turtle-neck.

''I know.'' He grinned. ''And unfortunately I have come to say goodbye. Tomorrow I leave, and tonight I must do some

Chamber of Commerce thing. So unless I can talk you into coming out to the airport tomorrow morning very early, before the sun even rises—''

I sat on the other chair. "I'm sorry about last night. Maggie wanted me to go to a party." I remembered then what I said last night: I probably would never see him again. While he was here, in the flesh, that seemed like bad luck. Bjarne grabbed my hand and began playing with my fingers. It was all I could do to draw it back into my lap. "I don't think I can take you to the airport—''

"No, no, Reineking has that duty. I just wanted to see you before I left." He frowned suddenly, looking away at my painting, the pile of pink While You Were Out slips, then back at his hands on the edge of the desk.

"Did you—um, did you have a good visit to Jackson?''

"Hmm? Oh, oh, sure." He didn't look at me, and his voice seemed different, sad.

Artie poked his head into the office then. "Sorry," he said, looking around eagerly as if hoping to catch us in flagrante. "This call came in while you were out. Guy had a bogus accent.''

He handed me a pink memo. I pressed it between my hands without looking at it. Artie went off to greet customers coming through the door. Bjarne stood up.

"Come here," he whispered, drawing me up into his arms. "Good luck.''

The hug was almost platonic, no kiss. He didn't look at me as he let go and hurried out. I watched him skip down the steps and look both ways for traffic before disappearing into the sidewalk crowds. So it was as I imagined, I told myself. He just wanted a little romp, a conquest for every ski town. But something told me, a warm spot in my heart, that his wasn't as cold as that.

I WAS ON the phone to Roscoe Penn before I looked at the message. Penn was giving me a little hypothetical legal advice about getting back something that is stolen from you when you didn't legally own it in the first place. He had a client some years back who had a large amount of very old Anasazi pottery stolen from his home. He had bought it from pothunters who pilfer on BLM and reservation land, although he denied knowing it was stolen. At any rate, he found out who stole his pots and had Roscoe sue the guy. He won them back but in the process attracted the attention of the law. He was arrested for receiving stolen goods and pothunting illegally, and his fine was more than the pots were worth. He forfeited the pottery too. Thanks to Roscoe's excellent legal negotiating, he avoided jail time.

"I'm off to L.A. tonight," Roscoe announced at the end of this instructional tale, which would not cheer anyone's heart around here. He'd be back as soon as he could to deal with Hank.

I would have been upset about his abandoning ship if I hadn't finally read the pink memo Artie gave me. It was from Peter Black. No number was given, only this message: "HAVE THEM. LEAVING." I hung up quickly.

"Artie?! What kind of a message is this?" I whispered loudly in the gallery. Two customers were examining a weaving, pointing out colors.

Artie threw up his hands. "That's what he said to write. He was very anxious about something, kind of stammering. Who is he, anyway?"

"Just tell me, what did he say about HAVE THEM?"

He shrugged. "Just that. 'Tell her I have them. She will know what I mean.' "

"The runes? Did he say he had the runes? And where is he going?"

Artie swore he knew no more. If I didn't think Peter knew more about what happened the night Glasius was killed, I would have been very tempted to think, even say, Fuck the runes. They weren't the big problem anymore. Glasius had wanted them, maybe even been killed over them. But what could they tell us now?

Maggie's laughter followed the tinkling of the front door behind us. She waved to someone on the boardwalk and came inside. Before I could say hello, she put her hands on her hips and gave a friendly frown.

"And where were you, young lady? Well, no matter. Gloria and I looked over the ice sculptures without you."

I looked at my watch: 4:30. *Shit.* "Sorry, Maggie. You and Gloria did it *together?*"

"Yeah, she's not so bad when you get to know her. She had to get back to the office, so we went on without you. You aren't mad, are you?"

"Mad? Are you kidding?" I said. "I'm grateful. You won't believe the kind of day I'm having."

"I figured. I thought I saw Bjarne a minute ago; did he come in here?"

I nodded, staring at the pink memo, trying to get it to talk. "Did you decide on prizes?"

"Yes, but, well, there's one sculpture you really have to see."

"Don't tell me."

All she would do was grin.

"We gave it the blue ribbon, first prize," Maggie was saying. "The transformation was just too complete."

Bundled up against the cold but wearing my clogs with too-thin socks, I stood with my mouth hanging open. Merle Tennepin had indeed transformed his obelisk of ice into something too fantastic. I glanced around at the other sculptures: the jackalope, the cornucopia, the elk head, the snowmobiler carved of ice. They were all unique, beautiful.

"Maybe it's because we thought it was a dick, I don't know. To have it turn into *this* is such a wonderful shock," Maggie said.

It was a shock. Merle Tennepin had taken the six-foot pointy-headed chunk of ice and made it into the most intricately carved totem pole, complete with food coloring dyes, eagle wings, gruesome masks, and animal heads. How it stood up with the heavy wings near the top, I didn't know. The snowballs were no longer at the base. Two spotlights on the ground shone up at the sculpture. A bank of hay bales kept admirers back.

"It's gorgeous," I whispered. It wouldn't make Merle Tennepin any more pleasant to get a blue ribbon. But damn it, he deserved it. "What a relief."

Maggie laughed. "And to think—well, it did come to a girl's mind."

MAGGIE WENT BACK to the apartment with me and whipped up some of her famous macaroni and cheese a la Velveeta. Luca came over to see Una, and we drank a little wine, ate some comfort food, and talked about the stone. I didn't think it needed to be a secret any longer, not with national news coverage. Una gave me a look of disbelief.

When I told them about her finding the stone at Fort Union, but after the subject was broached, and exclaimed about excitedly by my two friends, she looked relieved.

"Yes, yes, it *was* quite thrilling," Una admitted, almost in spite of herself. "When I fist saw those letters, well, I didn't know what to think."

"But who is this woman who says it is her own?" Luca asked, pouting.

"Fortune-teller," I said, wiggling my fingers in the air like a magician. "Full of spirits and bullshit."

"A thief," Una added. "And a liar."

"Not to mention a bad driver," Maggie said, glancing at Una's cast. She had already decorated it with sixties peace flowers, and her signature.

"She could have killed you!" Luca exclaimed.

Maggie nodded. "But how are you going to get it back?"

Quiet around the table. Una looked at the last macaroni elbow swimming in processed cheese and other artery-clogging agents on her plate. Luca raised her eyebrows at me. Maggie waved her fork around in the air and shrugged her shoulders. "Got any ideas?"

"Maybe we should just accept that it's lost to us," I said. Una jerked her head up and stared. "I know it won't be easy for Hank, or you. But I spoke to Roscoe Penn, and there really is no legal recourse. Technically, it didn't even belong to you. It belongs to the National Park Service, the federal government. You weren't supposed to take it out of the park."

Una looked as if I'd slapped her. Maggie put a hand on her good arm, soothing her.

Luca said, "For Mister Helgeson, just getting out of jail will be enough, no?"

"I should say so," I said.

Maggie glared at me. "But you can't just go on, letting her make up lies, take credit for finding it. You can't let her defraud the entire country, Alix."

"It's wrong," Una said weakly.

"It's our word against hers," I said. "And what difference does it make where it was found, really? The point is the same. If she makes everyone believe that Vikings discovered America before Columbus, then the deed is done. That is what Hank wants."

"But it's based on lies," Maggie said. "Sometime, someday, they'll find out she's a fraud, and the whole story will be debunked. She'll be discredited as a crackpot, and the stone itself will be dismissed as—"

"As a hoax," Una said.

"No one will believe the stone is real," Luca said.

"I'm not even sure the stone is real now," I said, and instantly regretted it. Una's face hardened at the words. "Mom, we don't have any expert opinions yet. This Breda fella from Wisconsin hasn't examined it, nobody really has."

"What about that expert the fortune-teller had?" Maggie said.

"He works for her, for chrissake. She's paying him to tell her that. And who knows, maybe he's not even an archaeologist."

"The newspeople would find out if he was just acting."

"You think they know the difference between a respected, credentialed expert who has in-depth knowledge and years of experience, and somebody with a Ph.D. who gets a lot of press because he's accessible and easy to quote?"

Maggie sat back in her chair, squinting at me. "What does *that* mean?"

"Not all experts are equal," I said.

"And reporters are stupid. Danny would love to hear you say that." Luca frowned at Maggie's words, and I remembered her new friend, the fat reporter.

"I didn't say that," I said. "I just mean they don't have time or the resources to check the background of every source, every expert. Besides, I've already talked to Danny about this. And I'm hoping he's not going to put it in the paper until he gets more documentation. Danny's not stupid. He doesn't want to get suckered by this woman.''

WE HAD COFFEE and cleared the table. Luca helped Una back to the couch, even though it seemed her ankle was much better. Maggie and I washed the dishes in silence, chewing on what seemed to me to be an impossible situation. More than anything I was trying to let it go, to focus back to Hank sitting in jail. We needed to get him out. That was our big problem. My mother loved him, he was her husband, and she might never live with him again if somebody didn't clear Hank's name. I wiped the plates and tried to think of somebody who could help. Peter Black had apparently bailed out. Maybe without his testimony the case against Hank would be less solid. That was something, but precious little.

By the time the dishes were done and put away, with Luca and Una talking quietly on the sofa in the warm glow of the floor lamp with the leafy paper shade, Maggie had her idea. By the time she left a half hour later, she'd talked me into it.

It might make everything right again, she said. It was dumb, it was foolish. Or maybe brilliant. It might solve nothing, it might make things worse. It might get us hurt, it might get us arrested.

But, by gum, we were doing it.

EIGHTEEN

Of his lashes the loving gods made
Midgard for sons of men;
from his brow they made the menacing clouds
which in the heavens hover.

HAVE YOU EVER noticed that the most improbable schemes seem doable if you break them down into small, bite-size units? We'd spent the evening on the phone biting off chunks. I could see the whole thing in my mind, and if I didn't think about it all together, but just in small pieces, I felt calm enough to do it. The morning had barely begun, even though the clock said 9:30, when I pushed through the fancy wood doors of the Wild-life Art Museum, built onto the side of the butte that faces the elk refuge. The driveway was long and slick in spots, but they had recently plowed it, so Maggie had no trouble getting her Wagoneer up. She was the designated driver. Somehow that should entitle me to get drunk, shouldn't it? But no, plans were such that I needed every ounce of courage and reflex.

The museum looked like a fortress, with a skin of mossy rock and the lumpy architecture of a castle. I glanced back and forth, trying to look as if I was interested in bugling elk this morning. I greeted the cashier with a small donation, kept my jacket on, and strolled idly down the exhibits. My hands itched, and the running shoes that seemed so apt earlier now squeaked on the polished floors.

At nine-forty-five Danny Bartholomew and Joel Lear entered the museum, chatting idly between themselves about the best spot to set up for photographs. Joel began to set up his tripod and camera in front of a huge photomural of the Grand Teton. The mural stood in for the real view, since the mountain sat behind the butte, out of sight. They clattered and laughed in the nearly deserted museum. Besides me one other customer roamed the hallways.

Isa was late, making me tense. I went into a corner and took some breaths, untwisted my gut. When she came in, dressed again in white wool, with the black boots and platinum-hard hair, she brought two bodyguards. That was a wrinkle we had only talked about, not exactly planned for. They weren't particularly intimidating, no linebackers. One looked like a bouncer but was paunchy and bald. The other was younger, maybe faster. I blinked hard behind the Karl Bodmer prints, my mind racing. Her voice, alive with false enthusiasm and condescension, carried easily across the floor.

"Put the table here, Lloyd," she instructed. "They want me up against the Tetons here. A beautiful backdrop of rock for another unique rock." She smiled at Danny, as if doing him a favor.

Lloyd, the older bodyguard, unfolded the legs of a small table at the spot Isa indicated. The younger man unfolded a blue velvet tablecloth, maybe the same one that had graced the Chamber of Commerce table at the news conference. I strolled across to a sculpture exhibit, herons and mountain lions and more elk in bronze. In the reflection off the glass I saw Lloyd lift the rock onto the velvet. Isa stood behind the table, eyeing it.

Danny began to talk to Isa, telling her that he was going to let Joel take some shots while they talked. We had discussed this earlier, the flashes distracting her. She shrugged her assent, rubbing her fingertips across the edge of the stone. I still hadn't seen it up close, wasn't sure how heavy it was. It didn't look too heavy, with about two inches of thick gray rock, about the size of a sheet of paper. Much smaller than the Kensington Runestone, which I'd managed to find an article about. That stone was more than thirty inches long and six inches thick.

Not wanting to attract attention, I decided to make myself scarce for a few minutes. Danny would be going through the basic stuff of the news conference, asking a few more questions, getting the facts. I could skip this. So I walked purposefully into the back corners of the museum, exchanging hellos with an elderly man in hiking togs who seemed fascinated by an exhibit of paintings of coyotes.

As I wandered back, pausing along the way, I heard a group

of schoolchildren enter the museum. Their laughing, pushing, and snorting caused a deep surge of panic for a second. I didn't want anything scary to happen with kids around. I tried to calm down. It wasn't as if shots were going to be fired—were they? I struggled to keep doubts from creeping into my thinking.

The children's high-pitched voices and excited whispers were good cover. I mingled with them as they raced from place to place, their teachers and chaperons asking time and again, "Please, walk. Quiet now." I couldn't hear what Danny and Isa were saying now, but she had her head cocked and waved her long, graceful fingers on one hand as if telling a story. Probably of her long, long walk to the Indian mounds.

Joel Lear snapped photographs, first with one camera that didn't use a flash, then with another that did. Isa blinked and tried to be professional, but it was obvious the flash bothered her. Go get her, Joel. She kept talking and posing with the stone. The bodyguards watched the kids running around and ogled Isa.

When Danny drew Isa aside to let Joel take close-ups of the stone, I moved to the exhibit next to the photomural, reading the sign next to it that explained the high-plains climate and habitat in much detail. I looked at the diorama, the different levels of soil, the altitude changes, and what animals lived where and why. Nice bobcat photos. Out of the corner of my eye I watched the two bodyguards. One was blocked from the table by Isa and Danny. The other, the heavy, older guy named Lloyd, stood like a sumo wrestler between me and the rock.

Joel took his time. He decided to set up some standing lights, the kind with little silver umbrellas. He opened his case, stood up a tripod, attached the light, fixed the umbrella in place. I moved closer to Lloyd. He turned his head toward me, probably saw my brother's ancient down jacket, took note of the duct tape patches, then continued watching Joel.

The photographer set up the second light, slowly and methodically. When he got it up, he turned toward his camera bag, picked it up, and spilled about a hundred filters in little square plastic cases all over the polished floor. They rattled and rolled, making a mess. Joel groaned and set the bag back down on the floor.

"Here's one, mister!" said a small boy in bright green hiking boots, carrying a filter case back to Joel. Lloyd smiled at the youngster as Joel took the case.

"Thank you, son. One down," Joel said, sighing.

"You need some help?" the boy asked.

"No, no," Joel replied, waving him off. "You better stay with your group." The boy skipped off.

Joel squatted down next to the camera bag and picked up a case, looking at it carefully as if he was going to alphabetize them as he put them away. Lloyd unfolded his arms. For a moment I thought he was going to let Joel do the whole job himself. But finally, he offered: "This going to take long?"

Joel looked up, his curly hair dangling in his eyes. "Want to help?"

Reluctantly Lloyd took a step forward. I had the feeling Lloyd made no moves that weren't reluctant. Joel pointed out a few cases behind the camera tripod for Lloyd to fetch. The big man squatted painfully onto his haunches, and I made my move.

Here's where I should say that time stood still, the earth paused in its rotation, that everything happened in slow motion or like I was walking through honey. But I'm hardheaded, so sue me. It wasn't like that. My heart was racing like a fire truck, almost as loud too. But I tried not to listen to it, and do what had to be done.

Without time to see if the other bodyguard was watching me, I grabbed the rock and ran for the door. I could only hope Danny would delay him long enough for me to get out the door. All the camera equipment was between me and them—that had been the plan. The stone was heavier than it looked, a solid chunk of smooth gray rock, not the kind of object one runs easily with. I hugged it to my chest, shoved—gently—a small child out of my path, and was pushing the inside doors open when I heard somebody yell, "Hey! Stop her!" A high-pitched scream, Isa's, followed.

Maggie had the Wagoneer running, the passenger door open. I tumbled in, and she took off down the driveway, slipping and sliding around parked cars in the snowy lot.

"Stay down!" she said. "You got it?"

Muffled in the seat, I answered, "Does the bear shit in the woods?" My heart was banging. The rock pressed against my ribs. I couldn't believe it had been so easy, just snatch and run. A cinch. I was sweating like a pig.

"Heee-haaaw!" She must have looked in her rearview mirror. "Here they come! The fat one's trying to run down the hill! He had the car keys too, I watched. There's the other one. They're hitting each other! The skinny one's down. God, this is too good."

"Watch the traffic on the highway, Maggie," I cautioned as I felt the Jeep turn.

"I know, but cripes. I wanted to see them beat the crap out of each other." She gunned the engine, the old V-8 rattling up to cruising speed. "The coast is clear."

I sat up, my hair in my face. "Is it over? Am I still breathing?"

Maggie grinned. "Gimme five, girl."

THE KITCHEN in Maggie's clapboard bungalow was big and warm, still decorated the way her mother had done it in 1954, same squatty refrigerator, same stained enamel sink, original chrome and swirled plastic table and chairs. Her mother had been fond of the color yellow in all its incarnations: sunflower, lemon, butter, sunshine. On cold winter days like this one, you could see why.

We split a bottle of Black Dog Ale to celebrate, not wanting to get too carried away since it wasn't even noon yet. I laid the stone on the yellow tabletop and examined it. The runic lettering was weathered and old. If someone had created it as a prank, they had done a thorough job of it, at the very least running water or rubbing sand over the stone until the edges were worn, the lettering dulled. No carbon dating on rock, so all the clues lay in the carvings. I ran my fingertips along the rough stone, trying to remember enough geology to identify the type. It felt like sandstone, like that along the Yellowstone River, but was gray, with small veins of blue-gray.

Struggling to remember the exact translation, I picked out some of the runic letters, then spied the closing: "AVM." These were Latin lettering, recognizable. Strange to see the two alphabets combined, just like on the Kensington Stone.

"You better call your mother," Maggie said, setting down

her empty glass. "She's probably worrying, and she's got enough to worry about."

"Yeah, in a sec." I sat back and drained my glass. What were we going to do next? Getting the rock back was one thing. But what to do with it was another. Maggie and I hadn't planned that far ahead, unsure of our success in reclaiming our status as rightful owners. In proxy for Una and Hank, of course. Hank was the one who should be called, I thought. But he didn't even know it had turned up in Isa's hands. Telling him everything would take a little time.

I frowned at the drops of ale in the bottom of my glass. Maggie used the bathroom. My stomach began to rumble, complaining for my skipping breakfast. I peeled a banana from the fruit bowl.

"Do you think we should just sit on this for a while? Let things blow over?" I asked Maggie when she sat down again across from me and began peeling her own banana.

"What if she reports it stolen? Sends the cops? She knows you, doesn't she?"

"We've never really met," I said. I got up to toss the banana peel in the trash, and paced a little. "She might know me. Danny and Joel will cover. So let's say she recognizes me. Or somebody else does. The cops come to my apartment and search it. It's their word against mine."

"What if they got my license plate?"

I stared at Maggie. We hadn't thought this out quite enough, obviously. "We've got to stash it somewhere."

"Safe-deposit box?"

"You've got one big enough?" She nodded. "But they can get a search warrant for those too."

Maggie got up and poured out brown sludge from the coffee maker's carafe into the sink. "You want coffee? I can make a new pot."

"You have any sandwich stuff?"

While Maggie threw together some sandwiches, I called Una. I dialed my number and listened to the phone ring three, four, five times, then the answering machine picked up. After listening to my own voice, then the beep, I stuttered, surprised: "Mom? Are you there? Are you in the bathroom? Pick up the phone. Mom?"

I hung up, waited thirty seconds, listening to Maggie hum the theme from *Mission Impossible,* then dialed again. Same thing, the answering machine picked up. "Mom? Pick up the phone, Mom. It's Alix. Mom?"

I slammed the phone down and cursed. "Give me your car keys."

Maggie looked up from her sandwiches. "What?"

"I've got to go home. I'm afraid something's wrong with Una."

She stared at me, then at the rock. "What about—?"

"I'll take it with me."

She thrust a turkey sandwich in my hand and grabbed her coat. "I'm coming with you." The phone started to ring beside me, but I ignored it. Maggie tucked the rock under her arm, tossed me the keys, and pushed me out the door.

THE DOOR TO the Second Sun Gallery, heavy wood and glass from an era when doors were made to last, hung open, swaying on its hinges. Maggie and I burst into the room. It was brightly lit, inviting if cold, but without customers or salesmen.

"Artie?!" I called, running to my office. He wasn't there. No one was in the gallery. "Shit. Artie!"

I headed for the stairs. "Lock the front door, Maggie," I called, taking the steps two at a time. I heard the bell jingle behind me, then her footsteps.

Hitting my door with the palm of my hand, I fell into the apartment, my breath heaving. "Mom? Mom!" I looked in the bathroom, my bedroom. I scanned the tabletops, the counters, for notes. What had happened? Had Artie taken her somewhere? Why had they left the doors standing open?

Maggie stood in the doorway, hugging the stone, eyes wide. Her breath was ragged. "Where is she?" she gasped.

"Where is everybody?" I slammed my palm against the counter, causing a cereal bowl to rattle. "I'm calling the hospital."

I picked up the receiver to call but didn't know the number. "Where's the damn phone book?"

Maggie set the stone down carefully on the coffee table and frowned at Una's reading glasses there. A mystery novel left open, facedown, sat next to them. She walked around the low pine table and stooped down. I saw Una's white tennis shoes in Maggie's hand.

"Does she have other shoes?" she asked.

"Boots." I checked the closet. Her pea coat, white fake fur hat, and boots were gone. "She went for a walk? With a bad ankle?" I searched Maggie's face for answers. "Find the phone book."

There it sat, under a pile of magazines on the floor by the sofa. Maggie dug it out. As she looked up the number of St. John's, the telephone rang. I jumped on it.

"Yes?"

"Alix Thorssen?" I grunted. "You have something that belongs to me." The voice was soft, almost gravelly, and female.

"Is my mother there? Is she all right?"

"She's here."

A shuffling noise, then Una's voice: "I'm so sorry, Alix, this is all—" She stopped abruptly, and a muffled squeal came over the line.

"Mom? Mom! Don't you hurt her. She had nothing to do with this. Please, don't hurt her!" I doubled over on the kitchen floor, sinking to a squatting position, sick to my stomach.

The woman—Isa, I presumed—came back on the line. "Bring the stone to this address." She recited a number on the highway near Wilson. "You have an hour."

"I'll be there."

I sank farther to the floor, burying my head in my hands. Maggie took the receiver.

"Was it her? Was it Una?" Maggie whispered, rubbing my shoulder. I nodded. "And the white witch?" Another nod. "Damn."

Maggie pulled me to my feet and pushed my hair off my face. "Well, we tried. Now we give it back. It'll be all right."

I straightened my shoulders and looked at her calm face. "That's right. I give it back." If it seemed so easy getting the damn stone, maybe giving it back would be simple too. Reasoning like this, I knew, could get you into trouble. If you weren't already in up to your eyebrows. "Me, just me. They don't know who you are, Maggie, or they would have gone to your house first. They know me, better than I suspected. There's no sense getting you involved."

Maggie shook her head. "I am involved. It was my insane idea to steal this rock. My fault that Una got kidnapped. I'm going with you."

"No, I can't let you. I think they just want the rock back. That's what they say. But what if there's more? No, you have to be there to tell Danny all about it. To tell the cops."

TWENTY MINUTES LATER I turned out of the alley onto Broadway, cruising west past the antler arches on the town square, the rock in an old towel on the seat of the Saab Sister beside me. Maggie hadn't been easy to convince; the argument went round and round until finally I had to tell her to shut up and go home. I had hurt her feelings by it, I knew. Strong and willful as she is, there is always a point where a person can be hurt. Was it the only way to stop her from coming? I didn't know, but I had stopped her. That was all that was important right now. I didn't want to endanger another person. I couldn't handle that on my conscience.

The day was overcast and grim, the mountains disappearing into the low, pregnant mist, white with snow crystals. What had they done with Artie? One more person to worry about. I hoped he was out here too, and we could exchange everyone for the rock and be done with it. I never wanted to be rid of a slab of stone so bad. I didn't want it, never did. A terrible mistake, I would tell her. Have your fifteen minutes of fame with it. Go for it. Be my guest.

The highway was clear of snow, a hard, gray twist dodging creeks and buttes. A pretty grove of aspen, the Snake River, iced up and sluggish like a kid with a bad cold. Past the turn to the ski area, where most people seemed to be coming or going. Ahead of me a beat-up VW bus, half green, half mottled with rust: *Peace Now, My Karma Ran Over Your Dogma.* They were in no hurry.

I drummed my hands, gloveless, against the steering wheel. This was just another day, I tried to convince myself. Then, finally, Nora's Fish Creek Inn came up on the left. The address was just past it, down a side road. I watched the VW bus turn into the post office, then found the road. It was unpaved, and rutted, as if it was very muddy in warm weather. The stone bumped on the seat next to me.

The first house was a small, white clapboard place right on the road. It was tiny, maybe two rooms, with an outhouse and smoke pouring from the chimney flue. A red pickup truck sat beside it. I drove on.

A string of tall bushes, leafless now, grew on the right, announcing the next dwelling. I peered down the driveway that appeared at the end of the gray twigs of the hedge. It was long. Behind several large trees a log house sat hugging the ground that swelled up toward the mountain. I stopped the car, found the number on a listing mailbox, a relic of years when Wilson had home delivery. My breath quickening, I pointed the Saab down the lane.

They stood on the porch, waiting for me. I wondered briefly who lived here, if they even knew what was going on outside their home. Then I saw my mother, her cast poking from the sleeve of her coat. Jesus, she looked scared, with that hulking bodyguard next to her, his hammy paw on her good arm. Next to him, the skinny bodyguard stood in a thin leather coat behind Isa Mardoll.

The White Queen of the Runes had the same determined set to her jaw that I'd seen all weekend. The same steely look in her eyes, the same unsmiling ferocity. She made me shiver. Her long navy coat was pulled tight across her body, the white turtleneck at her throat, the black boots on her feet. She was no Lara, I thought, remembering my first impression of her in that coat. No Lara jumping onto the tracks; Isa would be the one pushing her in front of the speeding train to get what she wanted.

I parked the car and turned it off. Swallowing hard, I took in the sight of them waiting for me. I scooped up the stone in the dull orange towel and pulled it against my chest. My kingdom for a stone. My kingdom—what was that? My family, my loved ones, my friends? They were the only kingdom I cared about, the only dear things in the world to me. This hunk, this slab, was meaningless in comparison to my dear, sweet mother who trembled just thirty feet away, afraid because I had tried to do what I thought she wanted. Had I even discussed the possibilities of the snatch with her? Had I even contemplated, admitted to myself the dangers? Obviously, so obviously, not.

The snow crunched under my feet, hard and brittle as the sky. I stopped halfway to the porch. The cold needled my face, my ears. My heartbeat was amazingly even, steady, as if I could control it with my breathing. Maybe I could. Maybe this would all be over soon.

Isa stepped out from the group, down one porch step, then two, but didn't come any closer. She eyed the orange towel coolly. "Let me see it," she said.

I took a step forward. She put up her hand like a traffic cop. "No. Open it there. I can see it." She stood ten feet away in dull light. I guess I didn't have time to make up a fake stone, that was her thinking. She didn't need a close-up examination. There was no time for papier-mâché or chisels.

Tilting the rock out on one forearm, I tugged off the towel wrapping, revealing the carved runes on the front of the stone. I lowered it an inch so Isa could see it. She looked, then turned to the skinny bodyguard. He stepped off the porch, walked up, and took the stone from me, letting the towel drop to the snowy lawn. As I stooped to pick up the towel, I heard the vehicle noise. A van pulling a small trailer moved out from behind the house, blocking the Saab. The driver turned off the big white conversion van and stepped out.

I stared, stunned. Bjarne Hansen looked sheepish as he walked toward me. No, he was walking toward Isa. He stopped next to her, and their arms circled each other's waist. I felt like a knife was twisting in my gut, and I fought to breathe.

The bodyguard beside me took my arm. Isa and Bjarne came forward, followed by the heavy man and Una. Isa spoke again: "You will understand, Miss Thorssen. We need some time. This stone is bigger than you can imagine. It proves everything that we have said for a century. We need the time to prove its legitimacy, though"—here she looked up at Bjarne and smiled, almost laughed—"though we know it is real. We know it in our bones."

I didn't understand what she was saying. And Bjarne so smug and straight, a self-righteous stoic who had us all fooled. Why hadn't I listened to my instincts? Why hadn't I known—in my bones, as Isa says—that he was dirty somehow? That he was toying with me? Was I so vain, so lonely, that I was blind?

I stumbled forward, where the bodyguard pulled me. He had given Isa the stone now, and dragged me toward the trailer. The other man pulled Una the same way. I blinked hard as they opened the back of the small trailer, no bigger than a single horse trailer but windowless, dark, and cold. I balked.

"Wait. What is this? What do you think you're doing?" I screeched, my voice ruined with emotion.

Una looked at me, her eyes wild with fright but her face expressionless. She couldn't speak, though her mouth opened and closed. She was too far away to hold.

"Put them in and tie them," Isa demanded. The men pushed us to the door. I put my foot on the metal floor, holding myself out of it, dreading the darkness, the future.

Bjarne turned to her and whispered. She listened, head down, shaking her head violently. He gestured, and whispered more. She looked at him, frowning. We couldn't hear him; their voices were too low, too far away. Was he bargaining for our lives? God, hope springs eternal.

They didn't tie us. That was the bargain. And we got Bjarne in the trailer, perched on the floor like an athlete ready to spring from the blocks. Una and I sat on a pile of moving pads, holding each other in the utter blackness. The doors slammed shut, latched. The van started up, doors closed. The rutty lane tossed us; the highway proved a smooth, if small, blessing.

NINETEEN

Seldom sleepeth the sense of wrong
nor, either, hate and heartache.
Both his wits and weapons
a warrior needs
Who would fain be foremost among folk.

AN HOUR LATER my mother lay back on the pads, her coat wrapped tightly, legs pulled up. I scooted over, put my hand on her side protectively, and told her to sleep. The road made you weak, if not tired, its rhythm and motion sapping you of everything you need to stay alive. In the dark I felt my senses shutting down. I needed to feel Una's coat to stay sane.

I couldn't see Bjarne, but sometimes I thought I heard him breathing. My shock wore off, and anger took its place. Finally I couldn't stop it from erupting.

"So did you burn Hank's boat too?" I said, my voice echoing in the trailer. In my mind's eye I could see the photograph Luca had taken, and see Bjarne there, in his long shaggy coat, torch in his hand.

No answer.

"You played me for a fool, didn't you? You bastard." I wanted to go on, lash out at him, but that would be admitting that I did feel something for him, even if it was only lust. The hot whispers in my ear—Jesus, I could still hear them, still feel his lips on mine. Still feel his warmth. I could only think of the hotel room, Carter's smirk, my pants around my knees, with hot shame. What a jerk I was. All along thinking he *liked* me. Waving so brightly from the float, twirling me around in the bar after his race, telling me so earnestly that he needed me. No wonder he seemed too good to be true.

"So what was the plan? Keep me panting after you, and I wouldn't—" Wait a minute. I met him before Glasius was killed. I had even introduced them. "Was it you? Did you kill Glasius?" I whispered.

"No." His voice was hard, clipped. "I did not kill anyone."

"But you know who did, don't you? Was it Isa?"

"Be quiet. Don't talk." He paused. "Please, Alix." His voice was different, pleading. *Oh, there I go, naive Alix again. So wanting to believe, I am.*

"Please Alix what? Please don't remind me I'm a lying bastard with no scruples? Please don't remind me my lover is a thief and a fraud? Please don't tell me—"

"Stop it! Now!"

There was a scuffling noise, and I turned my head away in case he was coming to hit me. I expected it, tensing, moving my hand off Una to shield my face. But there was nothing. The quiet settled in again. I felt my mother stir next to me. My hand lay again on her thigh. It was cold, damn cold.

ANOTHER HOUR or more passed, time drifting in blackness. The van and trailer slowed, stopped, moved forward again, stopped again. Car horns, a motorcycle. A town, I thought, trying to calculate which town it would be, some two or three hours from Jackson: Idaho Falls, Lander, Riverton, West Yellowstone, Rock Springs? I couldn't even be sure whether we'd gone right or left on the highway by the house.

Footsteps outside, then the latch on the door scraping. The metal door swung open, letting in dusky, electric-lit night air. How long had we been in here? I checked my watch. It was five-thirty. But when had we left?

The heavyset bodyguard leered into the darkness. He said nothing, just pointed at Bjarne and jabbed his thumb over his shoulder. Bjarne glanced at me for a split second, then climbed out. The door shut behind him. Una woke up.

"Where are we?" she mumbled, sitting up.

"Don't know. A town," I said. "I'm going to try the door." I knew it would be locked but, well, I had nothing better to do. I yanked at it fruitlessly. I pounded on the sides of the trailer a couple times and hollered, "Hey, anybody out there? Let us out!"

Una didn't move. She said nothing. She let me holler and

pound, then at last said, "Save your strength, honey. Somebody will get us out of here."

"Only it'll be *them*," I said, sinking to the floor of the trailer by the door. Maybe I could make a break for it when they came back. And leave Una behind? No.

Chin in hand, I waited fifteen minutes for someone to return. Bjarne opened the latch and pulled the door, holding two clear plastic trays of sandwiches in one hand. He handed them to me, his face grim. I looked beyond him, at a motel and a bar. The Sleepy Hollow, the sign said, with little white cabins trimmed in green. Where were we?

I handed Una a tray. I was famished, but the white bread looked soggy and unappetizing. My breath hung in the doorway, frozen.

"Alix, listen to me," Bjarne began, whispering. He looked over his shoulder nervously. "I don't like this. If she wasn't my—well, if I hadn't said I'd help her, I'd be gone. Never did I think—"He shook his head.

"Help us, Bjarne," I urged, throwing down the sandwich. I grabbed his arm. "Help us get out of here. She doesn't need us. She's got the rock, that's what she wanted, even though it isn't hers. Let her have it, but let us go."

He bit his lip, his blond hair disheveled. "She says she needs you quiet. Until the thing with the rock is settled. You know too much."

I took his hands, both of us freezing. "Look at me, Bjarne. Help us. My mother is a crippled old woman. She doesn't need to be riding in a trailer, and who knows? Shot, stabbed, dumped by the side of the road? Is that what she has in mind? Bjarne, if you ever meant one tiny thing you said to me... No, I know you didn't, I—"

"I have to tell you this," he said, taking my shoulders now in his hands. "She told me to do this, but I was willing. I liked you very much. When I kissed you, I felt it here—" He pounded his chest with a fist. "I was not making the fool of you. Alix, you must believe me."

I looked into those blue, blue eyes, impossible to read for their whispers of robin's eggs and oceans and the never-ending sky. Was he lying? Who the hell knows? But when he looked around again, motioned my mother out of the trailer, and told us to run, I didn't care.

We hadn't gotten half a block when I heard that now-familiar "Hey!" The fat bodyguard. I grabbed Una's arm to speed her, but her ankle buckled. Before I could figure out what to do, I looked back, saw Bjarne charging toward us. He scooped Una into his arms, and we began to run.

The corner loomed, around which we would at least not be in their line of sight. I looked around wildly for somewhere to hide, to duck into, a gas station, a store, a restaurant, anything. But everything was closed here, a short retail strip of gift shops, T-shirt stores, a pharmacy. Still the corner was near. We hobbled toward it, Bjarne doing the best he could with Una in his arms, she holding his neck for dear life.

Almost there—and the shot rang out. Bjarne cried out, sank to his knees, laying Una unceremoniously on the cement on her backside. I caught her shoulders.

"Oh, God—Bjarne," I moaned, seeing him hold his leg, the blood seeping through his fingers onto the snowy sidewalk. I pulled Una to her feet.

"Go, go," Bjarne croaked through his grimaces.

Una took a look at the bodyguards, running toward us now, guns drawn, and forgot she had a sprained ankle. I took her hand, and we dashed around the corner, relieved to see the lights of a motel ahead, a lobby. Another shot behind us. I screeched a little, flattened us against the motel, kept us moving. We were inside. The clerk was a little surprised that we crouched behind her desk, so we pulled her down with us. "Tell you in a sec," I whispered. The footsteps paused in front of the motel, then a voice far away shouted something unintelligible.

The door opened, tiny bells tinkling. His ragged breath filled the small reception area, grunting. I shrank against the wastebasket fresh with cigarette butts. The door closed again.

"Is there a back door?" I whispered after a long minute.

"That way," the clerk said, nodding to a door behind the counter. I grabbed Una's hand, pulled her to her feet, then put my hand on her head.

"Stay down." I crouched down and led her through one door, then another, past boxes of supplies, mops, and buckets, to an alley door. I cracked it, then stuck my head out. Nobody there. "Let's go."

I took her hand and began to run down the alley. We got halfway to the far street, and Una collapsed, groaning and holding her ankle. I pulled her up, put her arm around my neck, mine around her waist. "Come on. It's okay," I gasped.

The alley was slick with ice and chunks of snow. Garbage cans, Dumpsters, coffee grounds, and trash bags lay in snowy heaps. I didn't bother to try the doors back here—they would be locked. We made slow progress, linked together, my mother hopping on one foot.

We reached the sidewalk, eased out cautiously, and looked each way. Two snowmobiles ripped by on the snow-packed street, the streetlights glinting off chrome and helmets. The smell of their exhaust lingered, smoky and sharp. We were in West Yellowstone, I figured. West was the only town I knew where it was legal to snowmobile on the streets.

Across the street was a low, brick bank, then a small bridge abutment, a scattering of trees, and a snow-covered picnic table. I didn't want to go to the right; that was the direction of the van and the bodyguards. So with a deep breath I steered us down the buried curb, out across slick tire tracks and knobby snowmobile treads, onto the opposite sidewalk. The marquee lights of a small theater on the next block blazed yellow across the snow. A theater would be open at night.

"Stop, please," Una sputtered as we reached the bank's darkened drive-through lane. I took my arm off her but kept the other on her elbow, steadying. "I have to get my breath."

The streetlight above us made a pool of pink light. A green Chevy truck went by, rattling with chains. "Is it bad?" I asked, seeing her rub her ankle.

"I think I twisted it again," she said. "It's swelling up so that—"

The white van turned the corner behind us, still pulling the trailer. "Mom, run, come on!" I put my arm around her shoulder again, yanked her to her feet. She stumbled, almost falling on her face on the slick pavement as her heavy cast slammed against my ribs. "Shit, Mom, come on."

The low bridge abutment was on our right, a stone wall two feet above the sidewalk. I looked into the trees for something to shield us. A boulder, a sign, anything. But the trees were bare of leaves, and young, too small to hide behind.

"Stop!" The voice of the heavy bodyguard cut through my frantic thoughts. They were behind us, going slow, toying with us.

"Go down the bank, under the bridge," I whispered. "Slide down. Hurry." The bank beside the bridge was steep, leading to what was in the summer a small creek but now was just a low snowy place. Fat Lloyd wouldn't go down there. "Hide under the bridge." I pulled her off the sidewalk, pushed her down on her fanny. "Go. Go!"

The headlights swung across my legs as I let go of her, saw her slide into the shadows. I looked back. The van was easing up on the curb now, first one tire, then the next. Lloyd was hanging his hairy arm out the passenger-side window, gun in his hand.

I turned toward them and spread my hands. I even smiled. "Don't shoot," I said. "I'm not going anywhere."

The skinny bodyguard behind the wheel gave a harsh chuckle as he brought the van to a halt. Isa sat behind him, in the shadows, orchestrating this comic opera. I sucked in a breath, my senses keen. The van's exhaust hung like stringy, acid fog in the cold air. Voices from the direction of the theater drifted down the street. I dared not look to see if Mom had gotten down and out of sight. The skinny bodyguard stayed where he was, arms crossed. Was Bjarne in the van?

Lloyd pulled in his arm to pull the latch on the door, and I ran into the street, through the beams of the headlights, across the front of the van. Away from Una, was my thought. A car came barreling down from the direction of the theater, music blaring. A wailing horn and obscenities cut the air as it grazed me, sending me skidding and struggling for my balance. I stumbled up the curb. The bridge wall on the other side of the street was covered with a foot of snow, shaded by a huge spruce. I stepped up on the stone abutment, gauging the distance below me. Fifteen feet? Twenty? So much snow, I thought.

"Don't be stupid," Lloyd bellowed behind me. I looked back, saw him raising his gun again, and jumped.

The sound was so loud I thought it was gunshots, hundreds of them converging on me from all directions. I expected a soft landing and struggling through deep snow. I was confused. The darkness murky and thick with a blue glow. Then the cold hit me.

Water. Cold, cold water. I stretched my legs down, unbelieving. There was no bottom. My mind wrapped around this new reality. Water, a lake, ice. I felt the sharp edges of the ice against my arms for a second, then I went down, under it. My eyes refused to open against the freezing sheet plastering my face, my lips, my ears. My feet bicycled. The current was weak but flowing, especially at the bottom. I paddled against it, holding on to the icy break.

Then my hands tore against the roof of ice. I opened my eyes; it was so dark, a ghostly midnight blue. Already I was losing feeling. My hands and feet were numb. I tore away more at the ice above me with dull paws of fingers. My down jacket was still full of air pockets, bubbles escaping. Pearly strings of silver, leaving me here. Once I got a good enough grip to come up and take a breath full of snow, then the ice broke again.

My heavy clothes dragged me down, under. The jeans, wool sweater, pac boots, all imprisoning me. I couldn't think, I was just reacting, clawing, my lungs on fire. Confusing... Water, so friendly usually. Water, clean and clear. I loved water, rain, rivers, mist.... My thoughts drifted. I stuck my hand up through the hole as far as I could, thinking I should feel snow, or air, but feeling nothing, as the hand was gone. The arm was going. My shoulder ached, then stopped aching.

I was thinking about Houdini under the ice. Wasn't this one of his tricks? I thought about his chains and straitjackets. My clothes felt like that, heavy, leaden with water, my pac boots like weights. I kicked them off. I managed another gulp of air. I was still alive, wasn't I?

With that, I sank under more, the current dragging my feet downstream. My hand was still above, holding me at the hole. Would someone see it? No, no, my mind said. No one will see it. You must save yourself. Your wits and weapons, the warrior's tools. But how? No weapons. Wits in jeopardy. I was filled with despair. It filled my lungs, my head, my eyes, my mouth. Despair clung to my ribs, filled up my legs with sand. I closed my eyes and let the despair pull me down, down.

This was a new realm, a place past life, a place where there was rest. Rollie! I would see my father Rollie here. Gone these twenty years, would he recognize me? Sadness suffused me. My father doesn't know me. Then the sadness, the despair, all drifted away.

In the darkness was cold, and release.

TWENTY

*The warmth seeketh who hath wandered long
and is numb about the knees*

I WOKE UP coughing, my lungs strafed with firecrackers, and shivering. I blinked and opened my eyes. And coughed again. I lay on my side, under a mountain of blankets, in a bed with railings. Hospital bed. My body convulsed, shaking.

I took a painful breath. Christ, what had happened? What was this on my face? Oxygen? I pulled off the plastic mask and tried to sit up. The blankets were too heavy.

"So there's our ice miracle," a calm, pleasant voice said. A nurse appeared around the end of the bed, smiling. "How are you feeling?" She patiently put the oxygen mask back on me.

"Like I died," I said in the hollow mask.

She was short and round, with dark hair and kind eyes. Her eyebrows went up. "No wonder. You were under the ice for several minutes longer than you should have been. Let me look at your eyes now."

I let the nurse examine me, exhausted by the effort of trying to sit up. The ice. It came flooding back and hit me smack in the forehead. I must have groaned, because she asked if I wanted anything. I said aspirin and something hot. She returned in a few minutes, put the bed up and the rolling tray over my lap.

"Tea is perfect. Lots of hot liquids." She opened the teapot and poured hot water into the white china cup. "Your mother is here. I'll send her in."

I was wearing a hospital gown, but somebody had found long johns and put them on me too. In hospital green, lovely. My hair felt damp, stuck to my cheek. I pulled my arms out from under the blankets and wrapped my hands around the teacup. Una came in, still limping but at least walking.

"So, you are made of hardy Norwegian stock," she said, trying to smile.

I peered at her over the tea's steam. Her coat hung over her good arm, and a new ankle brace was fit over her foot. "Did you pull me out?"

"Good heavens, no!" She settled on the edge of the chair. "This is a nice little clinic, isn't it? Only three hospital beds, but still, it's perfectly adequate and the people are very nice." She wrung her hands a couple times. I popped in the aspirin and washed them down with tea.

"Are you going to tell me what happened?" I asked.

Una didn't look at me but seemed to be waiting for my cue to continue. "I was hiding over there, under the bridge, like you said. I didn't come up. I heard the gunshot, and I thought, oh!" She cleared her throat. "I didn't want to think it. I just huddled down. I heard the sirens, the police. Finally when I saw the ambulance I came out, but they already had you inside. It was hard climbing up again."

"So who got me out?"

"A man on a snowmobile. That's all they told me. Some man who saw you jump in."

"A Good Samaritan," I said. Una nodded. "Did they find Bjarne?"

She shook her head. "You shouldn't have jumped in there, Alix. How many times have I told you never to jump into something you don't know what's down there? You could have broken your neck, or drowned."

I felt the ire stiffen my back. Did she think this was necessary, customary parental behavior? I tried not to compose responses like, I could have gotten shot instead. I calmed myself with tea. Finally I said, "You know, I felt like I died under the water." Una looked at me with horror. "I didn't see angels or anything. No lighted tunnel. I didn't want to die. But still, it felt kind of good. Like sleep." My voice fell to a whisper. "I thought about Dad, and I was happy. When he was under the water in Flathead Lake…" My thought trailed off, undefined. I rubbed my cheeks with warm fingers.

Una swallowed and stared at me. "No angels?" she said at last.

I shook my head. "You didn't get hurt?"

"No, just the ankle. They said you would be okay, to watch your throat and lungs for a while." She fiddled with her coat hem. "I gave a statement to the deputy."

"Did you tell them about Bjarne?"

She nodded. "They got away. That woman. In the van."

I set down my tea. "What time is it?"

"Um, midnight or just." Una shook herself a little. "Maggie's coming—I called her. She should be here soon. The doctor said you should stay longer, but I knew you'd want to get home. I told him you'd see your doctor tomorrow in Jackson."

"Good. I have to get back." A niggling gnawed at the edges of my consciousness. I had to get back to the gallery, to Artie. What was I forgetting? The cold seemed to have made sludge of my brain.

The nurse brought us both more hot water and tea bags. Una and I drank in silence. Near drowning, how strange it was. I looked at my hands around the china cup, swollen with the freeze and thaw, red, sensitive. The burn on my palm seemed so fresh, but healed and new. Had I ever looked at my hands, my fingernails still purple, my fingers? Had I ever really been alive before? The miracle of movement, of feeling. For a moment it flooded over me. The miracle of thought, of tears.

I took a stinging breath and shut my eyes. I could see the black water, the force sucking me down. Was that the force that makes all that lives die? Was that God? Why would God want me to die? I wondered. No, the force was a natural balancing. My own life moving forward created a wake through time, a vacuum behind me. When I ceased moving forward, I was pulled into the wake. But what was it? Just a void, a black hole? Heaven? Hell? A pathway to another life, if I've been good? I sat back and sighed. People had been asking themselves these questions for thousands of years. Now I knew why. Death had a curiously seductive quality, a temptress to whose sins you know you will someday succumb.

The nurse, kind soul, brought us both pieces of apple pie that someone in the clinic had made. This was the first food we'd had since noon, and when she saw how fast we ate, she brought us two more. Satiated on sugar and tea, Una began to talk.

"Why did you have to say to Bjarne that I was a crippled old woman?" She pursed her lips. "You could have gone all day and all night without saying that."

"It was just talk, Mom," I said, leaning back on my pillows. "Something to get him to feel sorry for us."

"Well, I don't want people feeling sorry for me."

"So you didn't want to get out of that trailer?"

"I didn't say that," Una pouted. "I should call Hank. He'll be so worried. I didn't see him today, or yesterday. There he is in that horrible place. And his Viking Vindicator gone! He will be so upset." She stared into her cup for a minute, muttering more homilies about poor Hank, as if reminding herself of his troubles relieved her own fears. "I wish you hadn't exchanged me for that stone. Now we'll never get it back, and Hank will never forgive me for losing it."

I could only stare at her, disbelieving.

"You were always doing this when you were a girl. Doing first, doing whatever you thought the right thing was, and not thinking about the consequences," Una rattled on. "Morality, justice, was always so black and white for you. There wasn't another way to do it, just Alix's way. And if somebody got crushed in the process, well, they stood in the way of justice, and that was their own fault."

Stunned, hurt, I squinted at her through the greenish fluorescent light. "Justice had nothing to do with this. Okay, maybe taking back the stone, that was justice. Hank would have said so," I said, my throat hurting now. "I don't know what the right thing is, but what I feel here, Mom." I pounded my chest with my fist as Bjarne had. "My heart told me that I could never forgive myself if something happened to you. I couldn't lose another parent, especially by something I screwed up. I couldn't—wouldn't let that happen."

Her face was still twisted with indignation. "You take too many chances, Alix. I've always told you that."

"Mom, look at me. I love you. I would take any chance necessary to make sure you were safe."

My mother looked at me, hard, sucked her teeth for a moment. Then her eyes began to fill, and she cried a little. In a shaky, quiet voice she told me she loved me. I guess I was right. For some people it takes the scare of losing somebody before they can say what they really feel. It was true even of me. That shouldn't have surprised me. I was, after all, my mother's child.

JUST WEST OF Teton Pass, still in the land of russets—Idaho—I realized Maggie Barlow owned a cellular phone. She had it tucked under the seat, the coiled cord plugged into her dash lighter. The glow of the sun, even alpenglow, had long since disappeared from the western slopes of the Tetons. They were dark hulks in the night, shadows against the starless sky. It was past two, close to three A.M. I peered upward, remembering that I'd once seen the northern lights along here, far from city lights. A pulsating pink shower, streaks across the purple night—but not tonight. Clouds covered most of the heavens, obscuring everything but random vapor clinging to the peaks.

Una had let me tell Maggie most of the story. It was too painful for her, I think, the helplessness of being kidnapped, the humiliation of it all. I knew how she felt; there wasn't much to recommend being pulled like a human ice cube out of a frozen river. I also realized what her admission to me had cost her. It was no small thing to be rescued by your baby daughter, and then to have to admit gratitude. On top of that, not to be able to say you could reciprocate when the time came. I didn't blame her for not saving me, I never would have expected it. The indignities of age were bad enough. If you were a Norwegian, used to doing it all, it was devastating.

"Does your phone work over here?" I asked, after Maggie had dispensed most of her questions.

"Oh, yeah. The transmitter is up on a mountain somewhere." She reached down by her feet and handed up the cell phone. "Mountain climbers take them up the Grand all the time. Standard equipment these days."

"Do you mind if I call directory assistance?"

Maggie waved me onward. I asked for Danny Bartholomew's home number, hung up, then dialed again. He answered on the fourth ring.

"Christ, Alix, where have you been? I called your apartment all day, and I've been over to the gallery twice. Artie didn't have any idea where you were. What happened? You were supposed to call me when you got home with the stone. I can't sit on this story forever, you know."

I held the phone away from my ear so Maggie could hear his harangue. "Well, Danno, it didn't happen just the way we planned. I'll tell you about the whole thing tomorrow. But now—"

"You've got it, don't you?" he demanded. "I had to deal with those goons at the museum. They thought you had it. Do you?"

"Not exactly. No, that's not accurate. I definitely do not have it, nor do I ever want to see it again."

"What happened to it?"

I sighed. "I'll tell you later, I promise. But I've got one more little favor to ask you." He muttered and cursed; I knew he didn't want to do me any more favors. "You will get the scoop, I promise you, Danny. Just one more thing."

He exhaled loudly. "Do I have a choice?"

I smiled at Maggie. I felt so alive just then—my mind was back, my fingers were back. "Good. When does the paper hit the streets?"

"Four in the afternoon. Why?"

"I want you to print your article about Isa Mardoll. You can say whatever you want about the stone, that Leif Eriksson's blood is scoured into it, for all I care. Check it out with some scientists. Tell it the way she told it even. But here's the twist. I know this is stretching things. But I want you to say that Isa Mardoll checked back into the Wort Hotel—as she awaits the national media—or while she's waiting for more scientific documentation. Unconfirmed reports, something like that."

I could hear him scribbling; reporters must really carry those little spiral notebooks in their pockets all the time, even in their pajamas. He stopped. "Is this true?"

"You mean is she at the Wort? Let's just say it's possible."

"It's possible she's on the space shuttle docking up with the Russians too. Is this total bullshit or what?"

"Danny. I'm asking you, please. I will tell you the whole thing in the morning. I want you to be there when it all goes down. You *will* be there. Please, Danny."

"When what goes down? What's this about? The damn rock again?"

"Not the rock. I don't care what happens to that rock. This is something much more important than that."

He gave another exasperated sigh, then tapped the receiver with his pencil or something. "Okay. I'm coming by your place at eight in the morning, right after I file this. You be there this time."

"Thanks, Danny." I flipped the phone shut. Maggie was staring at me, waiting for an explanation. Una was asleep now, a ragged snore coming from the backseat. I sank down in the seat, shut my eyes, pulled Maggie's blanket tighter around me, and felt the shiver pass through me again.

They could wait until morning too.

TWENTY-ONE

No man so flawless but some fault he has,
nor so wicked to be of no worth.
Both foul and fair are found among men,
blended within their breasts.

THE MOON, only half full but bright, shone into the dark room of the Wort Hotel. Up over the trees towering in the square, over the buildings east of the hotel, the sky had a hard winter glow, cushioning the moon in a ring of snow mist. I lingered, pulling my hair out of its tight bun, before yanking the string to close the drapes.

Not her room, but it would do. I had hoped to get the exact room that Isa Mardoll had rented, despite the lingering malevolence of Glasius's death in it. I debated that for a while, not sure I wouldn't obsess about Glasius. In the end I thought the vibes from the room would help. God knew I needed it. But all the worry was for naught. Her room was still unrentable, sealed by the police.

Now I wished I hadn't even attempted a little disguise: hair pulled back, white turtleneck, black boots. Somehow I didn't possess a pair of white pants or a white skirt, so jeans had to suffice. The disguise wasn't necessary; the night clerk had hardly looked up.

It was eleven o'clock. I turned on the light on the dresser and looked into the mirror. Dark circles ringed my eyes. My winter paleness struck me as sickly. Nose red, cheeks blue. My hair was clean, bangs in my eyes. I pulled it back again into the bun. Not bad. A little longer, and it might actually work. I let my arms fall to my sides. My lungs held on to a low-grade ache from my minutes underwater, but otherwise my resurrection had been complete. Now a comfortable soreness in my shoulders made me smile. A rumble in my stomach: I was hungry. From

my backpack I extracted a sandwich my mother made me, tuna
on stale white bread. Sitting on the edge of the bed, I unwrapped
it and bit in.

The day had been full of argument. Despite my anticipation
that something would be revealed tonight, I had to spend the
day talking everyone else into it. First Danny, then my mother,
then Charlie Frye, who wouldn't at first send one of his officers.
He and I have never seen eye to eye. Being back in the Wort
with Charlie, after his threat last time, wasn't a hot idea for either
of us. But by the time I got to Charlie I had my argument so
well refined it shone like greased glass, and finally he agreed to
one of his off-duty men sitting in.

I finished the sandwich and a can of apple juice. My watch
said eleven-thirty. After dumping the trash and checking the
peephole, I picked up the phone. Maggie answered on the first
ring.

"What?" she whispered.

"Everything cool?"

"Hold on." A rustling pause, then she spoke normally. "I
had to go into an empty conference room. It's too weird talking
out loud in that lobby. *Everyone* listens. You okay?"

"Just tired. This bed is looking pretty inviting."

"Don't sleep, Alix. You don't know what kind of psycho you
might have attracted with that story. You might be completely
wrong, you know."

"It wouldn't be a first." I was hoping to be wrong, hoping
the bait didn't attract the right fish. I took a deep breath, feeling
a weariness, an inevitability in my gut. Tonight would play itself
out, one way or the other. *Please, let me be wrong.*

Maggie said, "Do you think she has more boyfriends hidden
around?"

More boyfriends. I was still worrying about Bjarne, going
over the last words he had said to me as if they were encoded
with meaning. *If she wasn't my*—If she wasn't my what? Lover,
I thought then, maybe even wife. Stranger things have happened.
But then he said, "If I hadn't said I'd help her, I'd be gone."
This was loyalty of a different sort. It didn't matter now. We
hadn't heard anything about Bjarne or Isa all day. I had called
the West Yellowstone deputy sheriff's number to find out if the
skier had been picked up or found dead or something. But they

knew nothing about a gunshot, just something about a woman jumping through the ice. Crazy broad.

"Alix, you there?"

"Yeah, I'm here. I was just thinking about Bjarne."

"Oh, yeah, soft-spot city." She made a noise out her nose. "He screwed you, girl. He set you up. I know you don't like that, nobody does. Hell, I feel like shit because I introduced you two. But you've got to believe he was just following orders from the white witch."

"I know."

She sighed. "Okay, tell me what he said again."

I lay back on the bed. The bedspread was red and gold and scratchy. "He was so sincere, Maggie. The way he said it, that he was willing. That he felt it deep in his chest."

"More likely deep in his loins."

"God, I just thought of something. Remember when I was under the trailer hitch, and it slipped off the blocks and almost crushed me?"

"You think Bjarne did that on purpose?"

I closed my eyes. Had he tried to kill me? Or at least put me in the hospital? And he was so sincere then, too. I breathed in and out, in and out, trying to purge myself of the lingering feelings I had for him. Whatever he was, he was weak to let Isa demand he do such things. "Maggie? You're going to call me if you see anyone, right? Anyone involved in this?"

"Right. You don't think she'll be back, do you?"

"No, not with what she's done. And she's got the stone now. That must mean everything to her." And to Hank, I thought. We still hadn't broken the news to him. "Strange how a slab of ordinary rock can make people nuts."

"You think she's seriously off balance? Because then she might come back for you, if she's mad enough."

"No, she won't come. She's got what she wants."

"So how long are we up for?" She yawned, making me yawn.

"As long as it takes. Listen, I'm not going to use the phone again. I'll just be waiting for your call," I said.

"I'm going to get coffee. Buster over there looks wiped. Nighty-night."

The policeman in plain clothes sat in the lobby with Maggie, the kind of guy who didn't really need a uniform to be recognized: ruddy complexion, buzz cut, big feet. He had pretended to be reading the paper when I went by, a likely story. He might as well have cut out little peepholes in the pages. At least Maggie was there with her cell phone.

I set the phone back on the hook and adjusted the lighting by the bed. The remote control for the television made it into my hand. Dave was throwing hams into the audience again; a plastic surgeon was showing Jay how he would look with a little time under the scalpel. I turned to The Weather Channel about one and watched cloud patterns go back and forth, back and forth. Fascinating stuff. I sat up and pulled off my boots, which were not as tall or as shiny as Miss Mardoll's. Could anybody hope to be so perfectly together, as single-minded, as ruthless and hungry, as the White Queen of the Runes?

Well, Queenie, things are about to get messy.

THE KNOCK WAS soft, as if a small bird had tapped its beak on the wooden door. I opened my eyes to a room ablaze with light, three pillows under my head. The television mute. Black-and-white pictures flashed on it: Cary Grant, Bette Davis, Ray Milland. In low-cut dresses and white tie, dancing. I stared at the set, and the knock came again, a little louder.

I put my feet on the floor and shook the feathers from my head. A deep breath, and I was up, then back to the bed to jab the remote control, turn off the set. My eye at the peephole—nothing, then a hand flashing by, another soft knock. I hadn't set the chain or deadbolt; now I twisted the knob, stepping back into the shadows behind the door.

I suppressed a shallow gasp as Peter Black stepped into the room. Quickly I shut the door, engaged the deadbolt. He turned staring at me. For a second he said nothing, as if registering my face. His own countenance kind, even gentle, a face once simple now tangled with contradictions. How I had wanted to be wrong

"Where is she?" His voice was barely above a whisper but a low rumble as always. He spun around, looking in the bathroom and around the room.

"What's that you've got, Peter?" I asked. He looked confused, then glanced at the wooden trunk under his arm, the case of fortune-telling runes. I said, "Are those for Isa?"

He wrapped his other arm around the trunk protectively and took a step away from me. He must have been carrying them with him everywhere, his constant companion, his connection to her. Did he come to return them to his mistress tonight?

"Where is she?" he said, desperation creeping into his voice. "Is she here?"

I walked to the small round table and flicked on the over-hanging light. "You know how to read the runes just as well as Mistress Isa, don't you, Peter?" I patted the table. "Set them here and read mine for me." He was between me and the door now. If he wanted to leave, there was little I could do to stop him. I kept eye contact, took a step closer to him, tugged on the sleeve of his thin red cotton jacket. His hair was still close-cropped but unkempt now. His dark eyes looked afraid, and weary, shifting from bed to chair to door, back to me. "Come, Peter. Sit down. I would love to get my fortune read. So many strange things have been happening to me, it would be great to know what else is coming."

He cocked his head. "Strange things?"

I sat on the wooden captain's chair, nodding. "If the runes can tell me what's going on, I'd sure be grateful."

He stiffened and shook his head from side to side, a violent *no* in slow motion. "You don't understand. Nobody under-stands. The runes do not tell you what will happen next. That is not your fortune. None of you understand!" He looked frantic at the thought. I stood up again, as close to him as I could without scaring him.

"I want to understand, Peter. Tell me."

He towered over me, at least six-three with that proud head, long, delicate fingers, still in the black tunic and pants, his uni-form for her. His short black boots were covered with slush and mud. The pink palms of his hands were chapped and raw. I noticed suddenly that he was shivering.

Over his shoulder, one way then the next, he looked wildly about the room. His gaze came to rest on me finally, as if giving in to gravity. He held my gaze, his dark eyes large and sad. He is lonely, I thought. Lonely and tired and cold.

"Peter—" I paused. "That's the name Isa gave you, isn't it?" He looked at his feet. "What's your real name?"

"Julio," he whispered, not looking up.

I whispered his name to myself. An old disco song with that title rose up from my subconscious, played over in my mind, "Who, who, Julio." An anxiety reaction: I pushed it back down. "Will you sit with me, Julio?"

We settled uneasily into the chairs, both of us tense, both of us waiting. I kept silent, biting my tongue. At last he eased the wooden box onto the tabletop, straightening it so that the brass latch faced him. His fingers rubbed the edges.

"It's a beautiful box," I said. "Were the runes always in it?"

He shook his head. "Isa had it made. She told me her uncle made it for her. He works with wood. A carpenter."

"He did a wonderful job."

Peter opened the lid of the trunk carefully, blocking my view of the interior. He moved one hand over the runes inside; I could see they had fallen to one end when he had the box under his arm. He straightened them, then turned the box ninety degrees. The silver-inlaid backs of the wooden pieces shone in the overhead light.

"May I?" I gestured toward the runes with my eyebrows. He nodded, solemn. I picked one near the center of the box, leaving an empty core to the assemblage. I fingered it in my hand, a cold, flat, irregular square of wood rubbed smooth by handling, the sharp edges of the silver inlay raised. I turned the piece over in my opposite palm.

Peter made a breathy noise deep in his throat, a purr. The ends of all his fingers lay on the edge of the table, twitching.

"I should remember this one," I said, my voice only a notch above a whisper as if these secrets shouldn't be told. "Is it Ehwaz?" The symbol in the wood looked like an *M*.

"Ehwaz, yes." Peter seemed unimpressed by my educated guess, as if everyone knows the runes. "The horse."

"I have a horse named Valkyrie," I said.

Peter startled, blinking. "Valkyrie? Your horse is a valkyrie?"

I shook my head. "It's only a name I gave her. She's not magical or anything. Just a horse." I tilted the rune piece up toward me in my hand and tried to intuit its meaning. "If I picked this piece in a reading, what would you say? Or what would Isa say?"

Peter's breathing calmed again as he focused on the rune. "A partnership perhaps. Marriage. It is a good sign for marriage."

I smiled. "I'm not getting married."

His eyes caught mine. "It can have other meanings." I waited. "Ehwaz often has a feminine meaning, your female energy, your mother, sisters." There it was: my mother. "Pick another rune," he said.

The next was Dagaz, which looked like a boxed *X*. It meant "day," I knew. I held it in my hand, next to the *M*.

"Opposites dissolving," he said. "The beginning of consciousness. Connecting the left and right sides of the brain, the eyes. Being whole."

"I always thought I was the opposite of my mother," I whispered, hardly aware I was talking aloud.

"Dagaz shows a connection, a bond between you. You and your mother are linked in many ways, from the time before you and the time after her. Infinity," he said, pointing to the symbol. With only small roundings, it was infinity.

"One more?" I asked, putting the runes on the tabletop. The last piece I chose looked like a double helix. "What is it?"

"Inguz. The god Frey," he said. "Something has come to a conclusion. You must combine it with the other runes to know. A transformation is at hand, even perhaps a dark night of searching and wondering."

I sat back in the chair. "This is my dark night, Julio." He didn't look up. I laid the piece next to the others. "I have been searching for an answer. Do you know what the question is?"

He sat perfectly still. I took several breaths, listening to both of us. The runes between us. A black man, a white woman, and the runes that separate us. Once, I might have said the runes that connect us. A magical language of the gods, of the breath of life, of the fiery depths of hell. Those beautiful runes that Glasius wanted so badly. Too badly.

"What happened here, in this hotel? What happened to a fine artist, a great man? That is my question," I said.

Peter's fingers began to twitch along the edge of the table. I could see the tension building across his shoulders, his neck. "Should I consult the runes?" I asked him. "Or does someone

know much more?'' I leaned into the light and whispered.
"What really happened that night? What did you hear?''

He stood up suddenly, knocking his chair backward. Two
steps to the side of the bed, jerky, stiff-legged. His back to me.
"I can't go back. They will kill me.''

"Who will kill you?''

"In Cuba. The soldiers. They killed my father, my brother.
Put them in jail, let them die. I won't go back.''

I stood up quietly. "You don't have to go back.''

He nodded ferociously. "They will send me back. If they
know.''

"If they know what?'' I could see his face in profile, head
bowed, hands clenched. "I know you love her, Peter—Julio.
What did she do that night?''

A low growl in his throat made his face turn toward the acous-
tic tile ceiling. He shut his eyes tight, grimacing as if in pain.
Then suddenly he collapsed, sinking to his heels, knees pressing
against the bed. His head fell forward against his arms, hands
clasped tightly on the folds of the spread.

I bent near him. "I want to help you. Let me. I want to be
your friend. But you must tell me the truth. Everything that
happened.''

"They will send me back,'' he repeated, stricken.

"We don't send people back. You must be a political refugee.
We don't send refugees back.''

"They will kill me in prison there. In Cuba.''

I didn't know how to further relieve that concern. Was he a
political refugee? Was he an illegal alien? Did working for a
fortune-teller qualify a person for a green card? I had to swallow
and let it go.

"Julio, I don't read fortunes or anything, but I can tell this is
troubling you. You can't take all this by yourself. You need a
friend, someone to help you. Isa is gone. She stole the stone
with the runes on it and left town. She won't be back for you.''

He lay bent over the bed, his head on his arms, face buried
in the red jacket. A low groan was the reply.

"Did she come back to the room that night? Did you hear
her?''

He bent his elbows, laid his face in his large, graceful hands.
Rubbed his eyes as he spoke: "With that man.''

"Glasius? Did she come back and talk to Glasius?"

"It was very late. The sounds had finished, and one person had gone. Then she came back."

I eased down on the bed next to him. "What did they talk about?"

"I followed them after supper. I saw them together."

"Isa and Glasius?"

He shook his head. "Her brother, half brother. They had been meeting in secret. But not secret from me." He glanced at me. "When you ask about him, then I know what you mean."

I asked about her brother? "Who—Bjarne? He is her brother?"

"Not real brother. She meets him, make him angry. She likes to keep me angry."

I frowned, remembering dinner at Luca's, the reception, kissing him in his room. "I was with Bjarne that night. Are you sure?"

"It was late, midnight. They always meet late. They think no one sees them. But I see."

"What did they do?" My voice squeaked; I had to know.

"Talk, whisper. I never hear them, but I can see."

"Then she came back to the hotel?"

"The two men show up a little before she gets back. That man stays. I thought he was gone, he is so quiet. But she finds him."

"What did she say?"

"I not hear all of it. They talk quiet. Then I hear her unlock the trunk."

"The trunk?"

"Big trunk. Like magicians escape from. She puts her clothes in it."

"Why would she unlock it for Glasius?"

He slumped against the red-and-gold bedspread again. "To give him the runes."

I blinked. "Just like that?"

He nodded. I could see he was crying now, tears staining his jacket sleeves. "She would give away the runes, *our* runes. They mean nothing to her. *I* mean nothing to her."

I set my hand on his shoulder. "It must have been an—an exchange," I mused aloud. Now we knew what she wanted more than the runes. And Glasius had that information. "Then what happened?"

He wiped his eyes against his sleeves. "All these thoughts were in my head, that she didn't love me, that she loved her brother, that she would throw me away like a piece of garbage, a toy, something she had grown tired of. I went out the door to the hall. Her door was locked. I went back in my room and unlocked the connecting door."

I held my breath. His own was getting quick as his pulse raced, remembering the hatred—and the love—he felt for Isa that night.

He raised his head, wet streaks down his cheeks, and stared at the far wall. "I never meant to hurt her. But there was something in my hand. I raised it. He was there, holding the box of runes. *Our runes*. She never said a word, I remember. Her face had the sweetness of an angel on it. I never meant to hurt him, but he was taking our runes, taking her from me. He fell, and she looked at me like I was a child. A stranger. I took the box from his hands and handed it back to her."

His voice choked. He began to sob again, all the spent emotion of the night his world fell apart running down the polyester bedspread. I sat on the edge of the bed, letting my hand slide from his shoulder, letting him cry. Five minutes passed before the connecting door to the next-door room opened, and Danny Bartholomew stepped in.

He looked as fatigued and satisfied, and yet as sad, as I was. He cocked his head, watching Peter cover his head with his hands and curl into a tighter ball, hoping to disappear, to contract and melt away so that the pain, the guilt, would end.

I raised my eyebrows to Danny, looking at the headphones with dangling wires he carried in one hand. Danny nodded silently. He had recorded it all. I looked around him, peering into the dimly lit hotel room. Where was the cop?

The telephone rang, making me jump. I circled the bed and sat down with my back to Peter. "Yeah?"

"Seen anything?" Maggie whispered.

"What do you mean? It's all over." Behind me Peter rose from the bed and walked to his box of runes, fingering them lovingly. Danny stood in the doorway still, leaning against the frame for support.

"You mean he's there?"

"You must have missed him. Although I don't see how. There aren't—"

I stopped as I heard the *oof!* sound. Danny falling backward, hands cycling, cords flipping up into his face.

"Hey!" I said and stood up. Peter's legs disappeared around the corner of the closet. "Wait!" I threw the phone down on the bed and rounded the closet in time to hear the clicks of the deadbolt. And to see him run out the door, the runes under his arm, the way he had come in.

"Peter! Julio!" I called in the hallway. "Wait!"

His long stride had him to the stairway entrance. I ran down the hall and threw open the heavy fire door. As I looked over the railing, the door on the landing below shut with a thud. I could run after him, but for what? I was in socks, it was January, and this was Wyoming. Danny heaved up behind me.

"He's gone," I said.

Danny gasped for breath, shaking his head. "Not for long."

EPILOGUE

PETER "JULIO" BLACK was picked up trudging along Interstate 80 near Rock Springs after being left at a truck stop by a semi driver with a load of cattle. The driver would have taken him to Omaha, but Peter turned out to be a vegetarian. When he found out the cattle were headed for slaughter, he began to walk. A mile along the interstate, crashing through crusty snow, pelted with mud and gravel by passing automobiles, cold and exhausted, he was almost grateful when the Wyoming Highway Patrol spotted his red jacket and took him into custody. Roscoe Penn agreed to take his case pro bono, and I took back everything I ever thought about the Flamboyant One. Roscoe thought Peter had a good chance for a second-degree or manslaughter plea, heat of passion and all that.

We heard about Bjarne two days later, in the evening while we huddled at Luca's house. She had been so kind as to take in Hank and Una, let them have her spare room and a little privacy to lick their wounds and rearrange their thinking about Vikings and the New World. Hank was still upset with me; he could hardly sputter out a word of thanks for rescuing Una. His chance at immortality, the Viking Vindicator, seemed lost forever. I tried to explain that if it was real, as he seemed to think it was, then truth would out. Isa would show it to experts, and he could tell where it was really found. It turned out he had at least some verification: one of the other volunteers on the Fort Union dig, a retired teacher from Kellogg, Idaho, had signed an affidavit that said she had seen the stone a day after it was found. It wasn't much, but it was something. When I remembered what I'd read about all the trouble the Kensington Stone caused for its finder, the teasing, the finger-pointing, the jokes, I was relieved for Hank. But I didn't think he'd agree.

Charlie Frye called about Bjarne that night at Luca's. The police chief had to apologize for the buffoon he'd placed in the lobby who had let Peter walk right past him while Maggie was in the ladies' rest room. Charlie was warming up to me again, although he had a few choice words about Danny's tape and my general arrogance. I was just glad he'd never heard my brother Erik say I had bigger balls than Odin.

Bjarne was delivered by nameless souls to an emergency room in Bozeman, Montana, with a ragged bullet wound to the thigh. He was delirious with pain when brought in; surgery was necessary. I wondered if he would ever ski again. With information from Bjarne and me, they were on the lookout for the white van, but when it was found a week later in an alley in Las Vegas, the bodyguards and Isa were gone.

Luca patted my arm as I hung up the phone. "Is everything okay?" Artie stood beside her, emotion flooding his face. He had been frightened off at gunpoint by the bodyguards that day and was still ashamed of not being able to help. His protective hovering now endeared him to me even more.

I nodded. "Bjarne's all right. He's going to be fine." Except, of course, they would probably miss him at the Olympics. That was his payment for involvement with Isa Mardoll.

She frowned. "Will they arrest him?"

"I don't know. I had to name him in the report about the— abduction, that's what they're calling it. The cops don't understand about the stone. They keep trying to get me to tell them more. Anyway, I felt guilty giving his name."

Luca smiled, sadly. "Because he saved you from her. From the guns?"

I nodded again. And swallowed down a lump in my throat, thinking of Bjarne alone in the hospital. Was she with him? No, she was somewhere planning her grand second act as the finder of the Isa Runestone. Sister, half sister, lover, whatever she was to him, she had used Bjarne just as she had Peter. As she used everyone.

THE NEXT MORNING Una sat behind Paolo's desk in the gallery, sipping coffee. She had come back to finish packing her things; they were going home tomorrow. The sun radiated off windshields of cars parked along the street by the square. Steam rose from hoods and roofs, the sound of cars passing through the slush made long shushing noises. Today was the day the ice sculptures would melt for good. I felt no sadness in that. Reminders of Nordic Nights could be gladly banished from sight.

Artie and I lifted the first of Glasius's murals off the wall and maneuvered it into a large wooden crate in the middle of the wood floor. Two customers who had been browsing scuttled out the door.

"The ambassadors, the Norwegian consulates, went home, did you hear?" I asked. Una and I were still picking at the edges of things, starting over. The embarrassment of revealing feelings had made us awkward.

"Yes. Nice gentlemen too, very refined." She sipped her coffee.

"They want me to take Glasius's murals back to Oslo."

She raised her eyebrows. "How nice for you. You're going?"

Artie lowered the lid of the crate into place and went to get a hammer. I crossed my arms and looked at her. "Do you think I should? It would be a long trip away from the gallery."

"It would depend on your employees, I guess. Artie seems very able," she said, awfully polite, as if I were a stranger she was advising.

"He is," I agreed. "And he wants me to go."

"Then go," she said.

I watched her for a moment and thought about ice and cold and winter and the end of it all, spring, when the world had another chance to make it right. "Would you go with me, Mom?"

Her blue eyes caught mine, then she set her coffee cup down on the desk. She looked at the sunlight and the row of drips cascading over the lip of the porch overhang. Her voice was softer when she answered. "I'd love to, Alix, but I can't leave Hank just now. Not with all he's been through. And there's my arm too."

I nodded, glad she hadn't invited Hank along. That was a gamble. "They want me to go next week." She nodded distractedly. Artie returned with his tools and knelt by the crate. "But there's something I have to do before I go."

"What's that?"

Artie began banging away on the nails that held the crate

together. I motioned Una back to my office. She sat in my desk chair, while I perched on the extra one.

She touched the box of runes on my desk, the handcrafted wooden trunk that had been rescued with Peter on I-80. "What's this?" She unlatched the trunk; her eyes widened at the intricate silver inlays on the backs of the pieces.

"The runes from Norway. The ones Glasius wanted. I'm taking them back with me too," I said. I reached over and shut the box, as if taking a toy away from a child. I knelt down and faced my mother. "Erik has been very worried about you. He called twice yesterday, three times the day before."

She stared at me, the corners of her mouth doing a minute twitch. Her silver hair gave her an angelic look, a halo. She turned away and said nothing.

"Mom," I whispered, leaning forward, "you have to call him."

She looked out the newly replaced plate-glass window at Artie, intent on his work. I got up and pulled the phone over to her. Picking up the heavy old receiver, I dialed the number.

"It's ringing." I held out the receiver. She took it with two hands as if it were a fragile thing, an eggshell, a bird's nest, a house of cards that might fall apart with the gentlest touch.

She jerked her chin down and cleared her throat. "Hello? Hello? Who is this?" She wouldn't look at me. "Is this Willie?"

I smiled, thinking of my little nephew, his favorite truck and blond mop of hair, his shrieks of delight. The next Thorssen, in a long line of fjord-sailors, searching for the winds that will take them the farthest, earn them Valhalla. The journey was all there was, I had decided. The tangled thread of life, extending from mother to daughter, son to grandson. The answers, the end of the thread? I had no answers on this day, and yet it was a good day, an honest day.

"Willie?" Una said. "This is—" She took a gasping breath. "This is your grandma."

She listened for a moment. Her eyes danced toward me. Her lips curled upward. "That's right, Grandma Una."

When she laughed, it sounded like a string of icicles tinkling to the hard ground, the warmth of the sun and a small boy's aim shattering their cold, cold heart.

AUTHOR'S NOTE

EVIDNECE OF Viking explorations in the New World is both indisputable and suspect. Ruins of ancient camps in Newfoundland, a swampy meadow near the village of L'Anse-aux-Meadows, have been verified as dating from around the year A.D. 1000. But all written Viking evidence has been disbelieved by some scientists even while proven authentic by others. The Vinland Map in the British Museum, an accurate drawing of Viking lands including the coast of North America, and dated A.D. 1440, has been debunked and, just recently, deemed authentic again by Yale researchers.

In 1898 a Minnesota farmer discovered a slab of rock covered with runic characters that reportedly proved that Vikings had been bushwhacked by local Indians in the year 1362. The stone became known as the Kensington Runestone and is now on display at a museum in Alexandria, Minnesota. My thanks to the museum for supplying me with information about the runestone. Controversy still swirls around the stone's authenticity.

Hoaxes about Viking explorers have a long history on the continent. The Viking Tower in Newport, Rhode Island, once owned by Benedict Arnold, was found to be built no earlier than 1640. In 1952 a drinking horn carved with figures and an inscription found on the shore of Lake Michigan was first thought to be from A.D. 1317. Later it was revealed to be a tourist trinket from the Reykjavik (Iceland) Museum.

Did the Vikings sail up the Red River and explore Middle America? Your guess is as good as mine. It's certainly possible.

For more information about runes, I suggest the book *Runes* by R. I. Page, published by the University of California Press in association with the British Museum.

Most verses heading chapters are from *The Poetic Edda,* a rich collection of Norse mythology, culture, and verse, attributed to Icelandic scholar Snorri Sturluson (11781241) and other chieftains, storytellers, and priests who kept the pagan traditions alive by writing them down. My translation is by Lee M. Hollander, University of Texas Press. Other quotations are from various Welsh, Scottish, and Scandinavian sources of traditional verses and songs.

Thanks to Kipp, Evan, and Nick, for keeping faith.

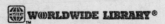

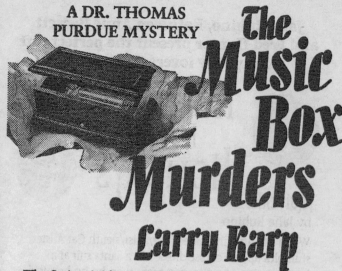

A DR. THOMAS PURDUE MYSTERY

The Music Box Murders

Larry Karp

The Swiss rigid notation music box is a rare, coveted masterpiece that collector Dr. Thomas Purdue would simply die for. Apparently he isn't alone. When the beautiful box is spotted at a local antique shop, Purdue races out to snag the mechanical marvel. Unfortunately, the price is murder.

Not only is the unscrupulous dealer shot and killed, but Purdue learns that the exquisite piece came from the collection of an acquaintance who recently died a most unnatural death. When the box disappears, Purdue follows a trail from New York to London in search of the elusive prize and its precious secrets.

Available November 2000 at your favorite retail outlet.

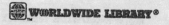

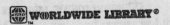